FireDrake

Look for these titles by
Bianca D'Arc

Now Available:

Wings of Change
Forever Valentine
Sweeter than Wine

Dragon Knights series
Maiden Flight (Book 1)
Border Lair (Book 2)
Ladies of the Lair—Dragon Knights 1 & 2 (print)
The Ice Dragon (Book 3)
Prince of Spies (Book 4)
FireDrake (Book 5)

Tales of Were series
Lords of the Were (Book 1)

Resonance Mates series
Hara's Legacy (Book 1)
Davin's Quest (Book 2)
Jaci's Experiment (Book 3)

Brotherhood of Blood
One and Only (Book 1)
Rare Vintage (Book 2)

Print Anthologies
I Dream of Dragons Vol 1
Caught By Cupid

Coming Soon:

Brotherhood of Blood
Phantom Desires (Book 3)

FireDrake

Bianca D'Arc

A S A M H A I N P U B L I S H I N G , L T D . publication.

Samhain Publishing, Ltd.
577 Mulberry Street, Suite 1520
Macon, GA 31201
www.samhainpublishing.com

FireDrake
Copyright © 2009 by Bianca D'Arc
Print ISBN: 978-1-60504-147-6
Digital ISBN: 1-59998-940-9

Editing by Angela James
Cover by Anne Cain

First Samhain Publishing, Ltd. electronic publication: May 2008
First Samhain Publishing, Ltd. print publication: March 2009

Dedication

To Jennifer Ray, who gave Drake his power.

And as always, to my family, who inspire me in so many ways.

Prologue

Prince Nico, Spymaster of Draconia, and now King-Consort of the Jinn Brotherhood walked the battlements. The high towers of the Draconian royal castle were his home, and among his most favored places. His keen eyes searched the wide expanse, built so high in the clouds, until he found the creature he'd come to see.

She was a juvenile dragon, only about twenty-five winters old, in an absolutely stunning gold, pink and soft orange color. That's what happened, Nico thought as he approached her, when a red and a golden dragon mated and were very, very lucky.

Jenet was one of the prettiest dragons Nico had ever seen, though she was often melancholy and refused to train with the knights and other dragons, since she had no knight. Nor would she choose a knight. She'd made her choice, she would reply when asked, and until the stubborn man died of old age without her, she would choose no other.

So Jenet served as a sort of royal babysitter, watching the younger princes when they flew as black dragons—something only a precious few males of the royal line, who could trace their lineage back to Draneth the Wise, could do. At the moment, Jenet was watching Nico's younger brother Wil and the younger set of twins making lazy loops in the sky. They were playing tag, but the activity also served to heighten their fledgling flying skills.

Nico walked over and sat next to Jenet, his human legs dangling over the sides of the high parapet. He had no fear of falling, for if he did, he would simply transform into the dragon that shared his soul and soar away on tar-colored wings.

"How goes it today?" Nico had known Lady Jenet all his life, so there was little need for formality between them.

"Passing fair, my liege."

"Please, Jen, just use my name. I'm sick to death of all this formality. It's even worse now that my new wife has been crowned Queen of the Jinn. Thank heaven it's mostly a ceremonial title." Nico spoke mind to mind with the dragon, as only a few people could do.

A dragonish chuckle, complete with a smoky, cinnamon-scented cloud, answered him as Jenet moved her large golden head to study him. Her jewel-like eyes blinked once, fixing her gaze on him.

"You never coveted your brother's throne, did you? Perhaps that's the reason the Mother of All saw fit to grant you one of your own, King Nico."

Nico groaned and clutched one hand to his chest in mock agony. *"You wound me, mistress, to remind me of my woes."*

Jenet laughed outright at that, filling the air with smoky dragonish laughter. *"To what do I owe the pleasure of your company this morn? As you can see, your little brothers are playing on the air currents above and all is secure."*

"I came to see you, actually. I have some news I thought you'd like to hear."

The fire opal eyes blinked once as she regarded him. *"And what is your news, Prince Tease?"*

Nico chuckled, relishing the moment. His news could change her life and would definitely brighten her mood, if he knew Jenet at all. He drew out the moment as long as he could, heightening the anticipation, but in the end there was just no way to say it but straight out.

"Drake's coming home."

"Drake!" Jenet jumped to her feet faster than Nico would have credited. She was a nimble little thing for all that she was as large as any healthy juvenile dragon. She crouched on all fours, her wings outstretched and trembling in a show of excited eagerness. Her large head crowded him as he stood. *"Is it true?"*

Nico smiled at her soft, almost frightened tone. "It's true. I had a special messenger from the Jinn arrive just this morning. Drake sent him ahead to make sure my brother Roland would stay put. Drake's coming to personally deliver a message from the Doge of Helios."

"Drake! Coming home!" Jenet rose up to stand on her hind legs and trumpeted her delight to the sky. Her magnificent pearl-like wings flapped happily, stirring up a joyful breeze as Nico watched, gratified and amused. It had been too long since Jenet had been this happy. It was good to see her so alive again.

And it was all because of Drake.

Drake had taken the eager light from her eyes when he'd left home fifteen years ago and she'd pined for him ever since. Now he was coming home, but for how long? Would he spurn her again? Or would he finally accept what was so obvious to everyone else who knew them?

Only time would tell.

Chapter One

Drake felt the weight of responsibility settling around his shoulders as he made his way to the throne room of the royal castle of Draconia. He'd sent the messenger at the last possible moment, but he knew the king would be expecting him. Drake wanted to make this visit as brief as possible. He didn't want to see anyone other than the king, if he could avoid it.

Coming back to Draconia after all these years was quite possibly the hardest thing he'd ever done, but it was necessary. Nothing less than the safety of the land, its people and dragons could have made him break his vow never to set foot in his homeland again, but it had come down to that, at the last.

Drake had a message to deliver that was too urgent to wait. It had to be him, much as he could have wished otherwise. He'd been closest to the borders of Draconia and there was no time to find another trusted operative to deliver the warning. This had to be done as quickly and covertly as possible so as not to alert their enemies.

The giant doors to the throne room were open and he could hear the soft murmur of voices from within. He'd hoped to catch the king alone, but it was not to be. Drake took a deep breath for courage and resigned himself before stepping through the dragon-sized portal.

Nico was there, closest to the doorway in the huge room.

Drake sketched him a saucy bow as he caught the new king of the Jinn's eye. Nico smiled and started toward him. They met in the center of the large chamber, exchanging a firm handclasp and a short, pounding hug of true welcome.

"Drake! You're here sooner than I expected. Your messenger only arrived yesterday."

Drake stepped back, his grin genuine, if a bit sheepish. "That was by design."

"Ah. Just enough time to recall Roland if he was elsewhere and not enough time for word to spread too far. You're a cagey one, Drake. Always were."

"*Has* word spread? I mean, does my family know I'm here?" He felt like a fool for asking, but he had to know, and Nico was as close as a brother to him, though he was in fact his liege lord twice over—once as Prince and Spymaster of Draconia, and again as King-Consort of the Jinn.

"You mean, does your blood-father know?" Nico cut to the heart of the matter. "If he does, he didn't hear it from me."

That should have set his mind at ease, but Drake knew Nico too well. His careful words were too vague for Drake's comfort, but he didn't have time to wrangle with the Prince of Spies about it. Roland had spotted them.

Few had the nerve to keep King Roland of Draconia waiting. Nico, of course, did but he was his brother. Drake, while having grown up alongside the royal princes, still couldn't claim that kind of kinship. And Roland was king now, after all.

Drake walked toward Roland, Nico beside him. When Drake would have fallen to one knee in respect for his king, Roland stopped him, grasping his hand and giving him a back-thumping hug, much as Nico had done.

"It's good to see you back home, Drake. We've missed you." Roland stepped back and nodded. That simple gesture of

13

approval said more than mere words to Drake, who'd known Roland and his understated ways since they were both youngsters. "Your work on our land's behalf has not gone unnoticed and I thank you."

Drake stood back, amazed by the welcome. He hadn't left under the best of circumstances, but all he'd done in the years he'd been away had been for the safety and security of the dragons and people of Draconia. Apparently Nico had told his older brother a bit about Drake's work as head of the Jinn Brotherhood's network of informants and spies. He didn't know quite what to do with praise of this kind. He'd heard so little of it in his life.

Drake bowed to the king. Roland's opinion mattered more to him than that of almost any man alive. Roland had been forced to assume the throne at a young age after the murder of his parents, and had always been a steady, solid influence on Drake while growing up. Later, after Roland had become king, Drake had been there, part of the royal court, younger than Roland, but not by much. He'd admired the young king as a friend and a leader even back then. Drake suddenly realized he'd missed Roland's strong personality and the influence of his presence in the years he'd been gone.

"It's good to be home, my liege."

Drake knew he had never spoken truer words.

A scuffle from behind caught all their attention as heavy, hurried, dragonish footsteps sounded through the large throne room. Drake's back was to the doorway, but he knew the sound of those particular dragon feet. He'd grown up hearing them and would never forget the rhythmic click of this dragon's claws on stone. A feeling of mixed dread and delight stirred in the pit of his stomach and he steeled himself before turning to face his destiny.

"Drake!"

The feel of her voice in his mind caused Drake's knees to weaken. It felt so good, so right. Drake had denied himself this feeling for far too long.

The peach-colored dragon approached him at full speed, her wings outstretched as she landed with a bounce in front of him. Without pause, she swept him into her wings and pulled him in against her smooth, scaled neck.

Jenet had grown since the last time he'd seen her. She was almost full size now, and so beautiful it made his heart ache.

"Sweetheart." Drake hugged her close, allowing himself the luxury of burying his head against her sinuous neck for a short moment. Jenet had been born when Drake was about five years old and they'd grown up together. They were closer than brother and sister. They loved each other deeply though they were of different species. *"It's good to see you again."*

Drake felt the tightness behind his eyes that he refused to humor. He had to keep firm control of his emotions here. He'd learned the hard way over the years he'd been gone to temper his feelings—for good or ill. His hot temper had cost him his family and home once before. He'd tried hard never to let his emotions get the better of him again.

Jenet stepped back, her wings withdrawing as Drake stood facing her. Her fiery jewel eyes focused on him as she sent her thoughts out to all in the room. *"I claim you, Drake, as my knight partner—"*

But Drake cut her off. "We'll have none of that, Jen. I told you before I left that it's just not meant to be. I'm no knight."

Gasps sounded from all around and Drake realized their audience had grown. He stepped back to see not only Roland and Nico, but his mother and her two mates, as well as their dragon partners had entered the room. They stood behind Jenet now, staring at him.

"Hello, Mother."

Of all the family now gathered in the room, his mother had been the least to blame for the blow up that had caused him to leave. She had tears running down her beautiful, pale face, and Drake opened his arms as she ran to him, enveloping her in a huge hug.

She hadn't changed much in the fifteen years since he'd stormed out of their home. Partnering with dragons expanded their humans' lifespans by hundreds of years, but Drake had given all that up when he took to the road fifteen years ago. He knew his own face showed every moment of the time that had passed.

His mother clung to him, her pale blonde hair glistening in the light from the overhead dome, vented to let out the dragon smoke. She was petite and seemed shorter than he remembered, but then he'd grown to his full size since leaving home as a teen. She wasn't shorter. He was taller. The thought gave him pause. What else about him had changed? And would it be so easily seen?

"I've missed you so much, Drake. I've dreamed of the day you'd return." His mother moved back, stroking his face with her delicate fingers. Drake loved his mother and had missed her, but he wouldn't allow emotions to overrule his better sense again.

"I've missed you too." Truer words had never been spoken.

A hard, masculine hand thumped his shoulder and Drake looked up to find his dark-haired father smiling at him. His mother moved away so the two men could share a quick hug and handclasp.

"You look good, my boy. You've filled out and wear your years well."

"Thanks, Ren. It's good to see you again."

A sparkling red female dragon dipped her head near. *"Hello, Drake. You're looking well."*

Drake reached up and scratched the dragon's eye ridges. "You're still as beautiful as ever, Lil."

He knew the dragon who had helped raise him wanted to say more, but the problems between Drake and his family had never had anything to do with Ren and Lil. They backed off to reveal a magnificent golden male dragon, with his blond-headed knight beside him. It was obvious to anyone with eyes in their head that this man was Drake's blood-father. They shared the same golden good looks, the same strong features, the same muscular build, height and keen intellect. The same impenetrable will was also broadcast by identical stubborn jaws.

It was a clash with this man that had caused the rift all those years ago.

Drake knew he had to face Declan head on. To avoid the confrontation would only diminish himself in all of their eyes as well as his own.

"You're looking well, Arlis." Drake addressed the huge gold dragon first, then dropped his gaze to the silent knight at his side. "Hello, Father."

Silence reigned as the older man strode forward, the dragon moving with him. When he drew close enough, Drake could see the battle going on behind the sky blue eyes, so much like his own.

"Is it true? Did Jenet try to claim you before you left?"

The question wasn't what Drake had expected—nor was the stricken look in his father's eyes. Drake recognized the hotheaded temper that mirrored his own, the wisdom that came with the passage of time...and the regret.

17

It was that last which struck him most. Never before had he seen his stern father show even the slightest crack in the armor that surrounded his heart. At least not around Drake. No, Sir Declan had always been a hard man, not given to patience with the son who was his very image. He'd demanded a lot of Drake as a child and never seemed satisfied with Drake's best attempts to live up to the Knights Creed.

Over the years, Drake had given up trying to please his demanding blood-father, opting instead to deal with his mother's other mate, the comparatively easy-going Ren. He'd found grinning approval from Ren and his mother Elena, and bloomed into a strong young man with their loving guidance while his father watched with quiet, measuring eyes. Drake had always felt the weight of that icy stare, always fearing in the back of his mind that he didn't quite measure up to the ideals of the Creed.

"I asked if it was true, boy." His blood-father's stern voice pulled him from his memories. "Did Jenet try to claim you before?"

Drake sighed, suddenly weary of all the drama. "Yes, Father. But don't worry. I didn't take her up on it then, and I won't now. She was only doing it to get me to stay and I wouldn't saddle her with an inferior knight when better men were available."

The older man looked stricken and for a moment, Drake grew concerned.

"Is that what you really believe?"

Feeling the failures of his youth once more, Drake nodded.

"Son," Ren's voice sounded from Drake's side, "you're an ass." Far from laughter, Ren's deep voice was laced with fury. "I thought we raised you better than that, but for all your skills and derring-do, you're a blind idiot." Ren's voice rose in true anger, shocking Drake. He could count on one hand how many times he'd seen Ren truly livid and this was definitely one.

"What?" Drake was surprised by the vehement anger directed at him.

Ren stepped right up to him and poked him in the chest with one hard finger. "A dragon speaks the words of Claim to you and you accept. You don't dither or keep her waiting for *fifteen years* while you play at being a spy."

"Ren." Elena put one hand on his arm, trying to calm him though her eyes were full of sadness and disapproval when she looked from Jenet to Drake.

"Jenet has pined for you all these years." Declan had moved closer while Ren was fuming and now stood only a few feet away, Arlis right behind. "And now I find it was my own pigheadedness—and yours, Drake—that caused it all. Sweetheart," Declan addressed the young female dragon behind Drake. "Can you ever forgive me?"

The peach-gold head dipped over Drake's shoulder and for just a moment it felt so natural to be sheltered in the coil of the dragon's long neck. Jenet nudged Declan in the chest with her nose.

"I love you, Papa Dec, even if you are as stubborn as your son."

Declan shocked Drake by laughing and reaching out to rub Jenet's pretty head with his big, battle-scarred hands. Maybe his father had mellowed in fifteen years, but Drake was reserving judgment.

When Jenet lifted away, the two men were left facing each other. Drake almost dreaded the serious look in his father's blue eyes.

"Son, I'm done trying to run your life. You're too old for that now anyway." The self-conscious chuckle, as well as the words, stunned Drake. "You were still just a boy when you left here, but even then I respected your willingness to stand up for yourself—to stand up to me. I'll admit I didn't always handle things between us as well as I ought. It took your leaving to make me realize that for all your youth, you were already a man. In the years since, Nico has been kind enough to let us know what you've been up to, though your mother still worried. It took me too long to realize you wouldn't come crawling back— that you'd made quite a bit of yourself—all on your own, and I couldn't be more proud, though I take none of the credit. You found your way in life despite my interference. You're a good man, Drake, and you've done your family proud, though I could've wished things had been different for Jenet's sake, and your mother's. They've missed you, son. And for the record, there is no man worthier to partner our little girl than you."

Stunned, Drake could do little more than return the fierce hug his father bestowed on him then, while the proud golden dragon who was his father's partner watched over from above. When, at length, Declan moved off, Drake was left facing Arlis, the mighty gold dragon who was also Jenet's sire.

"You've behaved like the idiot Ren named you, Drake," the dragon began, *"but you've also done good service to the dragons and people of this land, even from afar."* Drake didn't know where the somewhat austere dragon was going with his words and was even a little afraid of what Arlis might say next. Arlis had always been a quiet dragon—a deep thinker who spoke only after much deliberation—or on the odd occasion when his temper got the better of him. *"Welcome back."* Arlis's gleaming golden head dipped down so his jeweled topaz gaze could pin Drake. *"Work things out as you will, but don't hurt my girl again."*

Drake took the warning to heart. Dragons in general—and this dragon in particular—were not to be trifled with.

Displeasing a dragon could have dire consequences.

"I'll do my best, Arlis, but I'm only here to deliver a message. I'll be leaving again as soon as I've done so."

At this, the king stepped into the charged silence. "Do I have to issue a royal command to get you to visit your own family, Drake?" His tone was teasing, but King Roland's expression was serious.

"Not to worry, Rol." Prince Nico clapped his brother on the shoulder. "I'm sure I can think of some task to keep my Spymaster nearby for a bit. Perhaps he could help us with the influx of Jinn in the new town. He is one of their celebrities, you know."

"Excellent idea," Roland replied with a calculating grin.

Mention of the Jinn brought back to Drake the purpose of his journey. He turned pained eyes on his family. "I promise to see you all later, but right now I must complete my mission here."

It was Declan who motioned the family to withdraw. "We know you have important matters to discuss and we'll leave you to it, but it's good to see you, son. I'll expect you to keep your promise." Declan and Arlis turned to leave, Ren and Lilla not far behind.

Drake's mother hugged him before following. "I'll expect you for dinner tonight, if you finish your business in time. I'll make all your favorite dishes."

Drake couldn't say no and found himself sighing with relief as the room cleared. The thing he'd feared and dreaded most about his return to Draconia had just occurred and he was still standing. Perhaps this homecoming wouldn't be as bad as he'd always imagined. Turning back to the king, Drake was startled to see Jenet still there. She'd always followed him like a shadow since she'd first learned to toddle around, so he shouldn't have

21

been surprised, yet it was odd to have her around after all these years without her. Missing her.

"Jenet?" His gaze swept to Roland in question.

Roland nodded. "Lady Jenet is welcome here, Drake. She is companion to my younger brothers, and like family to me."

"Companion to the young princes?" Drake was taken aback by the synergy of events. "Then Jenet absolutely must hear what I have to report."

"Shall we adjourn to a more private room for our discussion?" Prince Nico led the way, Roland following with quick, decisive steps while Drake brought up the rear with Jenet. It felt good to have her at his side again, her warm presence heating the cold places in his heart.

Chapter Two

The meeting lasted most of the day. Drake imparted his message from the Doge of Helios as well as the intelligence the Jinn spies had been able to unearth regarding a threat to the younger set of twin princes. It was the threat that hung in the air now like a storm cloud. Since the return of Princess Adora of Kent and the discovery of her daughters, one of whom was now mated to Roland and had been crowned Queen of Draconia, they all took threats against royal children very seriously indeed.

Lana, the new queen, and her twin sister Riki, had been stolen from their mother, Adora, at a young age and forced into slavery. One had been enslaved in the enemy land of Skithdron and one in the frozen Northlands. Only years later were they discovered and restored to their family, both queens in their own right now. Lana was Queen of Draconia and Riki was the newly crowned Queen of the Jinn, married happily to Nico. Both women had also discovered within themselves the startling ability to transform into dragons. It was something not seen in Draconia in generations. Female shapeshifting black dragons were the rarest of the rare, but the two queens were becoming steadier on their wings each day.

New black dragons had also been discovered among Draconia's Jinn allies. More and more of the nomadic Jinn were arriving each day to settle the open plain on the other side of Castleton, the city at the base of the Draconian royal castle, which was built into the side of a mountain.

The new town was filling faster than anyone would have credited, as Jinn from all the far lands moved in to stay. They were massing like an army, Drake knew, gathering here in response to what they believed was the fulfillment of a prophecy. Those of the ruling Black Dragon Clan were training with the dragons and knights every day, learning how to fight as part of a group in preparation for a battle they believed was coming but hadn't developed yet.

Drake had to admire their conviction. He wasn't sold completely on the prophecy they lived by, though he'd come to the Jinn Brotherhood as a teen and hadn't been raised in their ways. Still, he held a high rank among them and respected their beliefs, if he didn't quite follow them himself.

"I'm sorry, Drake," King Roland broke into his thoughts. "You won't make that dinner with the family tonight. I need you to go down to the Jinn settlement and talk to them."

Nico shrugged. "They don't tell me everything, for all this King-Consort stuff. I think it actually prevents some of them from spilling what they know to me. They seem to be worried about insulting or angering me." Nico shook his head in clear disgust. "It was easier to get answers when I was just plain Nic."

Drake knew Prince Nico's alter-ego disguise quite well, having helped Nic gain acceptance among the Jinn and others during his time abroad. The persona had been invaluable in helping Nico accomplish great work as Spymaster of Draconia, but all the Jinn knew Nic was now wed to their new queen. The time of them speaking plainly to warrior Nic was clearly over.

Drake smiled. "Even as Nic, there was never anything plain about you, Nico."

All three men smiled as they rose from the table they'd been using. "I bet you're happy enough to postpone further confrontations with your family, though, right Drake?"

He sighed. "You'd win that bet. I confess to being—" he shot a look over to the gorgeous peach dragon sitting to one side, watching all, "—more than a bit overwhelmed."

Roland turned to Jenet. "Would you mind relaying my apologies through your parents? I need Drake at work tonight. He can join the family tomorrow."

"We're all happy to serve, my liege." Jenet stood and joined the men near the dragon-sized door. *"Though Mama Elena will undoubtedly be disappointed. Still, she's waited this long. One more day matters little."*

Drake heard a startling new maturity in the girl-dragon's words and tone. He'd have to remind himself she was no longer the baby dragon he'd left behind.

Drake crossed the oversized footbridge—one of many newly constructed to connect the old city of Castleton with the new Jinn settlement just on the other side of the river. Jenet had been convinced to stay behind, but Drake suspected she wasn't far away. She'd been his ever-present shadow since almost the day she'd been hatched and he'd felt an ache in his soul for the past fifteen years without her. He hadn't quite realized it until he'd seen her again. She fit at his side as if they'd never been parted and he was made to realize what had been missing from his life for the past years...Jenet.

It was a dangerous thought. Drake had turned his back on all that when he left home. His boyhood dreams of being a knight like his sires—being Jenet's knight—had died that day. So much had changed in the intervening years, Drake doubted he could ever go back. The fact that such a thought even crossed his mind indicated to him just how seriously being back in Draconia was already affecting his judgment.

The new town looked like nothing so much as a Jinn encampment, albeit on a grand scale. Drake felt instantly at home. Colorful banners, decorations and signs graced many of the newly built structures as well as the many tents that were still in use while more permanent quarters were under construction.

Already the familiar sounds of tavern bustle could be clearly heard, along with the unmistakable sound of Jinn music from almost every direction. These people had adopted Drake when he'd struck out on his own as a teen and they were his family as much as those he'd left behind in Draconia.

And now the Jinn were here, in his homeland. The wanderers were settling at last, at the base of Drake's childhood home, the royal castle of Draconia. Stranger things had happened, he was sure, but he didn't know when or where.

Drake looked around, spotting a likely place to begin his evening's work. He recognized the banner over the open flap of a very large tent. It belonged to a long-time friend and master spy named Devyn, who just also happened to be a brewer of excellent quality. Devyn had last plied his trade in a tavern deep in Skithdronian territory, but it looked like all the Jinn were pulling up stakes and gathering here in Draconia, even those with established businesses elsewhere.

Drake hitched the soft case that held his lute a bit higher on his back as he set off with a jaunty step. Traveling minstrels were the norm rather than the exception among the Jinn and few he passed looked at him with anything other than welcome. Drake of the Five Lands had made a name for himself with his musical talent, even among the gifted Jinn. His music would be welcome and his notoriety would work to his advantage.

At least, it always had in the past.

Shouldering through the open tent flap, Drake scanned the large common room. Newly made chairs congregated around tables that looked to be only temporary conveniences—just sawhorses with planks thrown across. The sounds of construction came from behind the bar area set up at the back of the tent and Drake guessed this would be the home of Devyn's next brewpub once the building was completed. It was a good choice of location, close by the main road from the footbridge and well upstream, where the water was clear and near enough the base of the mountain to be easily defensible.

But Devyn had always been a crafty man. Good in a fight, he was also a skilled elicitor of information. He had high standards for the ales and wines he both made and served, and hired only the best cooks he could find. A meal at Devyn's was guaranteed to be both wholesome and hearty.

Drake suddenly found himself famished. The wafting aromas of meat stew helped his hunger along and he decided to stop here for dinner. The time spent would serve several purposes. First, he'd have a great meal. Second, he'd have a chance to chat with Devyn and learn the lay of the land. Devyn was connected enough to be able to shorten Drake's search for certain informants considerably. Third, he'd undoubtedly be asked to sing, which in turn would spread word of his arrival in the new town. Keeping a high profile had been one of Drake's most useful tools as a spy. People always knew where to find him, and stray compliments and conversations with strangers were never remarked upon. Notoriety had its uses, he'd discovered quite early on in his covert career.

So Drake bellied up to the bar, placing his lute, in its padded case, next to him. It was early enough in the evening that the room was only half full and there was plenty of bar space to go around.

"Do my weary eyes behold Drake of the Five Lands?" Devyn's booming voice floated to Drake, eliciting a smile of satisfaction as he turned to greet the older man.

"They do indeed." Drake was at his showiest, bowing low before being swept into a quick, bone-crushing hug by Devyn. "It's good to see you again."

Devyn stepped back, his lined face wreathed in smiles. "And you, Drake! I hadn't thought you'd ever expand your travels to include a sixth land. What brings you to Draconia?"

Devyn walked around the bar as he spoke, his tone lowered so their conversation could be somewhat private. Drake weighed his response. Coming clean about his origins to a select few would harm nothing and might even help him now that the Jinn had decided to settle here.

"I was born here, you know."

Devyn's face showed his surprise. "Truly?" The barkeep poured a mug of his best ale and set it before Drake. "Now why in the world would anyone ever leave such a beautiful land as this? I always thought you were a bit daft, my boy." Devyn's teasing words were accompanied by a dramatic shake of his shaggy head and Drake had to chuckle.

"It's the old story. Disapproving parents and a stubborn child. I ran away from home in my teens and never came back."

"Until now." Devyn's wise face held understanding and the patient kindness that Drake had found in so many of the Jinn.

"Until now," he agreed, taking a long sip of Devyn's most excellent ale. "This is delicious," Drake complimented the man, changing the subject as he lowered the mug to the bar.

Devyn nodded, allowing himself to be redirected. "The air here is wonderful for my brews. This is the first batch that's been brewed since I started working on the new pub and even I am pleased with the results."

"So you've just opened for business?"

"Only just," the barkeeper agreed, "though I've been here quite a while. It takes time to get a business up and running, especially since I sold my last tavern lock, stock and barrel. I'm building everything from scratch here. The chairs came first, 'cause I figured people had to be able to sit on something. Tables will be next, though we've been working on the structure at the same time so we'll be able to move indoors before winter comes."

"Sounds like you have this all planned out."

Devyn nodded. "I've done this before, but never on this scale. It's been a challenge, but one I enjoy." He wiped down the bar and picked up the padded instrument case with a speculative gleam in his eye. "Will you play for us later?"

"Thought you'd never ask." Drake winked with a grin. "But is that mutton stew I smell?"

Devyn laughed good-naturedly as he placed the lute behind the bar in a safe place. "It is indeed. You can sing for your supper, just like in the old days."

"You have a deal, my friend."

Devyn returned a few moments later with a heaping portion of stew, a hunk of fine wheat bread and a selection of fresh fruits and cheese. More ale was poured as he placed the feast before Drake.

"Devyn, you've outdone yourself. I doubt I'll be able to sing enough to compensate you for this kind of abundance."

But Devyn only winked. "To tell you the truth, I'm getting the better end of this deal. Drake of the Five Lands is quite a draw. I've sent out runners to spread the word of your arrival." Devyn paused while Drake realized the man knew just why Drake had chosen his establishment to make his first public appearance. "I'm sure the place will fill up in short order and then we can get down to business—both of us."

Drake knew Devyn would make a good deal of coin from the night, but the old man probably realized Drake would set about establishing his contacts in full view of the entire bar. It was an ideal situation. Drake didn't have to go out and find his people. Knowing he was in town, most likely, they would come to him.

Drake dug into the tasty meal while Devyn went about his business. Already the place was starting to fill up as darkness began to fall. Food was served in large quantities and Drake noted the efficient serving girls Devyn had running about the place, filling mugs, stacking plates and keeping busy. Several of the bolder young women had sent him significant glances and Drake knew he wouldn't have to leave alone tonight, if he wished, but heavy thoughts weighed on his mind. The rumors of trouble brewing for the young princes, the drama with his family, the ever-present shadow of Jenet in his mind...all these things and more distracted Drake from even the idea of bedsport with any of these handsome maids.

Chapter Three

"Is this seat taken?"

The feminine voice was strong and not at all flirtatious, but Drake almost dreaded turning to find another of the cooing maids at his side. That the female had been able to sneak up on him at all was a testament to his distraction. With an inward sigh, Drake turned to face the woman.

And stopped dead.

This was no maid. This was a warrior woman, in the grey uniform tunic of the Castleton Guard. She was an enforcer of the law, a keeper of the peace, and she was clearly on duty, though apparently on her dinner break.

She looked tired. There were circles under her pretty grey eyes and a weary set to her shoulders.

"I was saving it just for you, my dear." Drake's charm was automatic and the fire that entered her eyes was his reward. It wasn't a spark of interest, but rather, of battle and Drake was intrigued. He looked at her more closely as she sat next to him at the now-crowded bar.

Her jaw was set in a stubborn line, and her features were strong. Some might say her features were unfeminine, but Drake would not. No, he'd always preferred strong-willed women over the more meek style many men seemed to favor. This girl was beautiful in a harsh sort of way that appealed to him greatly. Sleek muscles moved under her close-fitting tunic and she wore her badge of office with clear efficiency and pride.

She wasn't armed that he could see, but then that didn't mean much. Each of the town's Guards was armed in some way, carrying the weapon or weapons of their choice. For some, that was a sword or even a bow, but others had different specialties. He wondered idly what hers was while he finished off his meal.

The serving girl who'd replaced Devyn behind the bar greeted the woman with a friendly, familiar smile. Apparently this Guardswoman was known to the people in Devyn's employ and welcomed by them. That spoke volumes for her character as far as Drake was concerned. Jinn didn't usually accept outsiders easily. Drake read not only acceptance, but genuine friendship in the serving girl's words and actions toward the other woman. She served up a healthy portion of stew and a lighter beer that would leave the Guard with a relatively clear head after her hearty dinner.

Drake observed, not intruding on the bundle of feminine power sitting next to him while he finished his own meal. She ate with neat manners, though it appeared she was used to rough living, as most warriors were. Often, women didn't choose professions where they would be in the thick of a fight, though there were a good number of female Guards who worked in administrative ways or who dealt specifically with domestic issues and violence against women or female prisoners. This woman, however, showed every sign of being a patrolling Guard—one of the most dangerous of the Guard jobs.

"Quiet night so far?" Drake asked conversationally when it looked like she was finishing up her meal. It had been far smaller than his own, considering her much more petite size. She was trim and lithely muscular in a way that made his mouth water.

She looked at him with resignation and Drake got the distinct impression that she'd rather be left alone. Too bad. He had no intention of leaving the puzzling beauty to her own devices. He wanted to get to know her and then he wanted to bed her. It was that simple.

Suddenly, learning the feel of her body beneath his became of paramount importance. He had little doubt he could charm his way into her bed. He'd perfected his art over five lands, so why should his homeland be any different?

"It was a quiet day," she said with the beginnings of annoyance in her tone. "We've yet to see about the night."

"You've been on duty all day?" Drake was surprised and more than a little alarmed. No wonder she looked so tired. He felt a crazy impulse to protect her from the long and potentially dangerous night ahead.

She nodded wearily. "We're shorthanded with all the new sectors to patrol. Excuse me." Her gaze brightened as she slid from the stool and headed over to the far corner of the big tent. Drake followed her movements, his gaze glued to the enticing roll of her hips. She had a great ass from what he could see and he looked forward to seeing it bare and ready for his desire.

He was so entranced by the way she moved, he almost missed the action going on across the tent. A drunk was getting a little too forward with one of the serving girls. She was struggling to free herself from his groping hands, to no avail. Drake was on his feet and moving across the crowded room before he thought about his actions.

But by the time he got there, the Guardswoman already had the serving girl free and was escorting the unruly drunk outside. Drake followed hot on her heels. He didn't like the look of that drunkard and feared the man might not go peacefully on his way.

He was right. The ruffian was putting up a fight, but his attempts to knock the Guardswoman out were met by neat blocks and counterstrikes meant to disable the big man. But he was drunk and stronger than he ought to be with the pain-deadening effects of strong ale running through his system.

Drake stepped forward, into the man's line of sight. The woman's back was to him as he made sure to get the drunkard's attention with a quick flash of steel. Drake always had a blade or two hidden on his person for situations just like this.

"Clear off, man. This is your last warning." Drake used his trained voice to advantage, projecting to the drunk who'd seemed to give up the fight suddenly. The man's jaw went slack and his eyes grew round with fear as he stumbled away with nary a flicker of complaint.

Drake smiled in satisfaction as the drunk let the Guardswoman be. He felt smug as the woman turned to him, a trace of annoyed respect on her face. Then her eyes widened as she stepped forward.

Drake didn't quite understand why he apparently looked particularly fearsome tonight, but he wasn't asking questions. Whatever it was about him had scared off one ruffian and had the little Guardswoman looking at him with new respect as she moved closer. Moving closer was good. It was, in fact, much better than having her move away. He wanted to get much closer to her before the night was through.

She stopped a few yards from him and raised her gaze upwards as Drake's stomach sank. What a fool he'd been!

"Friend of yours?" Her eyes lit with humor as she stared at a spot well above his head.

Drake followed the woman's gaze upward though he could very well guess what he'd find waiting over his shoulder—or rather who.

"*Jenet.*" He tried to inject sternness into the thoughts he projected to the dragon, but it was no use. "*I thought we agreed I could handle this night's work on my own.*"

"*You said that nonsense, but I never agreed.*"

Drake sighed with exasperation, looking back at the beautiful woman still awaiting an answer.

"Lady Jenet." He made the introductions. "And what is your name, my lovely?"

The Guardswoman snorted with laughter, her easy manner delighting him anew. She looked up at the dragon and bowed low, though there was a smile on her full lips and her gaze never lowered.

"I'm Krysta of the Wayfarer Clan. It's an honor to meet you, Lady Jenet."

So she was Jinn. No wonder she'd been welcomed in Devyn's so easily. But what was she doing working as a Guard? Those answers would come later. He'd make certain of it.

Krysta scored big points with Jenet, Drake could tell, by her respectful words and actions. Dragons dwelt on tradition and respect, and favored humans who showed the same thoughtfulness, whether they could communicate with dragonkind or not.

"*She is very pretty for a human, isn't she, Drake?*"

Drake let the observation pass without comment. Jenet had sounded just a bit too hopeful there—almost like his mother when she was trying to matchmake.

"Wayfarer Clan?" Drake addressed the woman. "I had dealings with Rulu, the old clan leader, several seasons past, but I heard he retired in favor of his daughter, Malin."

"You heard right. Malin is gathering the remainder of our

clan and sending them here. Rulu is already in residence though. He set up camp on the southern boundary."

"I haven't gotten that far yet," Drake admitted with what he hoped was just the right amount of sorrow. "I only arrived today and haven't had a chance to explore yet." He moved a step closer, encouraged when she held her ground. "Perhaps you could give me a personal tour?"

One that he hoped ended in her bed, of course, though he would wait for this special beauty if he had to. Something told him she'd be well worth the time and effort.

"I'm sorry to disappoint you, but I'm on duty," she said in polite tones, though Drake wasn't convinced her words of regret were real. The thought irked him more than it should have, but he was beyond analyzing his strange reactions to this spitfire of a woman.

Krysta found it hard to catch her breath between the gorgeous dragon and the equally devastating man. Oh, she'd heard rumors about Drake of the Five Lands. What red-blooded Jinn woman hadn't, after all? But she'd never seen him in the flesh and had frankly doubted the reports of his charm. She knew now that every word she'd heard was true...and more.

The man was walking, talking, temptation. From the crown of golden blond hair that made her fingers literally itch to run through it, to the hard-muscled thighs that made her think of how he'd fit between hers. The man was dangerous indeed.

Add to that the real concern she'd read in his expression and the way he'd come to help her—though he stood back and let her do her job when it was apparent she could more than hold her own with the drunk troublemaker. She liked that Drake hadn't jumped in and tried to be the big man. Too many male Jinn would have tried something like that and gotten a good piece of her mind for it after the fact. No one underestimated her twice. Unless she wanted them to.

He was looking at her with real interest in his gorgeous blue eyes, but Krysta knew better than to get involved with a man like Drake of the Five Lands. He was a charmer. A seducer of the senses. And while she would enjoy every moment of attention he deigned to bestow, she knew he was the type that would use her and move on.

Krysta had vowed never to let that happen to her again and was wary of glib-tongued Jinn minstrels. Besides, she'd met a very respectable knight who'd shown a marked interest in her just the other day. Sir Mace was a much safer bet than Drake of the Five Lands. He was steadier and equally as handsome, but he didn't have that same unpredictable spark in his eye that made her want to risk all and follow where Drake led. No, Mace was altogether more mature in his outlook on the world. At least that's the impression she got. Only time would tell if her first impressions of the handsome knight would prove true.

But Drake was a known quantity. His reputation had spread far and wide. Krysta knew women from her own clan who'd bedded Drake in the past. They all smiled wistfully whenever his name was mentioned and it was clear he'd left a trail of broken hearts in his wake. Krysta would not be just one more in the long string of his conquests.

Devyn bustled outside to shake her hand just then, relieving her of a need to converse more with Drake. Devyn was grateful for her intervention with the drunk and turned away her coin when she would have paid for her dinner.

"I was in back or I would have tossed that ruffian out on his ear for molesting one of my girls. I thank you for doing the job, Krysta. You're a good woman." Devyn turned, doing a double take as he finally noticed the peachy-golden dragon looking down on the scene from behind Drake's shoulder. "Thank you as well, Drake. And you..." He looked up at the dragon, a little dumbfounded by her silent presence.

Drake came to the man's rescue. "Lady Jenet was just passing by," Drake said with a significant glance at the dragon.

Devyn bowed low with almost humorous respect. "I thank you, Lady Jenet. Please be welcome in my...uh...tavern yard anytime."

The dragon seemed to chuckle, sending a small stream of smoke upwards on the soft currents of night air. Her gaze sparkled and gleamed as she lowered her head in a nod of acknowledgement and Drake laughed.

"You may need to rethink your building plans, my friend, if you invite many more dragons to your door."

Devyn's gaze grew calculating. "I hear the king pays well for any livestock the dragons eat."

"There is a marking system," Drake told the tavern keeper. "If you keep a herd, you mark the ones eligible for the dragons and they will leave the rest of the herd be. It's a system that has worked in this land for generations."

"I've also heard the royal castle is teeming with dragonkind. All the rooms are rumored to be open to them, built on a scale appropriate for their size." Devyn was looking Lady Jenet over from the tip of her tail to the top of her head, obviously noting her size for future reference.

"That I can confirm as truth," Drake agreed. "Dragons are welcome everywhere within the castle."

"How do you know?" Krysta was intrigued enough to challenge the bard's assertions.

His blue-eyed gaze focused on her again and she felt the impact down to her toes. Accompanied by a slow smile, his expression was pure invitation. One she dared not accept.

Drake shrugged. "I grew up there. My fathers are members of the court. Jenet—" Drake reached nonchalantly up to stroke the dragon's glimmering neck with what looked like true affection, "—is my sister, of sorts. I was about five when she hatched."

"Your father is a knight?" Krysta had never heard such whisperings in all the gossip that constantly circulated about Drake.

Again he shrugged, but she could see a slight defensiveness enter his gaze. "Both of them are."

"Both?" Krysta found it hard to hide her surprise. Such things were spoken of, but she'd never met anyone who was part of such a union before.

"Ah, yes." Devyn nodded knowingly, grinning. "I've heard about knights and their mates. Two men share one woman." The older man shook his head. "It seems strange, but I've seen stranger yet in my travels."

"It's not so strange when you consider that few women can live with dragons. Not many are willing to share their lives and their homes with their husbands' dragon partners. Fewer still can communicate with dragonkind." Drake's expression grew shuttered and a bit mysterious. "There are other reasons as well, believe me. The dragons and knights are bonded on a very deep level. That bond affects every aspect of their lives, and their mate's life as well."

"Sir Declan." It came to Krysta in a flash, just who Drake's father must be. "You look just like him. He's your father, isn't he?"

Drake bowed his head in acknowledgment, though he didn't speak. Krysta had seen Sir Declan and his mighty golden dragon, Arlis, when she'd been sworn in as a Guard. They had come to the ceremony, along with their fighting partners, Sir Ren and the lovely red dragon named Lilla. Both knights had a special interest in the Castleton Guard corps and had personally welcomed each of the new recruits. Krysta had been impressed by the men at the time, and the dragons, of course. She thought she'd never see more beautiful creatures, but she'd been wrong. Lady Jenet was even more gorgeous than her parents, if Krysta's suspicions were correct.

Krysta stepped forward to address the dragon. "Your mother and father are Lady Lilla and Sir Arlis. Are they not?"

With a sparkle in her eye, the young female dragon nodded.

"I met them once," Krysta said in reverent tones to the beautiful creature. "You are the perfect blend of their colors. Amazing." Krysta couldn't help the soft note that came into her voice. The dragon before her was truly beautiful. "You're gorgeous, Lady Jenet."

The dragon shocked her by reaching down her big head and butting her with a gentle touch, in the abdomen.

"She likes it when you rub just behind her eye ridges," Drake said helpfully, a smile lighting his sinful eyes as he demonstrated, "like this."

Tentatively, Krysta lifted one hand to stroke the surprisingly smooth scale on the dragon's head. She'd never touched a dragon before and the experience was breathtaking.

"She also thanks you for the compliment, Krysta." Drake's voice was low, for her ears alone. Krysta's gaze shot up to his. With his words he'd just revealed something she doubted many others knew. Drake of the Five Lands could communicate with dragons!

Chapter Four

Drake didn't know what it was about this tough little woman that made it so easy to confide in her. Drake had made his living keeping secrets since he left home as a teen. Why then had he found it so easy to reveal such intimate details about himself to a woman he'd just met?

He'd had long-term lovers who didn't know as much about him. And that's the way he preferred it. Wasn't it?

Why did he suddenly feel an inexplicable longing inside for a woman to share his secrets...especially about Jenet, the most precious member of his family?

The thought rocked him.

"She has pretty manners," Jenet cooed in his mind, *"and not a little power of her own. She is a strong woman, able to hold her own in a fight."*

"Don't get too attached," he warned Jenet, not liking the way his thoughts were churning at all. *"She's only human, after all. You can't keep her as a pet, Jen."*

"And why can't I be friends with her?" Jenet blinked one jeweled eye at him. *"It's not unheard of, you know."*

"Friends?" The thought struck Drake as odd. And alarming.

Drake stopped rubbing the dragon's head as he stepped away. Krysta must have taken it as a sign to withdraw too, as she dropped her hand, but the smile still graced the luscious corners of her lips. Jenet rose a little, but kept her head low enough to be on a level with the humans who all watched her with varying degrees of awe, interest and indulgence.

"I will look into forming a yard," Devyn broke in on his thoughts, "where all those with animals to spare can collect them in one place. Down by the river, so there is also plentiful clean water." The spark of excitement was in the tavern owner's gaze. "This way, dragons who are in too much of a hurry to go out to the fields can stop here, within the city, for a quick snack. What say you to that idea, Lady Jenet?"

The dragon nodded vigorously, negating the need for Drake to betray his ability to hear her words to the barkeep. While it seemed as natural as breathing for Krysta to know one of his deepest secrets, Drake didn't feel the same way about sharing the knowledge with Devyn, old friend or not. Still, he could help the man without divulging his secret ability.

"Dragons enjoy fresh fruit too, like whole melons and bushels of apples. The royal treasury will reimburse you for those kinds of foodstuffs as well." Jenet nodded dutifully. "They like music and entertainment almost as much as we do, and would probably enjoy being included in the tavern itself. And dragons are an excellent heat source, so the increased draft from a larger door would be negated by the presence of a dragon inside during the winter. If they visited, you would need less coal and wood for your fires, that's for sure."

Devyn smiled broadly. "I'm glad to learn this before completion of my new building. We'll have to make an area where a dragon or two can sit inside with us to enjoy an evening's entertainment."

"Having a dragon around will cut down on the disorderly drunks as well, I'm sure," Krysta added with a wink. Her grey eyes sparkled as she gazed at the dragon, seeming unable to look away from Jenet's gleaming hide.

Devyn grinned from ear to ear. "I think you're right, Krysta. I saw how fast that bastard took off once he saw Lady Jenet rising over the scene." The tavern owner chuckled and bowed once more to the dragon. "Again, I thank you for your intervention." He opened his arms to gesture toward everyone in the small party. "All of you. And now, I must see to the rest of my guests. Drake, do you still feel up to a song? I daresay we could contrive an opening in the tent to make room for Lady Jenet. What do you say?"

"I, for one, wouldn't miss this for the world." Jenet's dry commentary was for Drake alone. *"I haven't heard you sing in fifteen years and I won't wait another day. I always loved your songs, Drake."*

"I'm always up for a song, Devyn. You know that." Drake sent the man one of his best smiles as the tavern keeper bowed once more to Jenet and bustled back into his domain. Jenet's words had touched him more than he could say.

He'd been a musical child, encouraged by Ren and his mother, who was also a gifted musician, but Declan thought it a frivolous pursuit and a waste of time. Still, he'd sung Jenet to sleep almost every night, playing the instruments his mother gave him for various occasions. There were few she couldn't play and she taught him all she knew.

Drake had learned much in his travels over the past fifteen years. Something inside him looked forward to showing his family just how good he truly was. That would start tonight, with Jenet, who'd been his best friend in the whole world during his youth. Funny how she fit right back into his life, even after the fifteen-year separation. It was like they'd never been apart.

"I'll sing for you tonight, Jenet." He felt an uncomfortable

43

lump in his throat. "Just for you."

The dragon moved to the side of the large tent where Devyn waited with several big men who were helping him lift the heavy canvas. Reaching out a wing, she made short work of sliding under the fabric, settling herself half in and half out of the big tent. Drake could just imagine what the mostly Jinn audience packed into the room thought about the appearance of a dragon in their midst.

"I should be going." Krysta was already backing away.

"Can't you stay for one song?" He found himself reluctant to let her go.

But she shook her head. "I'm on duty. I only stopped for dinner and now it's back to work." She was rejecting him again. Her smile held true regret this time though, which was a small victory at least.

She moved off down the street and he followed after. "Can I see you again?"

Damn, he hadn't sounded that desperate in years. What happened to Drake the Seducer? He was acting more like Drake the Dunce right now, but she didn't seem to mind. She smiled up at him and there was a new freedom in the lift of her lips that was more open than any smile she'd given him to that point. Perhaps this sharing of his deepest secrets was the key with this particular, special woman.

"I'm certain our paths will cross at some point, Drake of the Five Lands."

So she knew who he was. Suddenly he regretted the reputation he'd cultivated as a ladies' man and playboy. He didn't want her to think badly of him, or that he was just toying with her. This woman—in such a short amount of time—had become something precious to him. He didn't understand it, but he wasn't questioning it just then...at least not much. It was too important to secure a date with her before she disappeared into the night.

He wished he could follow her, but he too had work to do that night. It wouldn't do to disappoint his king on the first mission entrusted to him since his return. How would that look to the eyes of his family? His blood-father, Declan, in particular?

"When?" Drake touched her arm, stroking with a gentle, beseeching touch. "When will I see you again, Krysta? Will you join me for lunch tomorrow? At Devyn's? Or perhaps at the castle? I could give you a tour. You could meet some more dragons."

She laughed and his heart dropped into his stomach. "You don't have to bribe me with dragons, Drake. I enjoyed meeting your friend Jenet. She's lovely. But I have met other dragons before. One in particular, in fact." She stopped walking and turned to face him, true regret in her gaze this time. "I'm lunching with his knight tomorrow, so it wouldn't be fair to encourage you."

"You're involved with a knight?" Drake felt his stomach lurch once more as anger stirred. She couldn't be involved with a knight. Not when he'd given up his chance at that life in favor of his own road. It just wasn't fair.

Krysta shrugged. "A little. I met him a few days ago and we've shared one other meal. He's a cautious man." Her chin lifted. "And I'm a very cautious woman."

Drake lifted one hand to touch her hair. "A very beautiful woman as well." His words were soft as he drew closer, unable to keep from kissing her. She didn't move away, so he pressed his suit, dipping his head to touch his lips to hers. The kiss started out as a calm salute, but quickly escalated to a conflagration as he drew her into his arms.

45

Drake counseled himself to slowness, but his body wanted nothing more than to ravish her. But that wouldn't do. This woman was a warrior, a Guardswoman. She deserved respect. He'd never had a problem controlling himself with women in the past, but Krysta was different. From almost the moment he'd seen her, she'd called to him in a basic, yet complex, way. He wanted her. On many different levels. But he'd deal with the physical first.

She was fire in his arms, soft, womanly and full of spirit as she returned his kiss fully and eagerly. Drake pressed further, sweeping his tongue into her mouth, learning her taste and feel, delighting in the soft whimper that sounded in her throat as he swept his hands down her body, gripping the soft globes of her perfect ass and pulling her against his hardness.

Krysta moved into him as if she'd been made for him, but this had to stop. They were in the middle of a public street and people were waiting for them both to get on with their work. Drake drew back, little by little, though it was one of the hardest things he had ever done. He was breathing hard, just from her kiss, and his cock was as hard as a pike.

The woman packed a punch in more than one way. Drake was gratified to see the sleepy, sensuous look in her eyes as he moved back. She swayed a bit as he held her upright and a grin split his mouth. She was as affected as he was. That was something at least.

"Tell me your knight makes you feel like that and I'll leave you in peace."

Her eyes cleared abruptly and she pulled away.

"I can't tell you that because he hasn't kissed me yet."

Drake didn't like that "yet". If he had his way, the unknown knight would never get a chance to kiss her at all.

"Have lunch with me tomorrow."

"I can't. I made a promise to Sir Mace."

"Mace?" Drake cursed inwardly. He should have known. Any woman he found attractive just had to be spoken for by his childhood friend and rival. And it figured the bastard was a knight now, to boot.

"You know him?"

Drake paced away a bit, trying to hold his tongue. "I knew him as a child. We grew up together."

"Why do I get the idea you weren't friends?"

She saw too clearly, but he didn't want to leave her with the wrong impression. Drake sighed. "We were friends, but I did resent him. Mace was always so perfect, so predictably warrior-like. My father held him up as an example to me more than once and I grew to hate the phrase 'Why can't you be more like Mace?'"

"Oh, that's awful." Krysta placed her hand on his arm and Drake's spirits lifted a bit.

"Awful enough that you'll break your date with him and have lunch with me instead?" He waggled his eyebrows with a teasing grin though he knew her answer already.

Krystal chuckled. "It wouldn't be right. But—" Drake sensed an opening, but waited to hear what she'd propose. "I suppose I could have dinner with you. I'm not working tomorrow. It's my weekly day off."

Drake cursed fate once more. "I'm promised to my parents for dinner tomorrow night and I can't postpone again. I haven't eaten in their home in fifteen years and this promises to be a rather...difficult occasion, or I'd invite you to join us. Hell..." he ran an impatient hand through his shoulder-length hair, "...I'd love for you to come just to act as a buffer between me and them, but that's the coward's way out." He sighed. "I may be many things, but never a coward."

47

She smiled and the look in her pretty eyes was kind. "I've heard that about you, Drake, and I respect your reasoning. Perhaps another time."

"When?" He pounced verbally as she turned to go once more. "How about breakfast the day after tomorrow? Before you have to be at work."

She laughed as she moved off down the dimly lit street. "If you're up at dawn, meet me at Pritchard's Inn on the High Road in Castleton. All right?"

Drake whistled through his teeth as he watched her walk off. "It's a date, sweetheart. You can count on it."

"I won't hold my breath, but if you do show up, I won't throw you out either."

Drake watched her walk away, enjoying the sway of her hips and remembering the feel of her generous curves in his hands. She was explosive in his arms and he looked forward to feeling more of her fire. But first he had a job to do.

When she was out of sight, he turned back to the tavern and collected himself before entering. He could hear a lot of talk about the dragon now seated comfortably under one flap of the huge tent. People were throwing apples to Jenet as he entered, and she caught them in mid air with a resounding chomp that seemed to delight the crowd made up mostly of newly arrived Jinn.

"Enjoying yourself, milady?" Drake couldn't help but tease her. Like him, Jenet had always loved to be the center of attention wherever she went. Being such an odd, lustrous color had a lot to do with her notoriety of course, but her sweet, outgoing nature was just as important in her popularity with humans and dragons alike.

"These apples are tasty," she agreed as she plucked another one out of mid air.

Drake went to the bar and retrieved his lute from Devyn, taking a moment to unpack it from its traveling case and tune the strings. As usual, the crowd became aware of the imminent entertainment and he heard whispers as his name made the rounds of the tables. The excitement level in the room rose a notch as he moved to the space cleared next to Jenet. It was clear these folk weren't entirely comfortable with her in the room and had left her a wide area that was just perfect for his stage.

Shocking the assembly with his audacity, Drake seated himself on Jenet's bent knee, close in near the sinuous column of her neck. No one but Devyn knew of their prior relationship, and Drake trusted the older man not to speak of it unless he was specifically told it was all right to do so.

Drake started with a few runs on his lute, limbering up his fingers and teasing the audience to silence with the soft music. Jenet's ears perked up and a toothy grin lit her dragonish face. It was an expression Drake knew well, though few of the others in the room were able to read the face of a dragon as well as he.

When the room was silent, Drake began to sing. All his songs that night were for Jenet. He'd written many over the years with her in mind, and tonight she would hear them all. He'd stored up fifteen years' worth of tunes that he wanted to share with her, some that had become famous throughout the Five Lands he'd called home for far too long.

The crowd recognized many of the tunes and clapped or tapped their feet along with his rhythm. A few Jinn musicians even found enough courage to approach the cleared area around Jenet and set up their instruments to join in.

After twenty minutes, Drake had a regular little band formed complete with drums, pipes, flute and another lute as well as a young girl with a bell-like voice who sang clear, pure harmony with him. The tavern was packed to capacity and all within were clearly enjoying the rare talent of the Jinn musicians as they performed songs Drake had written and made famous.

Drake sang for Jenet and she seemed to love every moment of it. He could tell by her sparkling eyes and mobile facial features when a poignant line in one of his songs touched her tender heart, or when one of his little musical jokes struck her funny bone. The other musicians became more at ease with her presence as well, as did the inn's patrons, though few dared go any nearer than just a few feet away from her scaled body.

"So what do you think?" Drake couldn't help but ask after the first few songs. Jenet had been surprisingly quiet, listening intently, judging by the slight mobility of her ears.

"You were always gifted, Drake, but you are world-class now. I've heard some of these songs before. Traveling minstrels have played them for us in the castle from time to time, but I had no idea...I mean... You wrote them, didn't you?"

Drake felt a little uncomfortable. Jenet was never hesitant in her speech, except when she was emotionally overwrought. He didn't want to be responsible for making her sad or upset. He answered carefully. *"I wrote them, sweetheart."*

"Oh, Drake!" Jenet took a moment, raising her head a bit as she shifted just slightly. Drake knew it was a sign of her distress and his heart seized.

"What is it, honey? You know you can tell me anything."

Her jeweled eyes rolled back down to meet his gaze. *"You're even more famous than I thought you were, aren't you? You truly have a life in the lands beyond. Without me."* Her tone was flat, somewhat defeated, and Drake hated the sound of it, but was powerless to contradict the truths she spoke. *"I'm so proud of you, Drake. I knew no matter where you went or what you did, you'd succeed. Though I often wished I'd been able to go with you on your adventures. But a dragon's place is here, in Draconia. No matter how many times I contemplated flying off to find you, our parents reminded me it just wasn't that simple."*

"Oh, baby. I wish you could've come with me too. But I had to do it on my own. I had to learn who I was, outside of the duty I could never fulfill. I had to make my own way."

"I'm sorry you saw it that way, Drake. Truly."

The crowd cheered as the instrumental tune they were playing came to an end and Drake moved quickly into the introduction for a new song. He couldn't win this argument with his words, but perhaps he could express his feelings in one of the many songs he'd written over the years to explain the things he'd learned on the lonely road he'd chosen. The other musicians followed his lead and some of the crowd seemed to recognize the opening bars of one of his most poignant tunes. Sighs met the first clear notes of his voice as he sang the opening bars.

And he sang his song, "The Golden Beauty", finally, for the dragon he'd written it for, all those years ago.

When the song ended, the crowd was hushed for a long, sweet moment while the last clear notes rang through the room. Then a cheer erupted, louder than all that had come before, and coins were tossed toward the wide-brimmed hat one of the other musicians had placed on the floor in front of the make-shift group.

"'The Golden Beauty' isn't about a human woman, Jenet." Drake wanted her to know the truth. *"I wrote that song—and many others—just for you."*

Jenet sighed, a fine mist of cinnamony smoke wafting into the air above their heads as Drake saw her struggle with her emotions. When she reached down to butt him in the chest with her snout, soft chuckles came from a few in the crowd, but when a single, magical tear leaked from her eye to land in his palm, the crowd was silenced. This was magic. True magic, in their midst.

The dragon gifted him with the rarest of the rare—a tiny bit of her magic made real—a gem of the finest quality. A fire opal that flashed like the faceted fire in her eyes.

Drake was very conscious of the crowd sharing this special moment with them. He was still the Spymaster of the Jinn, and he had a reputation to uphold.

He displayed the rare gem, holding it up to the crowd. "A kingly gift for a poor troubadour." Drake stood and bowed low to the dragon. "I thank you, Lady Jenet, from the bottom of my heart."

Jenet bowed her head as well. *"You play nicely to the crowd, Drake. I loved your song. Almost as much as I love you."*

"And I you, sweetheart. No matter where I go or what I do, you are always in my heart."

Chapter Five

Mace was a handsome fellow, if a bit quiet. Krysta had taken to him right away, and enjoyed the solid camaraderie of the knight who seemed wise beyond his years. She guessed he was about the same age as she, but his eyes seemed older somehow. Perhaps, she thought not for the first time, there was some truth to the rumors about knights and how they stopped aging when they bonded with their dragon partners.

It was a well-known fact in Castleton that the royal family and the dragon knights outlived other people by many years, if they weren't killed in battle first. There was a price to pay for the added years—if you lived to see them. The price was a life-long duty to the dragons and the land named for them. A life-long promise to protect and serve Draconia's inhabitants.

But the trade off wasn't too bad. Increased lifespan and a dragon to call friend and partner. No, Krysta thought that was a pretty good deal, and if she'd been born male and had the ability to bespeak dragons, she'd pray to the mother goddess every night to grant her a dragon partner of her own. As it was, Krysta was female and not of this land she'd come to call home. It was highly unlikely she would discover a rogue gift of dragon speech at this late date, and even if she did, women were never chosen to be knights, no matter how skilled with a sword.

All in all, she didn't mind, though upon meeting Nellin,

Mace's dragon partner, she felt a pang of longing for the close bond she could sense between the two males. Wherever Mace went, Nellin was not far behind. Even now, while Mace and she enjoyed lunch in the small cafe, Nellin lounged outside in the square, entertaining curious children with puffs of warm air and waggling his wings to make them laugh. He was good with little ones in a way she hadn't expected. Who knew a fearsome fighting dragon could have a playful, almost paternal side?

"Nellin gets silly around children," Mace said, following the path of her gaze out the small window to the dragon. Mace seemed almost embarrassed, misunderstanding her interest.

"I think it's charming. I mean, it's obvious he can be fierce with such sharp talons and his large size, but I had no idea he could be gentle like that. I'm frankly amazed and altogether enchanted by him."

"You hear that?" Nellin said into Mace's mind, clearly eavesdropping with his keen dragon senses. *"She finds me enchanting."* Smug satisfaction filled his playful tone. *"Now if only she found you at least interesting, we might make a go of this."*

"Leave off, Nellin. Let me court her in my own way." Mace fought to suppress the annoyance he felt at Nellin's interference from showing on his face. Krysta didn't know how closely he and the dragon were linked, and he didn't want to scare her off just yet. She was far too lovely, too intriguing, too sexy, to let her scurry away from him and his dragon partner on the first date.

"Courting? Is that what you're doing? Could have fooled me."

"Everybody's a critic."

The serving boy came over to ask if they wanted a sweet roll to follow their meal and Krysta declined, opting instead for a hot drink. Mace held up a finger to indicate he'd have the same and the youngster left. Seizing the moment, Mace thought himself daring when he leaned across the table and took Krysta's hand in his.

"I've really enjoyed this lunch with you, Krysta."

"Whoa, a little too intense there, friend," Nellin coached him from the square. *"Ease off before you scare her."*

But Krysta smiled and folded her other hand over his. "I've enjoyed it too, Mace."

He rubbed his thumb lightly over her skin, liking the way she shivered and her smile deepened. He could have sworn her eyes even twinkled, but perhaps that was a trick of the afternoon sun, and his own overactive imagination.

"Enough to do it again? I mean," he stumbled a bit, "would you share another meal with me? Tomorrow, or the next day, perhaps? I really want to see you again."

She nodded, the lovely smile still in place on her plump lips, and his heart lifted. "I'd like that, but I'm on duty all day tomorrow. How about the day after? I could meet you for lunch again. Or dinner."

"Dinner!" Nellin counseled. *"After dinner you can take her for a moonlit stroll or a night flight, if she's game."*

"Dinner would be perfect. Shall we come for you at sunset? Nellin and I know a great little inn on the outskirts of Castleton where he can have as good a time as us, chasing his dinner with the other dragons who frequent the place."

"Pushing it, don't you think?" Nellin's worried voice sounded in Mace's mind. *"What if she's still afraid of me?"*

"She's not. You should see the way she looks at you. She wants to keep you as a pet, Nel. Trust me on this."

"You mean...ride on the dragon's back with you?"

Mace liked the way her eyes lit up as she shifted her gaze back to where Nellin lay, lounging in the sun with his flock of childish admirers.

"If you're not afraid. As you can see, Nellin and I are pretty much a pair. Where I go, he's usually not far behind." Mace tried to look sheepish, but the excitement in her gaze reassured him that his fears on this topic at least, had been unfounded.

"I'm not afraid of dragons," she said, and he inwardly crowed. "I haven't been around them much, I'll admit, but I'm not afraid of them. I'm actually kind of fascinated by them, I think." She turned to look straight at Mace with those lovely grey eyes of hers. "I'd love to fly with you and Nellin, if he's willing to carry me."

"Do you have to be anywhere this afternoon?" Mace pounced.

She shook her head. "I was just going to do some chores. Washing and such. But that can wait."

"Then how about we get the proprietor to pack two sweet rolls and some mead for us, and Nellin can fly us out to a little meadow we know where there's a nice shady grove by a bend in the river. We can have our dessert picnic style."

"And the little lady can get to know us better. Oh, you are much more nimble than I gave you credit for, Mace. Good work." Nellin's congratulatory words sounded in Mace's mind.

"I think that would be amazing. I'd love to go with you and Nellin." Once again Krysta peered out the window to the square, her gaze lighting on the reclining dragon with both admiration and awe. Mace thought it was a very good start indeed.

Who was this knight, after all? Just when Krysta thought

she had Mace figured out, he surprised her. She'd just about decided he was shy and somewhat staid when out of the blue he suggested a spontaneous picnic by the river and a dragon flight to get there. He'd surprised her in a totally wonderful way.

Not that she didn't like steady men. Krysta actually craved a bit of solidity after the years she'd spent roaming with her Jinn family, but there was something to be said for spontaneity as well. Still, she would never have pegged Mace for the type to come up with such a plan, and it thoroughly enchanted her.

He was such a dear man. So thoughtful and strong in character. That a dragon such as Nellin had chosen him spoke volumes about his commitment to duty and to serving the people and dragons of this land. All knights were special men, but Krysta had felt drawn to Mace from the moment she'd first seen him.

Tall, dark and handsome with a solid build and muscles that hinted at enormous strength, he had kind eyes and a tender manner with his dragon partner and his friends. He also moved well, like a well-trained warrior should, and she admired the fluidity of his steps. He'd be an excellent fighter...and a talented lover, if she were any judge.

They finished their after-meal drinks while the proprietor packed up dessert for them and Mace tipped the woman well for her good service. Within minutes, they were heading out into the square. To the waiting dragon.

Nellin rose to his haunches as Mace made the introductions. They'd met formally once before at the Guard House, but it had been a rushed occasion with many others around. This time, Krysta was well aware of the dragon's scrutiny as she bowed politely and he lowered his head in return.

"I'm pleased to see you again, Sir Nellin. Thank you for

consenting to let me fly with you and Sir Mace."

Mace cocked his head, smiling, apparently listening to the dragon before he turned to her. "Nellin says he likes your dress much better than your uniform, though the grey of the Guard's tunic does match your eyes." He looked over at the dragon. "Really, Nel. I never knew you were so keen on fashion." Krysta chuckled as Mace teased his dragon partner. "He also says he's happy to show you what it's like to fly." Mace winked at her. "He likes taking first-timers up in the sky. We spend a lot of our days off ferrying children around to give them a taste of the air currents. It's one of his favorite things to do, since he loves flying and feels sorry for those of us who don't have wings of our own."

Mace's tone was joking, but Krysta recognized the truth behind the teasing. With another bow, she addressed the dragon. "I think it's a beautiful thing to do. We who have no wings thank you, Sir Nellin."

Mace chuckled as Nellin dropped down to all fours so he could mount. "Save that for after you've been aloft. Some people hate it, while others can't get enough. We'll soon find out what kind you are." Mace swung up onto the dragon's back with practiced ease and held out a hand for her. "Use his elbow as a stepladder," he advised.

Krysta took Mace's big hand and stepped on the dragon's bent front limb. His scales were slippery under the leather of her boot, but solid and firm. Boosting up with the help of Mace's strong grip, she found herself seated before the knight, just over the dragon's shoulder, where his long neck met his wide body, the gorgeous wings stretching out behind. Already, she felt more alive than she ever had, but whether it was the dragon beneath her or the hard-muscled embrace of the man behind her, she knew not. Mace was proving to be every bit as exciting and unexpected as his dragon partner.

Still waters did indeed run deep with this complex man. Krysta couldn't wait to discover all his hidden facets.

Flying on the dragon's back was like nothing Krysta had ever experienced before. She'd thought she might feel a bit insecure with little to hold onto, but the ridge where shoulder met neck on the dragon made a natural saddle that felt more secure than she would have credited. Mace's strong arms around her added to the feeling of surety and Nellin flew with obvious care not to frighten her.

"What do you think?" Mace raised his voice to be heard over the rushing air as they leveled out over the city.

"This is amazing!" Krysta drank in the incredible view of the city far below, the maze of streets and lanes resolving into an intricate web from above. "It's beautiful!"

Mace pointed out a few of the sights as Nellin did a quick tour past the castle. Krysta saw things she never would have noticed—little architectural details that were only visible from the air—dragon perches, carved reliefs on the side of the great walls and hewn into the mountain itself on which the castle was built.

Awe filled her both at her first flight, and also at the beauty of the landscape and city spread out before her. She marveled at the chaotic symmetry of the city plan and realized for the first time the thought that had gone into its design both from a defensive stance, and an artistic point of view.

Before long though, they headed out along the curves of the river toward the meadow where Mace promised her a shady grove of trees awaited. The sun shone stronger against her skin now that she flew closer to it and the shade of those trees sounded delightful. The scent of the sweet rolls also wafted up from the small pouch the innkeeper had given them and it was very tempting. Krysta had always had something of a sweet tooth, but rarely had time or money to indulge.

"Hold on tight, now. The landings can be jarring with two aboard," Mace warned her as Nellin made his descent and his arms tightened around her waist, pulling her even closer against his hard-muscled chest.

The man was built like a warrior should be—hard where it counted but flexible. Krysta's mouth went dry as she contemplated the very real, thick hardness against her backside when the abrupt descent of the dragon threw her back against Mace. He was aroused.

Krysta tucked that information away with an inward grin, happy she wasn't the only one affected by the nearness. Mace smelled so good, she'd been salivating since the moment he'd pulled her up in front of him. And his arms felt so right around her. Not to mention his devastating masculinity, intelligence and hidden depths. He was a complete package and Krysta was more than attracted to him. She was perilously close to becoming hopelessly enamored of the young knight.

Nellin landed with a lighter step than she had expected and all too soon, Mace was hopping down. He turned back, reaching up to catch her as she too dismounted and she liked the way he held her against his hard body for just a moment. He wasn't fresh, but he was letting her know in subtle ways that he was as attracted as she was.

He was taking things slow, which suited her at the moment. Krysta had commitments to the Jinn he would need to understand and accept if she decided to take him as a lover. It didn't appear Mace knew much about the Jinn and she'd have to educate him a bit before this went any farther, but for the moment she was truly enjoying his slow, almost shy seduction.

It was altogether sweet and something she hadn't experienced in far too long.

Mace made her feel feminine. And treasured.

Krysta hadn't felt either of those sensations in years. It was only right to take a moment to bask in this honorable man's flattering attentions. There was time enough yet to grab him by the hair, wrestle him down to the ground and have her wicked way with him.

All in good time.

Mace didn't know exactly what was going on behind those lovely grey eyes, but he liked Krysta's reactions to Nellin and flying with the dragon for the first time. If Mace wanted to get serious with a woman, it was vital she accept his dragon partner. And Mace wanted to get very serious, indeed, with Krysta.

She was a woman of many facets and he liked each one he'd so far seen. She was a warrior, but she had a quiet femininity that appealed to him on a basic level. She didn't compete with men like so many female warriors always seemed to feel the need to do. No, Krysta was comfortable in her own skin, confident of her superior abilities and secure in her femininity.

The result was all too attractive for Mace to ignore. This was a woman to be admired—and won. Mace wanted to win her heart in the worst possible way. He wanted her as his lover, but if the Mother of All were smiling on him, he would have her also as his life partner. His wife.

Nellin liked her and she appeared to get along with the dragon. Now it was up to Mace to court her and pray that she found room in her heart for him, his dragon partner, and whoever Nellin's eventual mating brought into the circle of their family. For to be a knight's mate meant the woman must accept two knights into her life, and her bed.

It was the way of dragons and knights, though it was often difficult for women who hadn't been born and raised in Draconia to understand or accept. Still, Krysta was an exceptional woman in all ways. Perhaps she'd be more open to the idea than other women not of this land. Mace could only hope...and pray.

They sat on the soft moss under the promised leafy branches of a small grove of trees. From their vantage point they could see the lazy current of the river and hear its gentle trickling sounds. They could also see the meadow that was overgrown with colorful and fragrant wildflowers. The scent of the blossoms floated sweetly on the gentle breeze that soughed through the trees overhead.

The afternoon was perfect. It was magic.

Nellin rolled in the meadow, enjoying the idyllic setting in his own way, skipping through the river for a while, chasing and catching a few fish that he quickly gobbled up. Mace watched Krysta watch the dragon. All the signs were favorable. She seemed truly interested and not the least bit frightened of Nellin, which was all to the good.

"What made you want to be a knight?"

Krysta's words came to him out of the blue, it seemed, so intent had he been on his own observations.

"Nellin, of course. It's the dragon's choice. If the man can hear dragons, he is eligible, but the dragons choose who they will from the available candidates. Not all who can hear dragons become knights, though most do." Mace leaned back on one elbow, twirling a long stalk of grass between his fingers. "My fathers are knights and I grew up in the Castle Lair. Being like my fathers—being a knight—was all I ever wanted."

"You have two fathers?" Krysta seemed interested and Mace took it as a good sign. This was one of the most important things he had to reveal to her before taking this relationship any further.

"Well, Jir is my blood-father. I look just like him. But Kinnar is no less my father. They both raised me and I love and respect them both." He tried to be nonchalant, but this was the crux of it and he watched her expression carefully. "When dragons mate, their knights are caught up in the frenzy. It's the bond, you see. The bond between knight and dragon is very close and what one feels, the other inevitably feels as well. Which is why fighting dragons are not permitted to mate until their knights find a mate of their own."

"I've heard a little bit about this, but I'll admit I'm curious as to how a three-partnered relationship works."

Mace breathed just a tiny bit easier. She was curious. That was good.

"It works very well, indeed, and has for centuries in this land. It's the dragons that tie it all together and they claim the Mother of All plays a very large role in bringing the right people and dragons together." He trailed the grass stalk slowly down her arm as she leaned back just a few feet away. "When the dragons choose their mates, the knights form a fighting partnership as well. The two men train together and fight together, with their dragons, from that point on. They also share their mate."

"One woman for two knights?"

She didn't seem shocked, merely intrigued, which lifted Mace's spirits to a new level. He nodded in answer to her question, trying to hide his growing excitement. "One woman to share the love of two knights who will be devoted to her for the rest of their lives."

"Does it always work out so well?"

Mace shrugged. "Almost always. There are few unhappy trios in the Lair, and those that do have disagreements always seem to find a way to work it out when the dragon side of the family takes to the sky in a mating flight." He chuckled, remembering some of the more amusing instances of arguments being settled in just that way.

Mace was teasing her senses. He had a subtle way about him, vastly different from the in-your-face seduction of Drake. It was refreshing, but both men stirred her senses almost beyond bearing. Mace was a deep pool of dark water compared to Drake's bubbling clear brook, but the more she got to know of Mace, the more she wanted to know. He was intriguing, mysterious and altogether sexy.

He had a warrior's body and a strategist's mind. His conversation impressed her, and the attention he paid to her comfort was oddly endearing. Jinn women were protected, but seldom coddled. As a woman warrior, it had been a very long time indeed since Krysta had been taken care of with such solicitude. It ought to have annoyed her, but instead it made her feel intensely feminine in a way that was foreign to her.

Perhaps she'd spent too many years fighting and training. She feared she was losing her femininity as the years wore on, but one look from Mace's admiring gaze and all her fears were put to rest. Add Drake's rather obvious interest and Krysta was flying high on a wave of feminine confidence the likes of which she hadn't felt since she was a teen, newly discovering her female power.

Mace surprised her by leaning closer, his mouth hovering near hers. She sensed he was giving her the opportunity to deny him, but she had no intention of doing so. Reaching up, she wrapped one palm around the nape of his neck and drew him closer. Her gaze zeroed in on his firm lips, knowing what she wanted and knowing too that she'd soon have it.

She wanted Mace's kiss. She wanted to know his flavor and his passion. She wanted him like she'd wanted few men in her life, and now was the moment of discovery. Would he be as good a kisser as she hoped? Would he be as good a kisser as Drake?

Krysta tried to erase that last thought and concentrate on Mace, but it was there, niggling in the back of her mind, even as Mace's lips descended the final distance to hers. He was warm and firm, and his hot body crowded close as he pulled her into his arms. His lips pressed, then opened, and his tongue rubbed over the seam of her lips before she opened to let him in.

The feeling was incredible. Her hands went to his strong shoulders and drew him closer. All tentativeness was gone as he lowered her to the ground, his chest rubbing seductively over hers, his tongue tangling with hers, his body making hers sing. Mace was all man and all powerful. Any idea she might have harbored that he was just the slightest bit inexperienced was wiped away forever by the way he took command of her body and her senses.

He kissed like a dream. His hands were gentle but firm as he stroked over her, working at the ties of her simple dress to bare the skin beneath. He moved with deliberate slowness, giving her every chance to object, but Krysta had no intention of stopping him. What he was doing felt too damn good.

She slid her hands under the hem of his shirt, dragging upward to caress the sinewy muscles of his rock-solid abdomen. She felt powerful when his abs clenched under her exploring fingers and he pulled back, breaking their kiss.

"Do you want more?" His gaze mesmerized as he looked down at her.

Krysta licked her lips, liking the way his gaze followed the movement of her tongue. Smiling, she nodded with deliberate, seductive motions.

"I'll let you know if I want you to stop."

"I don't think I can take much more, milady. You're very potent." Mace tugged her closer, setting his hard thighs between hers on the soft, mossy ground.

"I can take all you've got, Sir Knight." She stroked his cheek with one hand. Boldly, she rocked her hips against his, loving the way he fit—even with their clothing still between them—into the notch of her legs. He felt huge and very hard, and she wanted that hardness inside her.

It had been too long since any man had made her feel this way. It had been years since Krysta's last intimate encounter, in fact. After the broken heart she'd suffered as a young girl, she kept her liaisons short and as unemotional as possible, preferring to concentrate on her work rather than the Jinn rogues who were constantly in her path.

Mace however, was a different story. The man was solid in every way. Grounded, mature, rock hard in all the right places, but still he had a sense of adventure and unexpected humor. He intrigued her and made her want to risk her heart—just a little—for the first time in years. She knew he was courting her with an eye to the future. Knights didn't bother coaxing short-term bedmates into accepting their dragon partners. No, this whole afternoon was a sure sign Sir Mace had a longer-term relationship in mind, and Krysta didn't mind that one bit.

She just plain liked Mace, and Nellin too. She wanted a steady man in her life now that she'd finally found a permanent home in Draconia and a place to use the skills she'd honed as a warrior of the Jinn. She was planting roots and making a home. If her new life in Draconia included Mace, so much the better.

She could do a lot worse than hook up with a knight like him.

"Are you sure?" Mace searched her eyes.

Krysta pushed his shirt off over his shoulders, drawing him down to meet her lips. "I'm certain, Mace. Make love to me."

The words were music to his ears. He hadn't planned on seducing her this afternoon, but she felt so right in his arms, he couldn't help himself. He wanted to take things slow, but his heart and body recognized its mate and it didn't want to wait.

Neither, apparently, did she.

Krysta tugged at his clothes and Mace pulled away long enough to rid himself of his boots. When he reached for her once more, she'd shucked her own soft, lace-up boots and he got his first glimpse of her shapely, bare calves.

He rubbed his hands over her lean, muscular legs, raising the skirt of her simple dress higher and higher. Her skin was so soft. Mace didn't think he'd ever experienced anything headier than the womanly scent of her or the strong muscles beneath her delicate, feminine skin. She was a wonder.

His lips trailed after his hands, kissing his way up from her ankles to her hip. He pushed the dress and undertunic up and away, taking it over her head and tossing it aside as he got his first look at her naked form.

She was lovely. Just incredibly lovely.

All the long hours of training showed in the sleek, lean muscles of her arms, legs and abdomen, but nothing could disguise the curves he found so appealing. Mace had never lain with a warrior woman before and after seeing her, he knew there was no going back.

Krysta was it for him. Possibly for the rest of his life.

Mace tucked that thought away as he moved over her. His

palms fit perfectly over her generous curves. He kissed her deeply as he learned her form by touch, his hands finally coming to rest on her surprisingly large breasts. She was perfect. Round, soft and peaking for him. Her nipples poked into his palms as she moaned against his mouth.

He dueled with her mobile tongue as his fingers teased hard nipples, drawing another light sound of pleasure from her lips. He was greedy. He wanted it all. Her sighs, her groans...her screams of passion. And he would have it, he vowed, or die trying.

His lips trailed down her neck, pausing here and there to nip and suck as she writhed against him. When his teeth raked her nipple, she lifted off the ground and Mace couldn't help but smile. She was very responsive. He liked that in a woman.

"You're beautiful, Krysta." He looked up into her eyes as his lips closed over one nipple and sucked with steady pressure. Her gaze was half-lidded, drugged with passion. He'd never seen anything sexier in his life.

"Mace!" She whispered his name over and over as he tongued her, his hands moving lower to tease the wet folds that waited. Her legs spread without much urging. She was eager and very nearly ready, which was good. Mace didn't think he could wait much longer himself.

"I want to make this good for you." Releasing her nipple, he moved down her body, to the apex of her strong thighs. Her eyes widened, but she made no move to stop him as he spread her wide, his blunt fingers sliding through the slick folds. She was excited, but he'd make her more so. He watched, rapt, as his finger skated around the opening to her body, pushing inward. It was a tight fit. Much tighter than he was used to. The thought gave him pause as a triumphant feeling of possession raged through him. Krysta wasn't a light skirt, giving her body to any man that asked. It had been a while since she'd had a lover judging by the slow yielding of her passage.

Mace would have to be careful at first, until she adapted to his girth. He wasn't a small man and he didn't want to hurt her.

No, pain was the furthest thing from his mind as he watched his finger disappear into her. She was wet, but he wanted her wetter. He needed to taste her cream and know every detail about her gorgeous body. Dipping his head, he licked at the little nubbin poking out of her folds, smugly satisfied when she jolted at the first, light contact of his tongue. Going back for another pass, he swept deeper this time, licking her cream and learning her taste.

She was divine.

He played with her that way for a few minutes, while his finger began to move, sliding in and out, building a rhythm and stroking her higher. Finally, he lowered his lips and latched onto her clit, sucking and using his tongue. It took only a few moments of this treatment for her to come beautifully against his mouth, drenching his finger with her release.

He sat back, watching carefully as he added another finger, stretching her wider. She'd have to be as ready as possible to take him without discomfort.

"Did you like that?" he teased.

"You know I did." Her voice was breathy with release. "Take off your leggings, Mace. I want to see you."

He'd left himself covered for good reason. He didn't want to scare her off as a few maids had been in the past. He also didn't think he would last long once he got his leggings off. He'd wanted her to be ready before he gave in to the incredible desire riding him.

"I want to lick you." Her low words sent a jolt through his cock. He knew he'd never last if she came anywhere near him this time. He was too needy.

"Hold that thought, sweet. Next time you can do anything you want, but right now, I'm too close to the edge." His gaze burned into hers as he felt her passions rise once more. Little movements of her hips told him she was eager for his possession. Soon, she would be ready. "I want to be inside you when I come. I want to feel you around me, milking my cock."

"I want that too." She moaned as he continued to tease her. She was very nearly ready. All he could think of was sinking into her and he knew he could wait no more.

Mace worked the lacings on his leggings, pushing them down and away. His cock sprang free, aiming for the place it most wanted to go.

"Are you with me, love?" He rose over her, tucking himself into the notch of her splayed thighs.

"Come into me now, Mace. I want you." She tugged on his shoulders as he lowered himself onto her...and into her.

She moaned as he took possession with slow, steady pressure, being careful to ease his way with short movements as he claimed her with his body. She was tighter than a fist and Mace knew he'd never felt anything like the clasp of her warm body. She was heaven itself.

Settling finally all the way inside, Mace took just a moment to enjoy the grip of her inner walls against his most sensitive skin. He dropped lower, bracing himself on his forearms as he leaned in to kiss her. Mirroring the slow stabbing movements of his tongue in her mouth, he began to move within her hot sheath as she writhed and moaned against him.

She was a vocal little thing and he loved every soft whimper from her elegant throat. He nipped at her lips, kissing his way down her body as his cock took over, demanding he fill her harshly, mark her and claim her as his woman. He was a little afraid of the powerful emotions riding him, but Krysta seemed to want as much as he would give.

This then, was how it felt to be with your mate. Mace knew for certain at that moment, he was looking at his destiny—if he could convince her to accept him—and Nellin. He would do all in his power to secure her agreement, and her love. He wanted her to love him, and Nellin, and eventually, the knight who was partner to Nellin's mate.

But all that could wait.

For now, he was experiencing the best sex of his life with a warm, willing woman. All thoughts fled as he sped his pace, gauging her reactions. She was eager for more, if the tugging on his shoulders was any clue. Her short nails dug into his skin and he liked it.

"More, Mace! Harder!" She whispered her need near his ear.

He gave her what they both wanted, speeding toward a hard, fast climax that sent them both into the sky. Crying out, he clung to her as his body seized with an orgasm unlike any he'd felt before, coming in her tight depths with pulsating spurts that went on and on, draining him and elating him at the same time. He lifted enough to watch her, ecstatic that he could read her gasping satisfaction on her beautiful face.

"Krysta," he sighed her name as he began the slow journey back to earth. Her hands rubbed at his back even as her sheath continued to contract around him in shimmers of delight. He'd heard her call out his name when she came and it was a sound he'd never forget.

At length when he pulled back, she was smiling. The beauty of her stole his breath as she touched his face.

"Thank you, my love." He kissed her with gentle motions, sated and fulfilled as he'd never been before.

"I think I should be thanking you." Her light skin flushed.

"That was incredible."

He chuckled and kissed her again. "For me too. Want to do it again?"

Chapter Six

Drake took the stairs to the Lair wing of the castle with a heavy heart. This part of the mountain fortress was where he'd been born and raised, among the knights and dragons that crowded the massive halls of the public areas. He saw many people he recognized from his youth though few now recognized him. Still, many did double-takes as he passed and he knew it was because he looked so like his blood-father.

He walked quickly, not allowing himself to be drawn into conversation with any of those who looked at him with questions in their eyes. Let them wonder. The evening ahead would be tough enough without questions from well-meaning childhood acquaintances to delay the inevitable confrontation between himself and Sir Declan.

Drake turned purposefully into the hall that led to the knights' and dragons' private quarters. This hall was one of many in the huge Lair, but Drake knew it well. This way led home.

He arrived in front of the massive entranceway much sooner than he could have wished. Drake stood a moment, taking in the ornate door inset with carved, painted dragons—representations of Lilla and Arlis, the red and gold dragons who lived within the large suite. It was beautiful work, done by one of the knights who'd been apprenticed as a young boy to a fine woodcarver before being chosen—much to his surprise—as a knight. He'd done it as a gift and much of his work now graced the already elegant castle. It was his hobby now, though it brought great joy to his friends and other recipients of his majestic gifts.

All of the family names were carved into the beautiful door. Drake stared at his own name for long moments...and the name directly next to his. Jenet.

There was room for more in the design, presumably for when Jenet chose a partner and mated. Drake had always wished deep in his heart of hearts it would be his name, linked with Jenet's as her knight partner.

But those were foolish, boyhood dreams. He loved Jenet too much to saddle her with a knight who was nowhere near good enough to even be a knight. No, Drake had learned well that his talents lay elsewhere. He was a grand spy, a lauded bard, and an all-around magnificent sneak. The more knightly skills were not for him. He'd left most of them behind when he left through this very door fifteen years before.

Drake had grown and changed a lot since then. He'd become comfortable in his skin, learning who he was without the specter of his blood-father looming large over his shoulder in everything he did. It had been rough at first, but Drake was satisfied now with the way it had all turned out. All...except for Jenet.

She was an ache in his heart that had never healed. Now, being near her again, he felt the happiness that had been missing from his life for so long. Now he felt complete. And it was entirely too dangerous a feeling.

He knew he still had to let her go when he left once more. This time though, the pain of separation just might kill him. He didn't want to make it any harder on her, so he had to keep his distance. It was the only way to protect her.

"Are you going to stand there all day, or work up the nerve to actually go in?" Lilla's amused voice sounded through Drake's mind. He turned his head to find the giant dragon who had been a second mother to him had somehow managed to sneak up on him in the wide hall. He'd been so distracted he'd been unaware of the massive creature's approach.

"I'm not sure, Mama Lil." Drake shook his head, chuckling at himself.

"It won't be so bad," Lilla encouraged him. *"You'll see."* Lilla moved closer and butted him in the chest lovingly with her head. It was a sign of affection and Drake returned it by rubbing behind her eye ridges in the way he knew she liked.

Without warning, the doors opened from within and Drake turned to find Ren and Elena there, watching him. Drake's blue gaze shot back to Lilla, her head rising now as she shuffled through the door, pushing Drake along with her.

"You alerted Ren, didn't you?"

"Well I couldn't let you stand out there in the hall all night while your dinner was getting cold."

Drake's mother grabbed him in a fierce hug, having to reach up now, though they'd been about the same height when he'd left.

"Drake, my darling boy! You're as tall as your fathers now, aren't you?" Elena stood back to look at him, tears of joy in her beautiful eyes.

"Or maybe you just got shorter?" He couldn't resist teasing her and she chuckled with that tinkling sound of joy he remembered so well. He'd always loved his mother deeply and the intervening years hadn't changed that at all.

Ren grasped his hand and pulled him in for a quick hug.

They were about the same size now, though Ren was just slightly shorter than Declan and now Drake as well.

"Come on in," Ren invited. "Supper's ready. We've been waiting for you." Ren ushered him further into the oval chamber that housed the dragons' large wallow. Arlis was there, gleaming and golden as ever, watching over Jenet who jumped up, spewing sand when she saw Drake. Within seconds she was at his side, rubbing her neck against him familiarly as she had when she was just a baby dragonet.

"I'm so glad you're back, Drake."

He didn't have the heart to crush the hope in Jenet's rare, heliotrope eyes. He scratched her scales and petted her neck. "It's good to be back, baby." Drake realized he meant it and the idea was startling. Never would he have thought his return would feel like this, though in the early years of his self-imposed exile he'd thought through the scene many times.

They walked together to the dining area, though Jenet remained outside the chamber itself, only craning her neck through the wide threshold, as did her parents. Declan was already seated at one head of the table, Ren took his place at the other, just as it had always been in their home. Drake's stomach clenched as Declan rose, meeting his gaze.

"Be welcome, Drake." Declan gestured to Drake's seat and Drake moved forward a bit awkwardly, first to seat his mother, as politeness demanded, then himself. The dinner was already on the large table and Drake saw that his mother had indeed made all his favorite dishes.

"This looks really wonderful, Mother. Thank you."

Declan cleared his throat, then said a quick, respectful prayer to the Mother of All to thank Her for Her bounty. Drake was shocked when his gruff blood-father added a line of thanks for returning their son to the family.

They began the meal in awkward silence until finally Drake couldn't take it anymore. There were things he wanted to say— things he needed to say to these people before they could begin to truly be a family again—if that's what they all really wanted. For himself, Drake wasn't so sure. He had his own life now and it was a good one. He was well known and respected in the five lands he claimed as home. He'd done good service for his true homeland and would continue to do so, regardless of how things stood with his family.

Drake set down his fork, his thoughts churning.

"Don't you like the green beans?" His mother watched his plate as carefully as she had when he was six and tried to con Jenet into eating his vegetables when his mother's back was turned.

"No, the beans are fine, Mother." He sent her a reassuring smile. "But there are a few things that need saying."

Everyone at the table set aside their utensils, Declan last of all. The knight raised his blue eyes and met Drake's gaze across the breadth of the table.

"You're right, son. Say your piece."

Drake's back went up, just as it so often had when he was younger. He didn't need Declan's permission to speak, but with the wisdom of years, Drake reined in his hot temper. He recognized the bold, dominant streak in Declan that he'd come to know in himself over the years. They both shared the need to be the alpha male, which was probably why they'd clashed so much as Drake grew into a man.

"Thank you, Father." Drake nodded, glad to see Declan start a little with surprise at his measured tones. "First, I want you to know that I'm only back for a short time. I have responsibilities in other lands and most especially to the Jinn Brotherhood. They took me in and I've worked behind the

77

scenes with them for a lot of years."

"I don't know much of the Jinn," Ren said quietly, his eyes narrowed in thought, "but I have heard they are more than they seem. Nico already told us you're more than just a traveling minstrel. He told us you were Spymaster of the Jinn."

Drake was surprised. He could count on one hand the people who knew his true position among the Jinn Brotherhood. Nico, as King-Consort of the Jinn, was his only superior. In a way, Drake was now Spymaster to the King of the Jinn, if the Brotherhood used such titles. It was a high honor and a weighty responsibility. To be the master of all the Jinn spies was daunting, to say the least, for every traveling minstrel among the nomadic Jinn was a spy of one sort or another.

"I guess I shouldn't be surprised Nico told you, but you must realize how important it is that you keep my true position to yourselves."

Declan scoffed, but with a good-natured smile Drake had rarely seen from his stern blood-father. "That goes without saying, son. None of us would ever compromise your safety or your mission."

Drake let that thought settle in his mind for a moment. This wasn't going as he'd expected, but perhaps it was better than he ever would have believed. His family seemed to not only accept the path he'd chosen, but to take some measure of pride in his elevated status. They actually seemed proud of him.

Slowly, Drake nodded. "Well, you'll understand that because of my position, I can't stay in Draconia for long. There are contacts I must make and keep outside these borders. Drake of the Five Lands has built up a certain reputation and a very large network that I must uphold."

His mother sighed. "Your fathers expected no less, but now that you've come home for a visit, I hope you'll return more often. I know Jenet wants you here as much as possible. As do I."

Drake reached out to cover his mother's small hand with his own. "I can visit, of course, but I can't stay. There is much work to be done."

"I get the idea you never would have returned if there weren't some grave plot afoot." Declan spoke shrewdly, his sparkling blue eyes narrowed on Drake. "Can you tell us?"

Drake shrugged as he thought fast. Of all the knights, Ren and Declan were ranked among the highest. If there was a threat to the royal family, they would need to know.

"I can tell you this. There is a substantial threat to the younger princes, the twins in particular. I thought it real enough to return here after all this time to warn them myself."

Jenet's head loomed over the family dinner table. *"We've already taken precautions,"* she said in soft tones, including them all in her thoughts. *"None of the royal family will be without escort until we determine the seriousness of the threat. We've devised a schedule. Nellin is with Wil right now. Jurak and Elinar are with the younger twins. They and their knights will sleep in the royal suites tonight and we'll switch off in the morning. Roland and Nico refused Guards, but we're watching them anyway."* She chuckled in her dragonish way, a little wisp of cinnamon-scented smoke rising above the table.

"You've been busy, sweetheart. Good work." The approval in Declan's voice made Drake start. Dec had indeed mellowed in the past fifteen years. He'd never spoken so gently in his life. Or perhaps Drake had just never recognized the deep caring in Declan's otherwise harsh voice.

"Is there anything we can do?" Ren leaned forward, seeking Drake's counsel in a way that surprised him. Roles had certainly reversed in the past fifteen years. His fathers were both looking at him the way his men often did—with respect and a willingness to listen and follow direction. It was a jarring, heady feeling.

"Having the dragons keep an eye on them is a good first step, but the information I have indicates the threat is greatest here, in the capital city and the castle. I recommended to Roland that his younger brothers either be confined here in the castle with multiple Guards or dispersed to the outlying Lairs where the number of people going in and out can be controlled."

"What is the nature of the threat, exactly?" Declan asked from the head of the table, all business now.

"Abduction." Drake's simple statement caused a stark reaction from everyone but Jenet. She'd heard his full report to the king and knew already what was at stake. "What my spies have heard indicates King Lucan of Skithdron wants to capture one of the royal princes. They say it has something to do with his own transformation and I fear he wants a half-dragon subject to experiment on. Nico and Riki saw first-hand what Lucan's done to himself."

"What's he done?" Drake's mother wanted to know, a fearful curiosity on her delicate features as she looked from one man to the other seated around her table. "What haven't you told me?"

Ren's eyes were grim, but he nodded at Drake to do the honors.

"King Lucan cut a deal with the northern warlord, Salomar. Lucan would ship diamond blades northward in return for two things. First, he wanted access to the North Witch, Loralie. He asked her to merge him—bodily—with the skiths that inhabit his land."

Elena gasped, shock and horror on her lovely face. Skiths were giant, venomous, snake-like creatures that killed all in their path. The only thing they were afraid of was fire, but even a dragon could be felled by their acidic venom spray and vicious bladed teeth. They weren't of very high intelligence and tended to be lone creatures, but just recently the king of Skithdron had found a way to mobilize and organize the skiths of his land into a sort of army.

"But that's crazy!" Elena's whispered words reached Drake's ear and he squeezed her small hand in reassurance.

"Lucan is insane. He's half-skith now. It's the reason he chained Riki at his side. He made her heal the constant injury to his body caused by the skith venom and blood, as the process of change continued. Without her healing power, he would have died at the very beginning of the transformation. We all assumed after she escaped he'd die a very slow and painful death, but he's still alive. My scouts confirmed it only a day or two ago." Drake ran one frustrated hand through his hair. "Either he's found a new healer somewhere—poor soul—or he's beyond the point in the change where he needs constant healing."

Declan sat back and all eyes turned to him. "What was the second thing Lucan bartered with Salomar for?"

Trust his father to remember the details. Drake would have smiled had the situation not been so grim. "Safe passage to the far north for search parties. Salomar didn't know what Lucan was looking for, other than some magical artifact, but some of my sources claim it was something from wizard times." Lilla reared up, as did the other dragons lying in the warm pit of sand some feet distant, but they said not a word, just listened intently while Drake continued. "One of my informants heard a name, but I don't trust the man completely and I only have his word on it."

"What was the name?" Arlis's great golden head loomed

near, over his knight's shoulder. There was urgency in his tone.

Drake surveyed the dragons, realizing there was something more here than met the eye, but he'd have to wait for a better time to ferret out just what the dragons knew. For now, he had bigger fish to fry and two princes to keep safe.

"The man spoke of something called the Citadel. He said that's what Lucan's men were looking for in the far north, but he didn't know whether or not they'd actually found anything."

The dragons bristled, but remained silent.

"Does this mean something to you, Arlis?" Declan asked of his dragon partner, suspicion in his gaze if Drake was reading his blood-father's expression correctly.

"It could," Arlis hedged, surprising Drake, *"but we must seek the Dragon Council. I will call them together tomorrow at first light. We must confer on this development before deciding how to proceed."*

Drake knew both Arlis and his mate were senior members of the Dragon Council. Only dragons met on the Council—their knights were not allowed within the vast chamber. The only humans allowed within were those of royal blood, who were also half-dragon. He'd often wondered what went on behind those closed doors, but that was one of the few areas into which even the Spymaster of the Jinn Brotherhood was not privy.

"Leaving that aside for now—" Declan sent his dragon partner a hard look, "—I'm impressed that you felt this threat strong enough to come here in person, Drake. It speaks both of your character and the seriousness of our current situation." Drake was shocked by Declan's words, but the older knight moved on without pause. "We'll need to augment the dragons' plans. Jenet, after dinner I want you to give us the details of the schedule you and the younger dragons have worked out. But for now, let's continue our meal." Declan lifted his glass and waited for those around him to do the same. "To our son, returned to us at last."

The toast was echoed by the rest of the family and Drake found himself drinking with a sense of unreality that puzzled him. How had Declan taken control of the situation yet again? And why wasn't Drake bristling as he always had when his blood-father took charge to bring them back to the matter at hand?

No, instead of anger, Drake felt something like relief that Declan had so easily steered the conversation away from such weighty matters. It was hard enough just being with his family after so many years. Discussing the dire threat to the Draconian royal family and the machinations of kings was better left to another day.

Drake watched as his family drank to his return, a sense of completeness enveloping him. He'd come full circle now. His blood-father was no longer the ogre he remembered and Drake had to ask himself if Declan really ever was quite as bad as Drake recalled.

Drake raised his glass when the others had finished sipping and gathered their attention. It was a heady feeling. They'd never paid such attention to him as a youngster, but he'd grown up and learned many things in his travels. How to play to a crowd was second nature to an accomplished Jinn troubadour such as himself.

"And to you all. The Mother of All knows you deserve special commendations for putting up with me as a teen." He shook his head ruefully. "I never expected to be welcomed back this way and I'm both humbled and grateful."

Drake drank deeply of the sweet wine, shocked to see tears gathered in not only his mother's eyes, but Ren's as well. Even Declan had a suspicious sparkle in his blue eyes, but Drake pretended not to notice the emotional response his words had conjured.

The rest of the meal passed with considerably less tension and Drake found himself enjoying the quiet meal with his family a lot more than he'd expected. So much had changed while he'd been away, yet much had stayed the same.

Drake bounded out of bed the next morning, feeling better than he had for a very long time. It was barely dawn when he ambled down the High Road in Castleton toward a quaint inn owned by the Pritchards. He remembered it from when he was a boy. They were famous for their confections and he was looking forward to learning if they still made the best sweet breakfast buns he'd ever tasted.

He entered the common room and spotted Krysta. She wore her grey Guard uniform, but her hair sparkled in the rising sun and her creamy complexion beckoned him to lick her skin, just to see if she tasted as good as she looked.

But that would come later.

For now, breakfast was the order of the day. Charming this special woman, the task at hand.

"Good morning, Krysta." His voice was his sharpest weapon, honed over years on the bardic road. He knew he could make a woman shiver with just the right inflection and it seemed Krysta was not immune. He saw her shoulders shimmy as his voice rolled over her and smiled in satisfaction.

"I wasn't sure you'd make it."

"When I make a promise, I keep it." He sat at the small table, brushing his knees against hers under the table.

"I'll remember that." She sipped at her steaming cup of tea, her grey eyes watching him through the mist.

The serving girl came over to them and Drake smiled at the youngster, placing his order. He learned that she was the youngest daughter of the house, Mary Pritchard, and by the time she left the table, she was grinning and promising to give his compliments to her father and mother.

"You certainly have a way with the ladies. Even the young ones."

Drake winked. "I used to charm honey buns from Mrs. Pritchard when I was a boy. She makes the best pastries I have ever tasted anywhere in all the lands."

"I know." Krysta looked a wee bit guilty. "I have a sweet tooth myself."

"Ah..." Drake sat back in his chair, watching her, "...so that's why you chose Pritchard's."

"I confess I have a weakness for Mrs. Pritchard's baking. Much to my chagrin. Eating here the past few months, I've gained at least five pounds, so I try to limit it to once a week."

Drake inspected her ultra-feminine form. "Well, I certainly can't tell." His gaze shifted to her. "I like a woman with curves."

She laughed outright, charming him with her candor. "You are such a rogue." She didn't flirt like the other women he'd known. She meant every word, and not in a teasing way. Drake sat up, eager to disprove his reputation for some reason, though he'd never felt the need to defend himself before.

"I've been many places and seen many things. I've done a lot I would never relate to my mother—" he paused to chuckle, "—but I've never played a woman false. I'm not quite a rogue, though I admit, I'm probably very close."

"Well at least you're honest." She leaned back, regarding

him. "I like that about you."

"Honest and true to my word." His eyes lit with a playful twinkle as he nodded. "You've learned that much about me already. What will you do when you discover I'm loyal, faithful and steadfast, I wonder?"

"Pat you on the head and toss a stick for you to fetch?"

He burst out laughing. "I'm not a dog, but around you I definitely feel frisky as a puppy." He pitched his voice low, to skate along her nerves. He knew he'd hit his mark when he saw her shiver.

He would have followed up on the small victory, but Mrs. Pritchard bustled over. Drake stood to receive her friendly hug as she marveled over how much he'd grown. The older woman had been one of his favorite people in Castleton, both for her excellent cooking and her understanding wisdom. Many times, he'd sought refuge here after one of his father's rebuffs. Mrs. Pritchard fussed over him, nearly coming to tears when he leaned down to kiss the motherly lady on the cheek.

It touched him deeply that she remembered him. He'd thought at the time he was just one of many youngsters who clamored after the woman, eager for one of her sticky buns. He was pleased to learn she'd felt genuine affection for the troubled boy he'd been and seemed proud of the man he'd become.

They talked for a few moments before the business of the inn called her away. When he sat back down at the table, Krysta was eyeing him.

"She loves you."

"I love her too. She's a very special woman." He tossed his napkin on his lap, trying to be nonchalant. The truth was, the woman's greeting had thrown him more than he liked. His emotions were much closer to the surface than usual. "She has a soft heart and a kindness for strays. Hmm. Maybe I am a dog after all." He chuckled, settling back in his chair as little Mary brought their breakfast on two metal plates.

They ate and chatted while Krysta fell a little more under Drake's spell. She felt the impact of his cultured voice and knew he was fully aware of how it affected people. Especially females.

Her insides jumped as she watched him lick the honey residue from the sticky buns off his elegant fingers. They were tapered and long, with little calluses from playing stringed instruments. The calluses were easy to see on the tips of his fingers as they moved, both nimble and dexterous. She wondered what such talented fingers would feel like on her skin. Would he play her body as skillfully as he played his lute?

A rush of disquiet filled her. She'd made love with Mace. She shouldn't be thinking of another man in a carnal way so soon after making a commitment to the young knight. It was disloyal, and it wasn't like her at all. She didn't indulge in casual sex. Sharing herself with Mace represented a very real step forward toward a relationship with him.

Krysta didn't rush into intimacy. Not since her foolish youth. But Mace was a different story. After only knowing him a short time, she felt strongly enough about him to trust him with her body. That was a big step for her and one she didn't take lightly. So why then was she feeling this unreasonable attraction for the roguish bard?

She knew full well Drake could have his pick of women and she'd be damned if she'd be just another notch in his belt. Still, Drake didn't strike her as insincere, and he certainly wasn't a cad. He was honest about his appreciation of women, regardless of their age. She'd seen him treat the young Pritchard girl with the same teasing respect he gave her mother, the same caring concern and desire to make them smile. He might be a rogue, but he was a kind one and that combination, Krysta discovered, was dangerous indeed.

"So what fills your days, Krysta? I know you're a Guard, but are you always on patrol or have you some other duty?"

The question drew her back to the moment and reminded her of her duty. Judging by the sun's position, she had only a short time left before she must begin her work day.

"I train the new recruits in weaponless fighting. Many of us share that duty, but in fact—" she wiped her mouth as she finished her breakfast, "—today it's my turn. I have a nice class of talented young men and women waiting for me."

"Ah, Jinn freehand fighting? That's a skill I learned many years ago, though I was too large for many of the more intricate movements—or so the armsmaster said."

"You might be at that." She looked him over with a considering eye. "I'd almost forgotten that Drake of the Five Lands was adopted of the Jinn. What clan are you?"

"Black Dragon." He said it casually, though they both knew the Black Dragon Clan ruled all of the many Jinn clans. They were the ones responsible for calling most of the wandering Jinn clans together here in Draconia. "I was lucky enough to have gained their notice when I was still just a boy, away from home for the first time with no knowledge of the wider world. Without their guidance, who knows where I'd be today?"

"I imagine you always land on your feet, Drake." She smiled at the picture he painted with his words of him as a youth.

He bowed his head in acknowledgement of her small praise. "It is a skill I've learned through much trial and painful error."

"Speaking of learning—" she glanced out the window again, "—I must go see to my students." She stood from the table and reached for the small purse at her belt, but Drake stayed her hand. His gentle touch jolted her, the warmth of his fingers causing little tingles on her skin.

"Allow me." He produced a silver coin from his own pocket, tossing it onto the table. It was much more than the simple fare was worth, but she knew he was probably leaving the extra for little Mary Pritchard, or trying to impress Krysta with his largess. Probably a little of both. Krysta smiled and thanked him as gracefully as she could manage.

Drake towered over her as they left the inn, reminding her of her femininity in a very basic way. Her limbs almost shook with the tingling heat of awareness. He was a tall man, but not brawny. No, he had the sleek muscles of the jungle cat, primed and ready to strike, though his loping stride was deceptively lazy.

"I'll walk you to the garrison, if you don't mind the company. I'm going that way and find I'm reluctant to see our time together end."

Oh, he *was* charming.

"I don't mind. But Drake..." her conscience rose to remind her of Mace, "...I have to tell you, I'm committed to Mace. I don't want to lead you on or give you false hope."

"Committed, huh?" He seemed to ponder her meaning. "Has he offered you marriage?"

"No." She shifted uncomfortably as they walked. "But I've committed to learning where the mutual attraction leads. I'm not in the market for a husband—or two."

"I'm glad you're aware what mating with a knight entails." She did, but only vaguely. Still, she wouldn't get into that discussion with Drake. Mace would tell her all about it, if they ever got to that point. "I'll be brutally honest with you, Krysta." He stopped walking, tugging on her wrist to make her face him. "I don't think I can stay away. You're unlike any woman I've ever known before and I want whatever time you'll give me."

"I won't stop seeing Mace."

"I didn't ask you to. But surely you can spare a few minutes to share a meal with me now and again? I won't deny your right to choose the man you want, but I'll do everything in my power to convince you I'm the right man."

He squeezed her hands, drawing her closer. She knew he was going to kiss her, and try as she might, she couldn't work up enough outrage to push him away.

His lips were gentle at first, coaxing a response. Desire flooded her as his tongue swept inward, invading, conquering, but in the most delightful way. He pulled her into his arms and she felt at home there. Dangerously so.

They were on a public thoroughfare but she was oblivious to the movement around them, the rest of the city just starting to stir from their homes and begin the day. Drake plundered her mouth, stirring her to passion even as his hands swept down to cup her backside. His hands were indeed talented and she longed to know what they'd feel like on her skin.

The thought roused her enough to push away. He let her go, drawing from her lips at the last possible moment. His blue gaze questioned, but she had no answers.

"I have to go, Drake." She patted his broad, muscular chest with open palms, then pushed back. "Thank you for breakfast."

She turned and ran off before he could say another word, the hounds of guilt and confusion snapping at her heels.

The garrison was built around a central courtyard that served as assembly area and training ground, among other uses. Drake arrived just as the new recruits were being put through their hand-to-hand training by none other than the talented Jinn warrioress, Krysta. He couldn't stay away. After that hot kiss, he knew there was something between them, though she tried to deny it.

He marveled at her lithe grace as she demonstrated take downs, avoidance techniques and strikes to the newer Guards. She drilled them with efficiency and taught with clear words and actions. He realized he was watching an expert at work as he lounged against a support column a floor above the courtyard, hidden by the shadows of the arching wall. The offices and a few of the living quarters were behind him, but the place was designed so that the inner wall was open to the courtyard—one long hall off which the outer rooms lay.

Curiosity had brought him here. That, and a desire to see Krysta that would not be denied. He had to make contact with some members of his network today, but first he couldn't resist visiting the garrison. He knew the building well and was able to find an out of the way place to spy on the mysterious woman who haunted his thoughts.

He watched her move, envious of the young men she taught, for they had all of her attention and focus. She touched elbows and patted shoulders as she passed each practicing pair, offering words of correction and praise in equal measure. She was a gifted teacher.

"You want her, don't you?" The deep male voice surprised him. A quick look to his side revealed his childhood friend Mace, now fully grown and much brawnier than Drake had expected. His old rival had changed since they were teens, but then, so had Drake.

Mace had somehow discovered Drake's hiding place, though he kept to the shadows himself. Drake spared him a glance, not liking the way the knight's eyes were trained on the lithe woman moving around below.

"Am I that obvious?"

"I intend to win her, so if you're just playing around, I'd appreciate it if you'd back off. Even when we were boys, I never stood a chance with a girl if you were interested in her too." Drake was floored by Mace's words, but the knight continued right on, not giving Drake a chance to speak. "This girl matters a lot to me, Drake. More than any other woman I've ever known."

Drake caught the note of dismay in Mace's tone, as well as the wonder. Could it be he'd found his mate? Drake could hardly believe it, though he knew knights often recognized their true mates within moments of meeting them. Still he refused to believe Krysta was meant for Mace. She was Drake's, dammit. Couldn't they see that?

The trouble was, Drake didn't know what to do about all these new feelings storming around inside him. He didn't want to settle down with just one woman. Did he?

He didn't recognize the indecisiveness in himself. Drake of the Five Lands was known for his steadfast character and quick turn of phrase. Why then was he reduced to a babbling idiot on this topic?

"I don't honestly know what it is about her, but I can't say I will withdraw from the field. It'll have to be up to her, Mace."

The other man sighed heavily. "I was afraid of that."

They watched her move in silence for some time, each lost in his own thoughts. Drake wasn't surprised Mace had realized his childhood ambition of becoming a dragon knight. He'd always lived up to the ideals of the Knights Creed—without even trying. Drake thought Mace had probably been born with the knightly traits of honor, bravery, strength, fairness and mercy. His skill with weapons and strategy seemed to come naturally, but he never lorded it over the other boys in the Lair. No, Mace didn't seem to have any vices at all—something Drake had both hated and admired about his former classmate.

Despite that, they'd been friends. They'd also been competitors in many ways, but always friendly about it. And now they seemed to be competing for the same woman.

"She's something, isn't she?" Drake marveled as Krysta completed a complex block-sweep sequence he'd never quite mastered himself.

"One of the best."

"You can say that again."

The men were left alone as she dismissed her class and disappeared into one of the rooms on the lower floor. Drake turned to study Mace.

"It's good to see you, Mace. My mother mentioned you'd been chosen. Congratulations." He held out the hand of friendship and Mace hesitated only slightly before returning the gesture.

When they were younger, theirs had been a constructive rivalry, with no hard feelings on either side. Drake knew Mace couldn't help the fact that Declan had often thrown Mace's accomplishments in Drake's face when he hadn't lived up to expectations. That wasn't Mace's fault. He'd always been better, brighter, and more diligent than Drake. It was just the way he was built.

Mace persevered. His character was such that if he didn't get something the first time, or even the second, he stuck with it, trying until he mastered it. Such thoroughness had led him to a level of skill in a wide variety of endeavors that Drake didn't have the patience or inclination to even try. Swordplay had been fun, so Drake excelled at that. Other weapons came to him easily as well, but the other things a knight was expected to know eluded him for the most part. Oh, he did well enough, but he didn't excel. Not the way Mace did.

Of course, Drake had an active social life, even back then. Mace had spent most of his evenings studying. Not for Drake was the life of a scholar. He far preferred common rooms filled with interesting characters with tall tales from far off lands. Much of Drake's real education had been earned on the road, talking to people and learning from the stories they told.

He'd turned his interest in people into songs and tales that paid his way from one inn or faire to the next until he'd joined up with the Jinn. They'd taken him in and nurtured his natural talents, taught him instruments and how to play in a group or solo. He'd loved every minute of it. Learning from the Jinn Brotherhood hadn't felt like work. Finally, he'd found a way to excel.

It had taken fifteen long years, though, to learn wisdom.

"Nellin is my dragon partner," Mace said with pride as they shook hands in the warrior style.

"I remember him. A fine dragon for a fine knight." Drake recalled the young dragonet, only a little older than Jenet. He'd been big for his age and promised to be a devil in the air, even back then.

"He's a handful, but we get along." Mace was being modest. They were highly ranked for such a young pair. Drake had heard about Mace's achievements from his family. "Have you eaten? I was going to get some lunch if you want to join me."

The invitation was polite and Drake accepted with some alacrity. They were rivals once again, this time for a beautiful, willful woman, so Drake fell into the role with which he was familiar. He envied Mace, almost as much as he respected him.

Lunch was pleasant enough and it had the added benefit of stalling his return to the castle until just before the evening meal. Mace brought Drake up to date on the happenings among their age group over the past fifteen years. Mace was as solid and steady as Drake remembered and he found he enjoyed catching up with Lair life more than he'd expected.

After a few companionable hours with the knight, Drake made his way back to the castle and his waiting family. Unlike the night before though, this second dinner with his family was much less tense and even somewhat enjoyable.

Rather than the long, drawn-out affair of the night before, this dinner was blessedly brief because the men had to report for duty soon after. That left Drake alone with his mother and Jenet for the rest of the evening. He talked about his adventures with the Jinn and the foreign lands he'd visited. His mother wanted to know all about his travels and Drake had even brought a few things to give her.

Once he'd made the decision to head home, Drake had picked up a few gifts for the family. In the tumult of the previous day he hadn't had much chance to give his mother the silk scarves, rare spices, colorful fabric and other things he'd acquired for her. He had a few items for Ren and Declan as well—master-crafted blades and small leather workings he thought they'd like—but he'd wait for a more opportune time to give them his gifts. They were small things, really, but Drake knew his family would enjoy them.

For Jenet, he'd brought a buttery soft, golden leather pouch she could wear around her neck if and when she finally chose a knight of her own. It matched the color of her scales and had pretty designs wrought on it. More importantly, it was made to fit comfortably against her hide and not get in the way as she flew. Drake had designed it himself and commissioned it from one of the master craftsmen of the Jinn.

He'd also brought some very special salves and creams for Jenet's scales. Dragons didn't need all that much in the way of skincare, but the delicate areas where their wings met their body could benefit from lubrication every once in a while. It was a knight's duty to see to the comfort of his dragon and though Jenet had no knight at the moment, Drake thought she would probably enjoy the gift.

"They all smell wonderful!" Jenet enthused as she slipped her head through the loop of the leather pouch Drake presented to her. She sniffed each jar, nosing through them with enjoyment sparkling in her eyes. *"Will you rub the one in the blue jar on my left wing joint?"*

Drake ducked as Jenet lifted her wing over his head. He stepped up, using the jar she'd sniffed out and the skills he'd learned as a youngster to soothe her irritated skin.

"You shouldn't have let this go so far, Jen. Your scales are ragged here."

"You could help me, like you did when we were little."

He knew that loaded suggestion was her way of nudging him about her desire to make him her knight—against all logic. Not answering her, he concentrated on his work.

He stepped back when he'd finished with her left wing and moved to inspect the right. He rubbed the scented cream into the joint until he was satisfied she was in good shape. Or at least as good as he could make her feel with only one treatment.

"I'll give you another rub-down tomorrow morning, Jen. The right side is all right, but the left needs a little more attention." He wiped his fingers on a cloth, then slipped the blue jar back into the pouch she still had around her neck. "You want me to put this with your things, Jen?"

But Jenet pulled away before he could remove the bag filled with jars of creams and ointments he'd given her. *"I want to keep it near for a while, Drake."* Her words seemed almost bashful as she backed away toward the sandy wallow where she slept. *"It smells good. And it reminds me you're really home."*

Drake worried at her words and her obvious attachment to him, but he didn't argue. He'd seldom seen Jenet so tentative, even as a young dragonet. The time would come soon enough when he'd have to leave her once again. Better to let it lie for now.

Chapter Seven

The sound of running feet in the dead of night was never a good sign. It took Drake only a moment to realize he was inside the castle, in his childhood home. He heard scurrying footsteps in the hall pause, then enter the suite. Drake got up, instantly alert to possible danger, or worse...bad news.

It wasn't long in coming. A knight he knew from his youth was knocking on his mother's door, the older man's face grim.

"Bertrand, what news?"

The man turned and peered through the dimly lit Lair. "Is that you, young Drake? I'd heard you were back. Just in time too. Your mother will need you."

"What's happened?" Elena opened her door, clutching the lapels of her robe in one hand, apprehension clear in the tight lines of her small shoulders.

"My fathers?" Drake asked, dreading what Sir Bertrand might say next.

"Arlis barely made it back. Dec is refusing treatment until Arlis is seen to. He won't let any of the healers near him and from what I saw, he's hurt bad."

Drake's jaw clenched as his mother sobbed silently, tears streaming down her face.

"What about Ren and Lilla?"

"Dec says they were in worse shape than he and Arlis, which is why they made for the Border Lair while Dec turned back to report to the king. Prince Wil's been kidnapped, right out from under them. It was an ambush, Dec said. They didn't stand a chance."

Elena sagged and Bertrand was there to support her. "Take me to them, please," she spoke in careful tones, regaining some composure as she straightened her spine. Drake marveled at the strength of his little mother. She was small, but she was mighty.

The older knight let Elena lean on him as they headed out of the suite, Drake following behind. Quietly, he sought more information.

"Are they up on the tower?"

"East platform, Drake." Bertrand nodded as they walked swiftly through the deserted halls.

"And Arlis is being treated?"

"They'd sent for the queen as I left them. She is a powerful dragon healer. If anyone can help Arlis, she can."

"Who have they got for Declan?"

"Jiris, Headmaster of the Healing Academy. He couldn't have finer, but he's refusing to let the man near."

Drake squared his shoulders as he struck off into a side passage that would lead him to the royal apartments.

"Where are you going?" Betrand called after him.

"I'm getting help. Do what you can until I get there." Drake had a plan in mind to outwit his stubborn father—all for his own good.

Arriving at his destination a moment later, Drake barely knocked on the door before entering Prince Nico's bedchamber. Nico and Riki were there, naked, but dozing after what Drake assumed had been just the beginning of a night of love. He knew first-hand how energetic the couple was in their lovemaking and how deeply they loved one another.

Nico glared at the sudden intrusion of light from the open doorway. "What is it? Can't it wait 'til morning?"

"I wouldn't ask if it weren't a matter of life and death." Drake moved into the room.

Riki blinked at him. "Drake? Is that you?"

"What's wrong?" Nico was alert and ready to act. Drake was never more glad of his friendship than at that moment.

"Declan is wounded and refusing treatment. Queen Lana has been summoned to treat Arlis, but Declan is as stubborn as ever. But he wouldn't dare refuse you, Riki. Please, would you come?"

Riki and Nico were out of bed and getting dressed in a flash. Drake silently thanked the goddess of the Jinn for their friendship and willingness to help.

"There is worse news still." Drake felt it only fair to tell them. "You may not wish to help Declan when you hear what's happened."

Nico looked over at him then and Drake knew the Prince of Spies had a good idea of what had occurred. The knowledge was in his dark eyes.

"Is Wil dead?"

Riki gasped, but Drake shook his head. "Kidnapped. Arlis and Declan were the least injured so they came here to alert us. Ren and Lilla flew for the Border Lair. We don't yet know if they made it."

Nico nodded once, his face grim as he placed one firm hand on Drake's shoulder. Silently, they commiserated for a short moment, each too filled with emotion to let the words out. Riki stepped between them and placed her small hand on her husband's arm, drawing him away. They all left the suite together, in worried silence. The three of them were out the door and heading for the east tower in under a minute.

"You were sending Wil away?" Drake asked as they climbed the stairs.

"We thought it best. The twins were sent to the Northern Lair two days ago and arrived safely. The entire Lair is watching over them and no one comes or goes from there except by dragon. It's easier to watch over them in such a place without the constant traffic of the castle." They rounded the corner to the last flight of stairs. They were almost there. "We sent Wil last night with your fathers as escort. He's big enough to fly most of the way on his own now, but he still has to rest periodically on such a long journey. We thought two dragons and knights would be enough to guard on the short breaks, yet not too many leaving together to raise suspicion."

"And they left at night so Wil's black dragon hide would be camouflaged in the dark." Drake nodded. "It was a sound plan."

"That somehow went horribly wrong." Nico turned to Drake, his eyes flinty hard. "We have to get him back, Drake. Either way. If he's dead, we need to know. But if he's alive—" His voice trembled with anger and turmoil, just the tiniest bit. "If he's alive, each moment is precious. We have to get to him as soon as possible."

"I'll see to it personally, Nico. You have my word."

They rounded the last corner and were thrust into the midst of turmoil. Arlis was down, panting smoke as Lana knelt at his side, just beginning to lay her powerful, healing hands on the huge golden dragon. Declan was leaning heavily against Bertrand on one side, Elena on the other, swearing roundly with each roar of pain from his dragon partner and batting away the poor healer who attempted to help him.

Nico stopped Drake with a powerful grip on his arm. "You get Wil back, Drake, and let us handle this for you." Nico hitched one shoulder toward the scene now before them.

Drake could have laughed when Riki, not waiting for her husband, marched right up to Declan and poked one finger into his chest. She got his attention without even raising her voice. Nico moved to stand directly behind her, backing his mate up with a dark, disapproving glower and his frowning presence.

Drake was glad to see he was right about Dec's inability to disobey a royal order. Within moments, he was being treated not only by old Jiris from the Healing Academy, but by Riki too. She was as gifted as her sister when it came to healing, and had spent years treating humans while her sister Lana dealt better with dragons.

Drake moved to his mother's side. She latched onto his arm and held on tight as they watched the agony begin to ease on Declan's face. Riki was a strong healer and her skill shone as she applied herself to Dec's worst wounds, working in tandem with the other healer. Drake didn't miss the gravely determined looks passing between the two as they worked.

"I'm so glad you're here." His mother whispered as she leaned against him. She felt so much smaller than he remembered, but then, he'd finished growing in a land faraway. He'd missed his mother and Ren, not to mention the dragons, terribly those first few years. And Declan. In some ways he missed his stern blood-father most of all. Each time he mastered a new skill or worked behind the scenes to protect the people and dragons of his homeland, he somehow wished he could share his successes with Declan. All his life, Declan's approval had meant so much more than anyone else's because it was so rarely given.

Drake hugged his mother. Both breathed a sigh of relief when Arlis's breathing steadied and he stopped thrashing his tail in pain. A moment later Queen Lana stepped away, leaning heavily on her husband. Lana walked straight over to Drake and his mother, reaching out to clasp Elena's hands in her own.

"Arlis will survive. It will take time for him to recover, but he'll be well and whole in a few months' time."

"Oh, thank you." Elena sobbed as the queen hugged her.

Lana's emerald eyes met Drake's and she smiled with gentle indulgence. This woman was so much like her twin—yet quite different. Lana seemed to be much more outgoing, though Drake hadn't truly met the new queen just yet. He knew Riki much better, having been instrumental in orchestrating Nico and Riki's escape from Skithdron a few months before.

Elena pulled back, thanking the new queen once more before moving to Arlis. Drake knew his mother would want to see for herself the extent of Arlis's injuries now that he was resting as comfortably as possible and it was safe to approach.

Drake faced the queen and Roland's calm presence just behind her.

"Thank you, milady, from the bottom of my heart."

"You're the image of your father," Lana said with a weary, almost dazed expression. She reached out one hand to brush a stray lock of his hair out of his eyes. There was healing in her touch and a compassion so deep, it humbled him. "My sister told me about you, of course, but I thought she must be exaggerating." Drake felt an unaccustomed flush rise up his cheeks as his eyes sought Roland's in alarm. But the king was smiling indulgently. Drake could see Roland was truly besotted with his new queen.

"Healing like that drains my lady wife to the point of exhaustion," Roland said in soothing tones, hugging the petite woman back against his chest as he stood behind her.

Drake lifted the queen's small hand to his lips, kissing the back in a gentle salute. "I am in your debt, my queen. Thank you for helping Arlis. He is another father to me, even though I lack wings."

"My sister says you have the voice of an angel. When everyone's better, will you sing for us? And play your lute? Riki's been playing some of the things you taught her and she's magnificent. She says you're hundreds of times better though. I love music. It's one of the things I missed most when Tor and I ran away."

Drake had heard the story of how the queen had lived on her own in the frozen Northlands with only a baby Ice Dragon for company. She'd fought off attacks and ongoing attempts to recapture her and her dragonet, Tor, for several years, living off the land. By all accounts, she was quite a woman. But then, Drake had always had great respect for Roland, who was only a little older than himself.

"I will sing and play for you, my queen, any time you wish."

"But first," Roland spoke quietly from behind Lana, "I want you to motivate your network of Jinn spies, Drake. I want my brother back with all possible speed."

"I've already given my vow to Nico, my liege. We'll find Prince Wil. This I promise you. I'll go after him myself as soon as I have word of his direction."

"See to your family now, Drake. Nico's already sent word to the leaders of his network in Castleton. Just be ready when they start to report back."

"I'm ready now, my liege." Drake glanced to Arlis and then to Dec. "If Arlis lives, so will my blood-father. He's too stubborn to allow it to be otherwise."

Tight smiles greeted his observation and Nico joined them.

"Riki says it's not as bad as it looks. Sir Declan will recover."

Drake winked at Lana. "What did I tell you?"

This time the smiles were a bit freer.

"I'm just going to check on my mother, then I'll be heading out to beat the streets, and knock a few heads if I must." Drake's eyes narrowed as he contemplated his next steps. "There's got to be someone on this end who saw them leave, so there must be someone—perhaps several—to question right here in the city or even the castle. There are some Jinn I'd like to bring into this. Their loyalty is beyond question and they walk the city streets. If there's anything to know here, they either already know it or they'll learn it."

Roland nodded. "Do it. Stop at the treasury on your way out of the castle if you need coin for bribes or payment. No price is too high to get Wil back."

"Most Jinn will help out of love for Riki and your family, and loyalty to dragonkind, but some others might need to be greased before they squeal." Drake's eyes took on a menacing cast as he thought through the possibilities and the steps he would take as soon as he got down to Castleton.

He stayed with his mother only until he was sure she would be all right. He even checked on Declan, surprised by the light of anger in his blood-father's tired eyes. The knight was mad as hell, but for once, it wasn't directed at Drake. Declan grabbed Drake's sleeve with more strength than he would have credited and told him the sequence of events in full detail as Nico and several other knights listened in with great interest.

The party made up of Declan, Arlis, Ren, Lil and Prince William had stopped for the final rest period near the last clear lake before the Border Lair. It was a predictable, but necessary, stop and the dragons and knights had checked the area carefully before setting down. What they hadn't spotted from the sky were the well-camouflaged, dug-out pits where a company of mercenaries lay in wait. They were a disciplined group, waiting for the perfect moment to spring their trap. They caught both dragons on the ground and separated the knights, threatening Wil, who was in human form at that moment, with Ren and Dec's deaths if he didn't surrender. They'd brought reinforced iron shackles sufficient to challenge even a full-grown royal black dragon shapeshifter. Wil was still a teen, barely out of his childhood years and still relatively new to flying and shifting from human to dragon and back.

"Drake—" Declan's grip tightened with urgency, "—you've got to get him back. He's just a boy. Only a little younger than you were when you left. I can't go through that again." Drake was shocked by the emotion on his blood-father's face. "Promise me, boy. Save him. I know you can do it. You're the only one I trust."

Drake took Declan's hand in his. This was a breakthrough moment in their relationship and he would treat it with all the reverence and seriousness it deserved.

"I've already promised Roland and Nico, and now I'll give you the same and more, Father." Drake fought past the lump in his throat. Declan was looking at him with such hope, such approval, such respect, he found it hard not to just stop and stare. "I'll find Wil and bring him home."

"And when you've done that," Declan pushed one step further, "I want you to come home to stay. I've missed you, boy. We all have."

Drake didn't want to think that far ahead. Events were spinning fast and furious out of his control and he needed to think long and hard before committing himself to such a life-altering course. "We'll cross that bridge when we come to it. For now, I've got work to do. You rest and heal. I'll find Wil and bring him back."

Declan lay back, drained. "You're a good man, Drake. I know if anyone can bring that boy back safely, it's you."

Stunned by his blood-father's confidence in him, Drake couldn't speak. He shared a nod of understanding with the man who was his image and backed away. He spared only a moment to check on his mother one last time before he left the castle. He had work to do.

As dawn broke over the stirring city of Castleton, Drake of the Five Lands set about the business he did best...collecting information any way he could.

Chapter Eight

Drake's steps led him to Rulu, former leader of the Wayfarer Clan, as the old man sat down to breakfast. Rulu didn't look all that surprised to see Drake at his door, which set him on edge. What's more, the old man wasn't alone. Seated at the long table with him was not only Krysta, but the Captain of the Guard, Edden Vonris, the most fearsome swordsman in all the land.

"We've been expecting you," Rulu spoke from the head of the table.

Drake entered the tent, taking the place already set for him at the low table. Edden's presence here meant one thing Drake had suspected for a long time. The Captain of the Guard of Castleton was also a member of the Jinn Brotherhood. But why was Krysta there?

"We know about Prince Wil," Edden said with a steely look in his grey eyes. Now that Drake saw them side by side, he noted the resemblance between Krysta and the Captain. No doubt they were related, probably brother and sister. But confirmation of that observation could wait. Wil's safety was the bigger issue at hand.

"How do you know?" Drake asked, his thoughts spinning to the possibilities even as he ate the food set before him. This would be a long day. He'd need his strength.

"Word came through our connections with the Mercenary Guild about an hour ago. One of their number went rogue and took a job they were advised to pass."

"Kidnapping Wil." Drake nodded as he ate steadily, barely tasting the hearty meal. "Who did it?"

"Shafir," Edden spat the name with obvious distaste. Drake knew of the mercenary leader and hadn't heard a single good thing about the man.

"Do you know who hired him and where they're headed?"

"Not yet," Edden said with deadly intent in his cold eyes, "but we will shortly." He nodded over to Krysta. "That's where my sister comes in."

Drake raised one eyebrow in the Guardswoman's direction. "Much as I admire her, just how does she fit into your scheme?"

"Drake, I'm the Wayfarer Clan's spymaster," Krysta said in a clear, firm voice.

Drake was surprised by the revelation. He'd dealt with the Wayfarer's master spy several times over the past few years, but always through Rulu, who acted as an intermediary. Now it all made sense. They were protecting not only the spymaster's identity, but also the very fact that she was female.

Drake sat back in his low chair and just stared at her for a moment. She watched him with wary eyes, probably wondering if he would get angry, or worse, laugh in her face. Drake did neither.

"I was just as blind as everyone else who placed bets on which Wayfarer male was the spymaster. Sweetheart, I'll admit you took me by surprise. I've long admired your work."

All in all, Krysta thought, he was taking the news of her secret identity much better than she would have imagined. She liked that he hadn't questioned the claim. Made in the presence of the Clan elder and the Captain of the Guard, the revelation had been accepted by Drake, just as it would have been had she been a man. She knew other men wouldn't be so open-minded and accepting. But then Drake had been special from the moment she'd met him.

Golden and good-looking, Drake was a definite charmer, but there were hidden depths in him that called out to her. She liked him. And she hadn't expected to like him.

The thought was faintly disturbing. Generally speaking, she didn't go for womanizers or Jinn bards with glib tongues, but there was something very special and not at all superficial about Drake. One felt his words were far more than just surface flattery and his eyes held an honesty and integrity she hadn't expected.

She was drawn to him, which didn't sit well, but Krysta was honest enough with herself to acknowledge the truth of her own feelings. Drake was gorgeous. Manly, masculine, with more than a hint of devil-may-care attitude and bad boy panache. He was also highly intelligent and sexy in a deep, mysterious way that was altogether alluring.

Krysta had to shake herself out of her contemplation. The man was just too distracting.

"You have information about Wil?" Drake's deep voice brought her back to the problem at hand.

"A lead. We'll see if it pans out, but if my source is as reliable as I believe, I didn't want to waste time summoning someone from the castle and it's obvious you're investigating this for them."

"I promised Roland and Nico I'd find Wil," Drake said, shrugging his broad shoulders as if such a momentous task was an everyday occurrence. But then, perhaps it was, Krysta thought. She knew full well that Drake was highly placed in the Jinn spy network.

It was significant to her that Drake was also on a first name basis with the king of Draconia and Prince of Spies, but she didn't let her surprise show. She sent a knowing look to her brother, who thankfully picked up on her silent signal.

"As Captain of the Guard, I'm assigning Krysta to this case exclusively until Prince William is found. I'm also authorizing travel and expenses to that end and giving her over to your care, Master Drake, for the duration."

Krysta thought that last was going a bit far, but didn't argue the point with her sometimes overprotective brother. The speculative look in Drake's blue eyes claimed her full attention.

"I could use her skills, I'm not too proud to admit. I've been away from home a long time and the city's changed a great deal. I'll be glad of your assistance, Krysta."

She warmed under the true respect she saw in his expression. But this was not time to moon over his handsome face. No, there was work to be done.

"Good." She stood decisively. "Then if you're finished eating, there's a man we need to see before he finishes packing."

Drake stood, nodding to the men as he followed Krysta out the door. "Packing?"

"He's an outland trader who's let it be known he plans to depart the city this very afternoon."

"How convenient."

"Quite." Krysta stopped at one of the barrels where an oiled canvas coat lay airing and shrugged into it. It looked like it might rain later.

"You think he'll stick to his publicized plan?"

"I do. It will rouse less suspicion if he does, but even if he tries to flee, half the Wayfarer Clan is watching his every move at this very moment."

"Very nice," Drake commented as she led him to two horses, already saddled and waiting. Krysta had tried to plan for every contingency when she'd heard about the kidnapping in the middle of the night.

The square was one of the larger public spaces, just over the farthest bridge, on the fringes of the old city of Castleton. There they found nothing seemingly amiss, though the bustle for the early morning was a little livelier than one might expect. For one thing, there were more than the usual number of patrons sitting at the three outdoor cafes that sat on the square, and they were unusually vigilant as they watched one particular traveling peddler pack up his wagon and clear out his small space in the square's central market.

Krysta and Drake flanked the wiry man as he looked up from his packing.

"What can I do for you, friends? As you see, most of my wares are packed and I'm on my way out of town, but perhaps there is something I can find to please you." An oily smile and waving hands accompanied his slick talk.

Drake moved closer.

"We aren't looking for goods. Merely information."

The man's shifty eyes narrowed, seeking over Drake's shoulder, possibly for an escape route. Drake knew the man's helpers were otherwise engaged by the Jinn who'd stood at Krysta's subtle signal, to surround the merchant on all sides.

"What is it you're looking for?"

Drake smiled as the man's eyes refocused on him. It wasn't

a pleasant smile.

"Actually, I'm looking for Prince William, and I have it on good authority—" Drake seized the man by the collar and lifted him with one hand, "—you know who's taken him."

The man protested, but Drake would have none of it.

"Tell me now and I might spare your life."

"Who are you to threaten me?" The man started blustering, looking to Krysta—and her grey Guard's uniform—for help.

Bless her, Krysta perched on the side of an apple cart, picked up a ripe piece of fruit and polished it on her tunic. She flipped the owner of the cart a coin and bit into the juicy apple with a satisfying crunch.

"I'm the man who will break both your legs if you don't start talking."

"Guard!" the man called to Krysta. "You can't let him do this!"

"Actually," she replied calmly, "I can, and I will. You messed with the wrong people when you decided to assist in the prince's abduction."

"Come now." Drake shook the man. "I'm growing impatient. Tell me what you know."

The man kept protesting his innocence until suddenly his eyes widened and he went stiff with fear. Drake could smell the terror sweating from his pores as he stared over Drake's shoulder.

Drake felt the whoosh of air against his back and heard the distinctive clacking of dragon claws on cobblestone. He knew without looking that Jenet had decided to assist yet again. This time though, he didn't mind in the least. He'd use every advantage to discover where Wil had been taken. He dropped the shaking man and stepped back, making room for the dragon.

Jenet took a menacing step forward, brandishing her sharp talons in a way that impressed even Drake. His little dragonet had certainly grown into a fearsome creature while he'd been away. Drake hardly recognized the aggressive dragoness as his own little Jenet, but he had to admit she was quite effective.

The merchant crumpled in fear, cowering away from the fiery dragon.

"Tipolir! They took him to Tipolir!" The man cried out in terror as Jenet's smoky breath streamed over his face and her shining talons drew closer to his trembling skin. "That's all I know. I swear! That's all I know."

Drake looked at Krysta, raising one eyebrow in question. She nodded almost imperceptibly. She too felt the truth of the coward's words.

"Back off, sweetheart. You did a good job," Drake said to Jenet privately as he moved in to bind the man's wrists with Krysta's able assistance. As a Guard, she had lengths of rope as part of her kit for just such purpose. The dragon moved back, but kept a wary eye on the proceedings.

Krysta whistled loudly and more Guards appeared, from where Drake could only guess, but they seemed to know Krysta well enough and took charge of the prisoner with tidy movements. The man was bundled into a cart brought out from a side alley with almost frightening efficiency and Drake had to hand it to Krysta. She certainly had prepared for all contingencies.

"I've got to get to Tipolir." Drake was thinking out loud as Krysta stood at his elbow, nodding. He knew the city of Tipolir was near the southern border, on the coast. If his abductors managed to get Wil on a boat, the trail would be lost. There was practically no way to track them over water.

"We can't be more than a day or two behind them and on dragonback, you might be able to overtake them before they get to the sea."

Drake turned to the dragon who was never far from his side since he'd returned to his homeland. "Jenet, will you take me on this journey? It could be dangerous, but—"

"I will do anything to find William. You could not keep me here."

"I'm going too." Krysta walked right up to the dragon. "Will you take me, Lady Jenet? Or must I make my way over land?"

Drake turned to her. "I thank you for your help, Krysta, but this journey is mine to make. You should stay here."

"I disagree. I can still be of help. I have connections all over this land and you've not been here for fifteen years. You need me, Drake."

"She speaks the truth," Jenet offered, *"but I'm still too young to carry you both the breadth of the land."*

Drake sighed, studying both females. Why did they have to make things so difficult? Krysta was right. She had the contacts here, not him. She had to go, but she couldn't go alone, and Jenet might have grown up quite a bit in those intervening years, but he remembered well the way she would tire from flying long distances as she grew. He didn't want to put too much stress on Jenet. There was no help for it.

"Send for help from the Castle Lair." Drake asked Jenet to relay the message.

"Already done. He's on his way."

"Who?"

"Nellin." The way Jenet practically purred the other dragon's name gave Drake pause. Then he thought of Nellin's partner.

"And Mace."

"And Mace," Jenet agreed rather smugly. *"They have taken Krysta aloft before. I thought it would be easier for her to fly with a team she knew."*

Drake had to concede to the young dragon's wisdom. *"Good. There's no time to waste."*

He turned to Krysta. "Are you ready to fly?"

She moved away to speak in a low voice with another Guardsman. Turning back to Drake, her face was set in determined lines. "I'm ready. My men will carry back news of where we've gone to the Guards and the castle."

"You'll fly with Mace and Nellin. They'll be here shortly."

As if on cue, Nellin trumpeted from above and the bystanders cleared a space for the massive dragon to land. Drake had to admire the skill Nellin displayed in setting down in such tight quarters with perfect precision. Nellin too, it seemed, had grown from the youngster Drake had once known.

Mace jumped down and jogged over to them, greeting Krysta first, then nodding to Drake. "Nellin told me what Jenet relayed to him. We're up for the flight whenever you're ready."

"Krysta will fly with you." Drake didn't like the tiny spark of satisfaction that edged into the knight's eyes when he looked at Krysta, but there was no hope for it. Jenet was still too young to carry him and Krysta riding double, however much Drake would have preferred to hold Krysta close to him. No, he had to trust her care to Mace.

And if truth be told, Drake did trust Mace to take the best possible care of Krysta. He was an able knight and the boy he'd known had been steady, respectful and wise beyond his years, even back then. Drake knew too that Mace had strong feelings for the Guardswoman. Krysta could have no better knight looking out for her on this potentially hazardous and long flight.

That didn't mean Drake had to like it.

"It will be our pleasure," Mace replied, his admiring gaze for Krysta alone.

Drake scowled. "We don't have time to waste if we want to catch them before they reach the coast." Mace's attention focused back on Drake, for which he was glad.

"We'll catch them, Drake. Don't doubt it. We'll flame the gryphons themselves if we have to, but we'll get Wil back. No matter what."

Drake was pleased to hear the same determination that flared in his own heart in Mace's words. Drake clasped hands with the knight before turning to Jenet.

"Let's be off."

With little fanfare, the humans found their way to their respective mounts, climbing nimbly onto the dragons' backs and then taking to the sky. It had been years since Drake had last ridden on Jenet's back, and even back then, he hadn't done it often. Jenet had been a petite dragonet and Drake had grown quickly. He'd never flown with Jenet for longer than an hour or so, not wanting to overburden her, though she was always game for more. Still, he loved her and looked out for her back then, just as much as he wanted to now.

But Jenet was nearly fully grown, with a juvenile dragon's seemingly unending supply of energy. She could fly for longer than even most adult dragons with the added metabolism of the adolescent. She could support his big frame easily now, and Drake was glad he wouldn't be too much for her to carry over the long distance that awaited them.

Drake had second thoughts about the wisdom of their headlong flight, but something within him refused to give up the chase to others. He'd made a promise to Roland, Nico and his own father. He'd find Wil. It was his task. His quest.

No other would fulfill it.

Drake didn't dare examine why his thinking was so adamant on that score. It was not his nature to interfere where others with more skill would be better suited to a task, but this was one mission on which his normal routines did not seem to apply. No, in this duty, Drake was charting new territory for himself both as a man and as a citizen of Draconia.

Perhaps this was the beginning of his true homecoming. Perhaps this was the act that would redeem him—if only in his own eyes—and allow him to return to his land and family with his head held high. Only time would tell. And such thoughts were mere idle speculation. The real task was retrieving Prince Wil safe and sound. Nothing else truly mattered. Only Wil's safety.

Jenet took to the air with three strong wingbeats and all other thoughts dropped from Drake's mind as the ground dropped away beneath them. He'd often enjoyed flights with Jenet's parents when he was small, but to be on Jenet's back again was something that defied description. The sense of rightness, the feeling of belonging was nearly overwhelming. As was the beauty of seeing the city—new and old—spread out before him. It was breathtaking.

On one side the new Jinn settlement was growing. Rough planked buildings vied with colorful tents, flapping pennants in every color of the rainbow marking various clans or establishments. It was organized chaos of the most lovely design.

On the other side of the river, over newly constructed footbridges, was the old city of Castleton. Sleeping at the foot of the castle mountain, Castleton was a study in lovely stone and wood architecture, combining the best designs of nature with the most attractive creations of man.

And out beyond the city, the pasturelands and farmlands spread as far as the eye could see. Within moments they were away from the city and up higher than he'd ever flown before. He could just make out the mountains in the distance and the endless terrain over which they would fly to reach their goal. He was struck momentarily speechless, taking it all in.

"You've gained weight since last we flew together, Drake."

Jenet's voice in his mind pulled Drake from his reverie. *"So have you, sweetheart, but in all the right places. Did I tell you yet how gorgeous you are?"* Drake knew dragons—and women— well enough to know that females of all kinds loved compliments. And in Jenet's case, he meant every single word. *"I missed you so much."* He hadn't meant to add that last bit, but the words slipped past his guard as he admired the view from just under the low-hanging clouds.

"I missed this, Drake. I missed flying with you all those years. Think how much we could have shared." Jenet sighed a stream of thin smoke out behind them. *"But they tell me not to dwell on the past. What's done is done. What matters is that you're with me now and we're together."*

Drake didn't like the possessive tone in her words, but he was powerless to fight it. He knew Jenet was right, even if he did have to leave her again once this adventure was over. Perhaps she'd come to understand his reasons on this quest. Perhaps she'd learn first-hand how bad he'd be as a knight— how bad he'd be as *her* knight. And then, when it came time to leave, she wouldn't be hurt. Only *his* heart would break this time.

It was time to focus on the matter at hand. *"Can you do a low pass over the place Wil was kidnapped? I want to see if we can follow their trail. If so, perhaps we can overtake them on the road."*

119

"*Good idea.*" Jenet was silent a moment as she conferred with Nellin. "*I've never been to the spot, but Nellin has and he'll lead us there.*"

Chapter Nine

As it turned out, Prince Wil had been kidnapped several hours from the capital city, well south and east from where they started. The dragons pushed ahead, stopping only once to drink from a small lake and hunt from among the small herd kept nearby and clearly marked for dragon consumption. They would need their strength on this long journey.

The sun was still strong in the sky when the dragons dropped down to do a quick skim over the site. Mace took the lead now, with Nellin in front. They'd been trained in aerial reconnaissance and Drake knew when to let an expert do their work. They made several low sweeps over the site, where it was obvious a serious scuffle had taken place. There was blood, and lots of it, dried now, into the pale dirt. Dragons and knights alike had bled here—Drake's family.

Fire burned in his veins as he took in the evidence of what had happened here. He recognized the deep red of dragon blood, mixed with the sandy soil. Lilla and Arlis's blood. And Ren and Declan's blood.

Drake worried for Ren and Lil. As he'd left that morning, word still hadn't come from the Border Lair of their arrival or condition. For all he knew, they were still gravely injured and in danger. He didn't actually think they were dead. Drake felt he would know if either Ren or Lilla left this realm. Undoubtedly

Jenet would know too, in that magical way of dragons, if her mother passed on.

So there was hope. But worry as well.

Mace signaled with an upraised fist and both dragons descended to the ground. There were a lot of hand signals used between knights that Drake remembered seeing in his youth, that came back to him as they flew. The dragons relayed messages between themselves and their knights, but the complex system of hand signals was faster in many cases than waiting for the dragons to speak back and forth and then pass on information.

Unfortunately, while Mace and Nellin had been training for the past ten or fifteen years, Drake and Jenet had not. Drake knew only the things he'd seen his fathers do in his youth, but he hadn't studied the ways of knights and dragons with any real seriousness. As a result, he had to rely on Jenet's communications with Nellin more than he thought most knights would, but then, he wasn't a knight, and that fact was driven home at every turn.

Drake slid down from Jenet's back, careful not to disturb the ground a few feet distant where clear marks had been left by men, horses and injured dragons. Those marks held a story and Drake would read it well, now that he was on the ground, where he was more used to tracking.

Mace walked over to him, stretching the kinks in his muscles as he moved. "They went off in a straight line to the south, but Krysta wanted a look around before we press on and I thought we could all probably use a little break."

Krysta moved up beside Mace and headed straight for the outskirts of the tracks, moving carefully, Drake was interested to note. She knew something of tracking.

"Five men waited here, under the soil," Krysta said, walking with short, sure steps as she studied the ground. Drake moved up beside her.

"And another four right over there, past the scrubweed line."

Krysta looked up at him with agreement in her expression. Agreement and respect. "Small pockets lay in wait all over this area. It was an ambush, but one of the most elaborate I've ever seen."

"I agree." Drake studied one of the larger bloodstains. He looked over his shoulder, knowing Jenet would crane her neck to him if he beckoned. *"Are you up to this, little one?"*

"Anything to find William." Jenet lifted her head clear over Drake's tall form and sniffed at the ground near the soaked-in blood. *"This is where they hurt Papa."*

Drake padded around the site, skirting the perimeter as he walked with Jenet to the next large stain. His hand continually caressed her neck as she shivered with emotion. He hated to subject her to this trauma, but she knew her parents better than any other dragon and could help them decipher what had happened here on the ground better than anyone.

They reached the next stain and she stopped, using her long, sinuous neck to sniff at the spot. *"This is Mama's blood."*

"I'm sorry, baby." Drake consoled her as best he could, feeling her pain as if it were his own. *"Just one more thing. We need to know if you scent Prince Wil's blood anywhere here. We need to know if they hurt him."*

Jenet walked the perimeter of the site, craning her neck over to the various bloodstains. Krysta stood next to Drake as they watched the brave young dragoness do her work.

"This is where they took Lilla down, and that first area is where Arlis was attacked." Drake clarified the scene for Krysta as they watched Jenet go about her scent study of the area. "So far, Jenet hasn't detected any of Wil's blood, though she definitely scents his presence."

"That's good news," Krysta agreed.

"How so? They could still have hurt him after they took him." Mace had come up to join them while Nellin cooled off in the nearby lake.

Drake raised one eyebrow at Krysta, suspecting she understood his thinking better, it appeared, than Mace did. She turned to the knight and explained. "If they weren't willing to hurt him during the capture, it means they want him as close to unharmed as possible. It's a good indicator that they won't kill him or seriously injure him elsewhere on the journey."

"And when he tries to escape, they probably won't hurt him too badly if he doesn't manage to get free," Drake added. If Wil was anything like his older brothers, he'd attempt escape at the earliest opportunity.

"Wil was in human form when he left," Jenet reported as she finished her circuit of the site, *"and not bleeding. They left on horseback."*

Drake patted her neck and sent her off to drink and cool off with Nellin.

"They were on horseback," Drake said shortly, turning to Krysta and Mace to confer. "We should be able to catch them, even with the head-start."

"We're already making good time." Mace scanned the sky, probably noting the position of the sun. "We could reach the southern mountains by nightfall at least."

"But we'll need to fly lower now. We should follow the trail as closely as possible," Krysta said, while Drake nodded in agreement.

"Shouldn't be too hard with their horses kicking up the

ground."

"We'll follow your lead in the air, Mace." Drake felt he needed to be clear on that point. Mace had always been a very deliberate young man and it looked like he'd become a steady, if a bit sedate, knight. "You and Nellin can recognize and follow the trail better than either me or Jenet."

"We've trained for aerial recognition, but it's easy to see you and Krysta have the advantage on the ground. If the trail forks at any point we'll land and you two can use your tracking skills. I remember how good you were at tracking game, even when we were children, Drake."

Mace's smile was complimentary—even friendly—and Drake suddenly recalled all those adventures the young boys of the Lair had gone on when out of their parents' sight. Mace and Drake had always been part of a larger group, but often the two of them were paired off on one escapade or another. For one thing, Mace and he were of a size when they were younger, and very close in age. The other boys had been either older or younger and most didn't care to follow fanciful Drake on one or another of his imaginary quests. But Mace had been a good sport. He'd played sidekick to Drake on many a boyhood adventure.

It was nice to see that camaraderie translate into adulthood. Even over the many years, that early knowledge and respect for each other remained, and it pleased Drake to know he had the good opinion of this knight who had once been his childhood friend.

They set out not long after. The dragons had found wild game and taken a moment to cool down and drink from the nearby lake. Nellin even shared a few fish he'd caught with Jenet in a kind gesture that Mace found somewhat telling. If he weren't much mistaken, his dragon partner was attracted to the spectacularly colored female. Too bad Jenet didn't have a knight yet. Nellin couldn't mate her until she had a knight of her own and the two knights had found their mate.

It was the way of dragons and knights, but Mace felt a pang for his dragon partner. It seemed unfair that Nellin had to wait to claim his lady love, but Mace was glad for the dragon's control. If Nellin ever mated, bonded as he was to Mace, the dragon's lust would drive Mace crazy with a need that could only be fulfilled by his true mate. It was the main reason fighting dragons did not mate unless their knights had already found their own females to share their lives and their lusts.

When the dragon's passion rose, Mace would be swept along in the fury that only a love partner could assuage. No mere casual sex partner would do. Only a mate, bonded by love, could slake the carnal thirst that would otherwise drive Mace insane.

He wasn't completely sure, but Mace had a very strong feeling Krysta was it. She was the woman he wanted to share his life with, but he had a long row to hoe to convince her to become his wife. And she'd have to be prepared to accept the knight who partnered the dragoness Nellin eventually mated with as well. It wasn't an easy thing to find a woman who could accept such an arrangement, but Krysta already seemed comfortable around Nellin and the dragon liked her as well.

She felt really good in his arms too. This trip was all very serious business, but Mace couldn't help but feel the tiniest bit of glee at the fact that Krysta was snuggled up against him for hours on end. Sure, he had the hard-on from hell to prove her nearness, but it was a sweet sort of torture.

"Can you follow the trail from up here?" Krysta leaned back to speak near his ear, shocking him to an even fuller awareness of the soft woman in his arms.

He pressed forward, tightening his hold around her waist as he leaned close to her neck. "Easily. Nellin's eyesight is much better than mine, but even I can see the telltale marks of the company's passage from this height."

She nodded, but Mace couldn't move away from the tempting softness of her skin. Giving into temptation, he licked just under her ear, nuzzling in closer as he tasted the salt of her skin and breathed in the essence of her. She was delicious on so many levels.

"Mace?"

One hand rose over her breast, squeezing gently as he tested her response. He could feel the increase in her breathing as she leaned into him, pressing herself into his palm. He tucked his other hand downward, insinuating it between the dragon's hide and her hot core, clothed in her soft, well-worn uniform trousers.

"Mace, stop. We can't."

"Just let me hold you like this, Krysta." He nuzzled her neck from behind. "I've dreamed of you since our time together. Every single night."

Dragons were exhibitionists and that proclivity tended to rub off on their knights, so Mace didn't particularly care if Drake and Jenet could see what he was doing. In fact, he felt a primitive urge to publicly stake his claim on this woman. If Krysta was meant to share his life, she'd have to get used to the idea of another man watching—and even joining—in her rapture, but he didn't want to push her too far yet.

Mace hadn't planned to touch her like this, but for once in his life, he decided to go with the moment. He was taking a page out of Drake's book, being spontaneous and impulsive.

Drake definitely had the right idea if this pleasure was the reward for breaking with Mace's carefully laid plans. Krysta shifted, rubbing her taut ass against his straining erection and he bit back a groan. She was fire in his arms and he never wanted to let go.

"Do you dream of me, Krysta? Did you enjoy our time together as much as I did?"

"You know I liked it, Mace, but we can't do this now. Drake might see and I don't want to hurt his feelings."

Krysta couldn't get over the feel of Mace's strong hands on her body. She'd been in turmoil since almost the first moment she'd climbed on Nellin's back, and she'd been seated for hours now in front of the strong knight as they flew in pursuit of the lost prince.

Mace was a special man. Already, he'd claimed a piece of her heart she would never get back, though she hadn't told him yet. She wasn't sure if she'd ever tell him. Things were so unclear to her about the future—as they'd never been before.

There was Mace. And there was Drake. How could she reconcile the growing feelings she had for both men? Unless things changed in a drastic way, the scenario could only lead to heartache and personal disaster. But she felt powerless to stop it all.

And now this. This slap-dash flight across the land after a stolen prince. And both men working together, with her, to save the boy that meant so much to their land.

Mace pressed her further, his fingers igniting little fires of need through her body. She grabbed his wrist, stilling his motion, though the flame in her core sparked higher. She couldn't do this. She didn't want to hurt either of these brave men.

"No. Mace, I'm sorry."

"I'm sorry too. I lose my head when I'm around you, Krysta." He removed the hand from between her legs, returning it to her waist, but his other hand remained just under her breast, cupping her. He kissed her neck, nuzzling close as he spoke into her ear. "You're the most beautiful woman I've ever known—inside and out."

"Flatterer."

"You're easy to flatter, Krysta. You truly are the most amazing woman." He squeezed her around the middle, and Krysta felt the affection in his words. He was such a good man.

But then, Drake had been charming her for days now and she felt torn. How in the world could she choose between them? Something in her heart would be ripped apart if she hurt Mace, but she didn't want to hurt Drake either. There was a depth to the bard she hadn't expected. He was an honorable man too, with skill and bravery he kept hidden most of the time. He loved his family too, especially the dragon who so obviously adored him. That spoke well for him. Dragons were judges of men. Only very special men were befriended by dragons and that Drake and Mace both had gained the trust and respect of two such noble dragons argued well for them both.

So the problem remained and only grew more complex the more she learned of both men. How was she to choose?

Chapter Ten

Drake seethed, watching Mace hold Krysta on Nellin's back as they led the way across the sky. Nellin followed the kidnappers' path, keeping his sharp dragon eyes on the telltale signs dug into the surface of the earth below.

Drake had little say in the matter when Jenet decided to speed up a bit, bringing them alongside the other dragon. They pulled even just in time to watch Mace cup one of Krysta's spectacular breasts in his hand. Drake could have happily cut off the knight's arm just then, had they been on the ground.

Drake had never been a jealous man, but in that moment, he was never more envious of his friend. Mace had the woman of Drake's dreams in his arms, and Drake could do nothing but watch. And want.

When Krysta drew away, Drake silently applauded.

Drake's mouth watered, thinking about getting Krysta alone. He hadn't had much opportunity to woo her or touch her as he longed to do. He wanted her desperately. Like he'd never wanted another woman in his entire life.

The thought was sobering. And frightening.

"Looks like they're getting along." Jenet's wry voice sounded through his mind.

Drake growled low in his throat. *"We don't have time for*

this. Finding Wil is our priority."

Jenet perked her neck up, chastised. *"You don't have to remind me, you big grump. But we've a long way to fly first and there's nothing you humans can do but be baggage until we find the kidnappers."*

Drake knew he was being unreasonable, but seeing Mace cuddling the woman he wanted above all others set his jaw on edge. It also—strangely—set him afire. Krysta looked...right...in Mace's arms. Somewhere, deep inside, Drake registered that realization, even as his unaccustomed jealousy reared its ugly head.

"You know, you could have her too, if you became my knight." Jenet's smug voice intruded on his troubling thoughts.

"What are you talking about?" Drake felt the bottom of his stomach drop. *"Are you planning on mating with Nellin?"*

"Nellin is my mate, it's true. But we'll wait for Mace to find his own mate—and for you to come to your senses and accept me as your partner."

"You've got to be kidding!"

"No, Drake. Search your heart. You hear the truth of my words. You know I was born for you. You've been my knight since the moment I hatched and as long as you live, I will have no other. I love you."

Drake felt the truth of her words all the way down to his soul. He remembered the precious little creature that had busted out of a giant shell after hours of labor, and the first meeting of their eyes. He remembered talking to the baby inside the shell long before she hatched, making friends with her even before she was free to roam about the Lair with him, his constant companion. He remembered too their parents' indulgent smiles and encouragement.

All except for Declan.

131

The man whose opinion mattered most in Drake's young life had always seemed to expect more of him than he could give. Declan had demanded perfection when Drake could give only mediocrity. He'd failed time and again at the tasks Declan had set for him, meeting with grim disapproval and reminders that he'd never be good enough for Jenet if he didn't work harder.

Declan had said those actual words only once, but Drake had taken his sire's warning to heart. Drake loved Jenet too much to stick her with an inferior knight, and Drake knew he was inferior in every way to the star pupils like Mace.

Steady, strong, staid Mace. He never put a toe wrong and excelled at all the knightly skills. Drake wanted to hate the boy, but had found an odd camaraderie with the quiet lad instead. They'd even parted as friends the day Drake struck off to find his own path. Mace had seen him leaving the castle and had walked a short way with him, down the road into Castleton. They'd parted with kind words and good wishes between them and Drake had made Mace promise to keep an eye out for Jenet, which he was sure the young knight-hopeful would do without falter. He was just that dependable.

"I hate to disappoint you, sweetheart—" Drake's tone was full of frustration, *"—but your plan will never work. I'm still leaving Draconia as soon as this mission is over. I have responsibilities in other lands to which I'm much better suited. I learned the hard way I can never be the knight you need, Jenet. You have to give up this crazy idea."*

"I will never give up on you, Drake. You're mine as much as I am yours. The bond between us can never be undone. It is only for you to accept and let it grow stronger."

"I can never be what you deserve, Jenet." The words were torn from his soul, barely whispered into her mind.

"You are already more than I'll ever need and all that I want. It is only for you to recognize that truth and accept your destiny."

Drake would have replied, but at that moment, the sky turned grey and a light rain started to soak through his meager city clothing. Wonderful. The weather matched his glum mood, even as his shirt soaked clear through. His leather breeches were in somewhat better shape, but they were old and starting to soak up water in places around the knees and crotch. Just great. This would be a soggy, miserable trip to match his sullen mood.

Drake spared a moment to look over at Nellin and noted that Mace—ever prepared—had pulled an oilcloth from his pack and spread it over himself and Krysta. At least they would be dry, but the knight's preparedness just drove home to Drake how un-knightly he was himself. He'd gone off on a quest without the most basic of necessities.

All Jenet had was the leather pouch Drake had given her, filled with lotions and creams for her wings. No oil cloth. No food. Nothing that could be useful on a cross-country journey.

A knight would have prepared.

Which only went to prove, Drake of the Five Lands was no dragon's knight.

Before it got too dark to see, Mace signaled a halt and the dragons started angling downward to find a place to weather the storm and get some sleep before they carried on the search.

Dragons could literally sniff out caves. It was part of their basic survival instincts. Even though both Jenet and Nellin had been born and raised in the safety of the Castle Lair, they'd been trained since a young age to rely on their natural abilities. Still, both dragons claimed there was not one suitable cave in the area for their human friends to spend the night.

So the three curled up on the ground at the base of a relatively dry granite cliff. The dragons arranged themselves on either side and held Mace's tarp between them, making a little tent area for the humans, though it was small.

"I've got a dry shirt you can wear and some food in my pack. It's not much, but we won't go hungry tonight."

"Thanks for the loan. I just took off, not thinking about provisions—or dry clothes."

"Don't be so hard on yourself, Drake. You're not trained as a knight, after all."

Drake paused in the act of accepting the dry shirt from his friend. Mace thought he read hurt in the other man's eyes for a moment and realized his words might've come out differently than intended.

"Look, Drake—"

"No. You're right." Drake reached out to snap up the shirt. "I'll never live up to my father's example. It's why I left." He shrugged as he tugged the shirt on. "I knew I'd never be good enough for Jenet." There was real pain in Drake's voice and he wouldn't meet Mace's eyes. "This only proves, once again, that I was right."

Mace was stunned. He'd always admired Drake and the easy way skills like archery and swordplay had come to him. By contrast, Mace had to work hard for every small step forward when they were boys, training and learning together. To Drake, everything had come naturally, yet he'd never lorded it over the younger or less skilled. Drake had always pushed himself harder than anyone else could have. He demanded a lot from himself. Almost too much.

But he'd had a wild side. Drake had been a prankster and often got in trouble for the mostly harmless jokes he played on

134

his classmates. When that happened, Sir Declan came down hard on the boy he clearly thought was far too frivolous.

Mace knew that was finally why Drake had left. There were few in the Castle Lair who hadn't seen the way Drake took every condemnation and word of correction from Declan to heart. Few were really surprised when Drake took off for parts unknown. But Mace had missed him. They'd been friends of a sort.

"You were always good enough. Drake, you were better than all the others in our age group, but you never saw it."

"You're deluded. I couldn't put a foot right. Jenet will be better off when she finds a man who is worthy of her."

"If you truly believe that," Mace said at length, "you really are a fool."

"Look—" Drake turned on him, "—I appreciate the sentiment, but I have my own life now. Away from Draconia. Away from my family. I've found my niche and it's working for me."

"But what about Jenet?"

Drake sighed. "Like I said, she needs to find a knight who is her equal. That's not me."

"I think you're wrong, but we'll let it rest for now. At least until after we eat."

Krysta was sorting through the food in Mace's pack, divvying up the meager rations. She handed each of the men a portion that was noticeably larger than what she kept for herself. Distracted by her beauty, Mace let the matter go as he moved to sit beside her.

The tension in the air wasn't lost on Krysta. Drake bristled when Mace settled at her side. She feared a confrontation of some kind was next on the agenda and the men didn't disappoint. Apparently even among knights—or near-knights— the male mind still had the same basic possessiveness.

Too bad she'd have to end such a long day by teaching these males a thing or two about women.

Krysta sighed as she set aside her meal to look at the men. Drake was frowning as he chewed mechanically and swallowed. Mace seemed oblivious to Drake's temper—*seemed* being the operative word. She knew darn well he was fully aware of the response his actions had provoked in his counterpart. The dragons watched all, saying nothing.

It wasn't long before Drake couldn't hold his tongue any longer.

"You two look cozy."

She should have seen it coming, but was still annoyed when Mace put his arm around her shoulders and drew her against his side. Drake's eyes narrowed and Krysta hated the way they'd put her between them, like a bone for two dogs to fight over. But this was something more than just male posturing. There were dragons involved and all the tantalizing possibilities of knighthood. Krysta wanted to see just how far they'd go in their one-upmanship and learn where she stood in the bargain.

She hadn't become a master spy by playing her cards too early, after all.

"It's no secret Krysta and I have a relationship." Mace almost sounded as if he was gloating, but he was too sober a man to actually gloat. Or so she thought.

"Funny—" Drake stood and tossed a scrap of crust away into the brush, "—I thought Krysta and *I* had a relationship. Guess I was wrong."

"You know full well we could both have what we want if you'd just wake up and accept what Jenet offers." Mace's words were tinged with surprising anger and she saw an answering flush of emotion on Drake's face as he spun to confront the knight.

It was time to step in. Elbowing her way free, she stood, as did Mace, to face Drake.

"What about what I want?" She had their attention now. "Did either of you ever ask me if I'd be interested in something more permanent? Did either of you give me any reason to believe you want me for *me* and not just because I'm a convenient woman you both happen to like?"

"I more than just *like* you, honey," Drake was quick to point out.

"Spare me your rogue's ways, Drake." She turned her attention to the dragons. "And you two." She marched right up to Nellin and Jenet, facing them down as they blinked at her in surprise. "I'm pretty sure you're trying to orchestrate this behind the scenes. I get the idea you two want to be together and the way I understand it, you can't be until Jenet bonds with a knight and the two knights find a woman willing to put up with them both. If you ask me, that will require a miracle if these are the two men in question." She gestured grandly, turning back to the men. "Oh, but that's right. No one asked my opinion. Far be it from me to have any say whatsoever in what you all have planned for my future. You know what?" She paused, eyeing them all with a steely glance. "Just count me out. I've heard a lot about convenience here, but nothing about genuine feelings. I've been down that road before and I swore I would never willingly travel it again. Unless and until any of you can convince me otherwise, you'll have to look elsewhere for a *convenient* woman who isn't too picky about spending the rest of her life playing the fool for you all."

Tears threatened, surprising the hell out of her, but she

sucked them back. No way would she let them see her cry. She'd be damned if she let on how much she'd come to care for all of them, only to realize from the tone of their conversation that she meant less than nothing to any of them. She'd hoped Mace, at least, had come to feel something for her on a personal level. She'd hoped for...love.

But she'd been a fool again. Thinking back, not one word of love had been spoken to her by either of the men. And here she'd thought to guard herself only around Drake. At least she'd known enough not to take anything the glib-tongued bard said to heart. She hadn't had any such caution with Mace, expecting the somber knight to be more honest in his feelings.

Too bad he didn't seem to have any at all.

It shouldn't hurt so badly, but it did.

Krysta moved a short distance away, needing space. No one followed, for which she was glad. She needed time alone to gather her composure and refocus her energies on the task at hand. All this personal garbage had to be put on hold while Wil was still out there, in need of their help.

"You could ask her to ride with you tomorrow," Jenet suggested as Drake watched Krysta's rigid back. *"Then you could talk during the flight and bring her around."*

"But you said you couldn't carry us both." Drake immediately grew suspicious.

Jenet's voice grew small. *"I lied."*

Drake just stared at her for a moment, then started to chuckle. "I'll be damned. Krysta was right. You and Nellin have been working this all behind the scenes, haven't you?"

"It's no crime to want to see you happy."

Drake sighed and patted her neck. *"Or to want happiness*

for yourself." He looked over at the male dragon. *"So Nellin is the one for you, eh? Are you sure, sweetheart?"*

"Oh, yes. I'm sure."

Drake reached up and hugged her with one arm. "I'm happy for you both, then. Nellin's always been a superior dragon. And Mace is a good man. He'll be a good second-father to your offspring—steady and fair."

"He'd be a good fighting partner for you too, Drake, if you'd consent to being my knight."

"Sweetheart." Drake's heart felt so heavy it might break. *"I love you and it was always my fondest boyhood dream to be worthy of you, but you know my reasons. You deserve better than a man who would run off across the breadth of the land without even a change of clothes. I'd be a miserable failure as a knight. This latest fiasco only proves it."*

"You may think so, Drake." Jenet sighed a thin stream of smoke. *"But there's more to being a knight than remembering your pack. It's your heart that led me to choose you when we were both just children. It's true, brave and strong. That's what I want in the man I will fight beside and live with all his days. You don't see it in yourself, I know, but it's there—your nobility and courage. You're all I've ever wanted, Drake."*

Something in her words wanted to sink into his mind, but he refused to consider it at the moment. Right now, he was wallowing in self-pity and anger over his own stupidity. He hadn't felt this bad about himself since he'd left home. He should have known coming back to Draconia would bring back all that crippling self-doubt.

"That's because I'm all you ever knew. There are many more worthy men out there, Jen. I hoped you'd have found one in the time I was gone and the fact that you waited and pined for me only makes me feel worse. I've been nothing but bad for you

since the moment you hatched, but I can't help loving you. Please don't make this any harder than it already is."

Jenet backed away, clearly hurt. *"I'll leave it for now, but I'll never stop hoping, Drake. You don't see yourself clearly, but I do. I see to the heart of you, and it's you I want."*

Great, Drake thought, only two women around for miles and they're both upset with me. So much for the fabled bard's charm.

Sometime in the dark of the night, Krysta had snuggled against Drake. There wasn't a lot of room between the dragons and under the tarp, and though the dragons kept the area warm, Krysta undoubtedly felt the night air's chill, even positioned as she was between Drake and Mace. She'd returned to the group silently as they prepared for sleep, giving in to the necessity of sharing body heat to stay warm as the rain continued to pour down in a steady stream.

Drake felt the soft, feminine touch on his chest under the loose shirt Mace had loaned him and came instantly awake. Krysta was still sleeping, her face nestled into the crook of his arm, her body turned to his, burrowing into his side. Drake saw the way she shivered in the chill air and drew her closer, wrapping his arms around her.

She settled into a deeper sleep, her hand trapped between them, under his shirt, her palm resting over his heart like a promise. Drake felt the rightness of having her there, in his arms, but was powerless against the drag of fatigue on his tired body. He fell back asleep, only to dream of the moment when they would finally make love.

The first rays of dawn touched the land when Drake woke again. Krysta was still in his embrace, her lithe body entwined with his. Their legs had tangled in the night so that his morning erection nestled snuggly between her thighs, resting against the place it most wanted to go. Her lips grazed his neck, raising gooseflesh where they touched as her soft breath rasped across his skin.

Drake relished the feel of her for a long, pleasurable moment before the slight motion on her other side roused him to open his eyes once more. Mace was watching them.

He read envy and a little regret in the knight's eyes, but strangely, no trace of anger. Drake wondered at that. He thought for certain any man would be incensed to find the woman he wanted had turned to another for comfort in the dark of the night. But then, this was Mace. The quiet knight seldom reacted as others did.

Krysta stirred against him, slowly coming awake.

When her eyes popped open, confusion reigned there for only a moment before she tried to pull away. Drake wouldn't let her. There was something he needed from her first, something he had to know.

Slowly, he lowered his lips to hers, seeking the warmth of her kiss, knowing full well Mace watched every move. She didn't resist as his mouth claimed hers, lips and tongues tangling with the familiarity of long-lost lovers though they hadn't yet shared more than a kiss and a snuggle.

She felt so right in his arms. Surely Mace could see the truth of it. This woman was meant for Drake and he was making the point the only way he could think of at the moment.

He turned her, settling her on the ground beneath him, his cock settling into the welcoming cradle of her thighs as she spread them easily for him, as if he was always meant to be there. Stars! He couldn't wait to get inside her, but he'd bide his time until they were alone.

Sense overriding passion, Drake eased up, lifting his head to look down at her passion-glazed eyes.

"Good morning, sweetheart."

Her breathing was ragged, just the way he liked it. "Good morning."

"I'm sorry about last night. I had a long talk with Jenet and you were right about everything. The nosey little matchmakers were manipulating us all." He moved off her, helping her rise while Mace stood and folded the tarp they'd used for cover. Drake saw the instant Krysta realized Mace had witnessed their kiss as color flooded her cheeks.

The dragons stood, going off in search of water and perhaps something to nibble on while the humans readied themselves for the journey ahead. Drake felt them leave, but didn't spare a glance for anyone but Krysta.

"Let's just forget it, Drake."

He bowed his head, never taking his eyes from her. "As you wish."

"There's a little left for breakfast," Mace said, moving to place his pack between them. He straightened and yanked Krysta into his arms, planting an almost bruising kiss on her parted lips. Drake half expected her to floor him, but instead, she responded, sinking into the knight's kiss with what looked like genuine abandon.

Dammit. Drake felt a little of what Mace must've been feeling a few minutes ago. Regret that this woman would choose another, envy at the way she was kissing Mace, but Drake also felt the anger he'd expected. It wasn't anger directed at her for choosing Mace, but rather anger at himself, that he couldn't be a part of their pleasure. Now that was odd.

Drake squatted by the pack and busied himself with the rations Mace had brought. There wasn't much left, but it would do until they could find a town or time to hunt. He concentrated on that problem rather than the unsettling thoughts watching Mace kiss Krysta had stirred up.

He heard them break apart and couldn't help but look up, disappointed to see the same dazed look on Krysta's lovely face. She responded to Mace in much the same way she'd responded to Drake, though he knew she'd have decked anybody else who dared to kiss her without invitation. She wasn't easy. Far from it.

Drake expected Mace to be wearing a smug grin, but as usual, the knight confounded him. Mace looked...vindicated was the only word that sprung to mind. As if he'd just proved a point of some kind, and Drake was half afraid he knew just what point Mace had wanted to prove. Nellin and Jenet wanted to be together. Mace was bonded to Nellin and would therefore have to accept the man Jenet chose as her knight to share a wife with. Mace seemed to want to prove the point that not only would Krysta be compatible with both of them, but that Drake would be a good choice as Jenet's fighting partner for that reason.

Drake knew it was all too neat and tidy. For one thing, he'd make a terrible knight. For another, the Mother of All only knew if Krysta wanted to be shared between two knights. She seemed to like both of them well enough, but on a permanent basis? Who knew?

Drake shook his head and set to eating his meager breakfast as Mace did the same. He could feel Krysta watching them both, but he didn't have any answers for her, so he kept his eyes on his food and his thoughts to himself.

Krysta couldn't believe it. The two idiots were posturing over her again. Pawing her in the early morning, to prove something to each other. Damn them!

And she'd fallen in with their plans, meekly accepting their kisses and even enjoying them. Had her brains taken a holiday? What was she thinking?

Obviously she *wasn't* thinking, or she would've kneed them both in the balls and have done with it. She wasn't any man's plaything. Sure, she'd already bedded Mace, so he'd probably expected a good morning kiss, but that...*assault*...he'd just made on her person was far from a good morning peck. And Drake—well, she didn't know where the ballsy bard got the notion he could kiss her like his last breath depended on it, but being honest with herself, she admitted she'd enjoyed every last minute of it. The man knew how to kiss. As did Mace. Dammit.

It was annoying to find they'd only been kissing her to prove some kind of manly point to each other. She grabbed her ration of food and ate breakfast quickly, saying not a word.

She mounted Nellin with Mace, still not speaking to anyone, but over the hours of flight, her anger mellowed. After a while, she found she could actually laugh at their theatrics. They were such *men.* Competing over the silliest things. This morning it had been her. She shrugged inwardly. She had to forgive them. After all, they were only living up to their nature.

She wasn't quite sure when it had happened, but Krysta came to the startling revelation that she was well and truly in love with Mace. Drake too, though she hadn't let him close enough to seal their growing attraction with lovemaking yet. It was a romantic kind of love, but it was also the kind of love that endured long after the heat of passion burned to an ember.

She respected them both, admired their courage, their skills, the different way they approached life. The two men complimented each other so well, yet they went about things in completely different ways. Mace was a planner, Drake a seat-of-the-pants improviser. Yet they both were incredibly effective in whatever they set out to do. This journey had only raised them both in her estimation.

They could easily have become rivals—even enemies—but the way they worked together and complimented each other's skills was something rare and remarkable. The way they both set about wooing her also made her chuckle. Mace was deliberate and yet surprisingly spontaneous, able to plan on the fly and roll with the punches. He'd surprised her by inviting her on the spur of the moment flight and she'd challenged him, she knew, by making love to him so soon.

But she couldn't have waited. She'd wanted him too much. She still did, as a matter of fact. Oddly, she found the same want within her when Drake smiled in that charming way at her. She wanted Drake too, and respected him just as much. He'd proven an able warrior and a man of deep integrity, contrary to all her expectations and experiences with rogues. Oh, he had a rogue's reputation and way with the ladies, to be sure, but Krysta knew deep down, the reputation wasn't earned. Drake wasn't a cad. He'd never lied to her or played her false. True, they'd known each other only a short time, but she recognized the light in his soul and the fire in his being. He was a good man. As good as Mace, in his own way.

They were well matched and if the dragons had their way, they'd be fighting partners one day, sharing a mate between them. Somehow Krysta thought Jenet wouldn't give up until Drake was her knight. Which left Krysta with only one startling thought—did she really want to be the woman for them both?

In order to keep Mace in her life, Krysta would eventually have to accept Jenet's knight as well. Right now, Drake was the less encumbered of the two men, but Krysta suspected he wouldn't be for long. Jenet was as cunning as any woman, and Krysta had deep respect for the dragon who'd waited on the stubborn bard for so many years.

So if she chose Drake, in order to keep him, sooner or later, Mace would come into the relationship again. She really had no choice. It was either both of them or neither. The question remained, did she believe herself up to sharing her life with two knights...and two dragons?

Krysta wasn't sure and for the first time in her life, she agonized over her future. She didn't want to give up Mace or Drake, but how could she commit to such a strange relationship? Worse, would they even ask her? Neither man had spoken of love. So far, it seemed, only her heart was on the line. Krysta prayed to the Mother of All she wouldn't be the one to walk away from this with a heartbreak she doubted would ever mend.

Chapter Eleven

Mace called a halt later in the day, his hand signal clear enough to Drake, though he'd never trained with knights. They were to land and proceed with caution.

"Nellin sees something," Jenet told Drake as they circled and dropped altitude. *"The trail ends abruptly. Mace sees it now too and Nellin says he's upset."*

"Upset how?" Drake asked as they neared the ground. He braced himself for landing as he'd been taught as a youngster in the Lair.

"He's furious!"

They hit the ground with a jarring thump and Mace jumped off Nellin's back before he'd even come to a full stop. Krysta was left to scramble down as best she could, but Drake vaulted from Jenet's back and caught Krysta when she jumped down from Nellin's tall knee.

"What's wrong with him? He started grumbling about traitors and took off." Krysta's tone was both curious and concerned. "I've never seen him like this. He's livid."

Drake looked to where the knight was stomping around the edges of the trail, kicking at stones, though he was careful to aim his irritation away from the signs he studied. Drake shook his head.

"I have. Mace is normally the steadiest of men, but when something pushes him past his limits, watch out. He sees something about this trail that has him in an uproar and we need to find out what it is."

Drake approached Mace cautiously. He could hear the knight almost growling under his breath. A habit he'd probably picked up from his dragon, Drake thought. Nellin didn't look all that happy either, come to think of it.

"Mace?" Krysta approached him with sure steps, though her voice was calm in the face of his obvious fury. "What is it?"

The knight whirled on them. "What is it? Damn it to the nine hells! This is beyond anything I've ever seen!"

"What, brother?" Drake asked quietly, hoping to calm his friend. "What did you see from the air that we didn't?"

Mace walked briskly off, pointing to the ground. "This!" He cursed viciously. "The trail ends here."

"Ends?" Drake met Mace and looked at the ground. Seeing things from this vantage point, the tracks started to make sense. "I see. They left by air."

"Dragons?" Krysta asked, incredulous. "Dragons participated in Prince Wil's kidnapping? How could this be?"

"It could not. No dragon would harm a royal black. It goes against everything we are." Nellin spoke as he moved forward with Jenet beside him. She nodded as well, though her expression was sad and more than a little confused.

"It wasn't a dragon," Drake said into the tense silence. He moved off to stand beside a large print in the sandy soil. "See this?" The rest of them came near to view the depression in the earth. "This is no dragon claw. This is a paw. See the pads? Like a cat's paw, but on a grand scale."

He walked forward a few feet, his entourage following. "And

this?" He pointed out a deep scratch in the surface of the land. "This is not a dragon mark either. It's a bird's claw."

"What bird could grow to such a size?" Mace wanted to know.

"In all the lands the Jinn roam, I've never heard of a bird that would carry people on its back. Or even in its grasp," Krysta said quietly, "Or a giant, flying cat, that would do the same."

"But I have," Drake insisted. "This creature is neither bird nor cat. It's both. And neither." Drake stepped back to view the two sets of prints together. "We're dealing with a gryphon. Probably more than one."

"Gryphons!" Nellin roared. *"By the Mother, they shall pay for this!"*

"But they're very rare, aren't they? And not inclined to deal with humans, or so I've heard," Krysta questioned.

Drake nodded. "Not usually. But I knew two gryphons who dealt quite well with people in the court of the Doge of Helios. They were bound protectors of the royal line and had lived among people for many generations. I knew them well, which is why I recognize these prints beyond the shadow of a doubt." Drake nodded with grim confidence. "Somehow gryphons have been enlisted to aid in the kidnapping of a royal prince of Draconia."

"It makes sense in a sinister sort of way," Nellin said, *"only their great magic could even hope to stop a black dragon in human form from changing and flying away. If Prince William somehow managed to change, the gryphons could always fly him down, but their brand of magic could probably prevent him from shifting form at all. They are very potent against humans, but have little impact on dragons."*

"Their magic and ours negate each other. At least that's

what the elders say," Jenet agreed. *"But they are said to be powerful indeed."*

"The worst part of this though," Drake bent to examine the earth, finding the tracks many hours old to his trained eye, "is that we have no hope of catching them before they reach the sea now. If they fly as fast as a dragon, they're already at the coast."

"We fly faster," Nellin said with determination.

"But probably not by much." Jenet was more honest, craning her neck over so she could touch her head comfortingly against Drake's chest. *"Drake,"* she said quietly, *"how are we going to get Wil back now?"*

The lost tone touched his heart. Drake knew Jenet was closer perhaps than any dragon to the young prince, and she worried for him. Drake reached out and stroked her head, hugging her for a short moment as he tried to reassure her.

"The gryphons didn't bother to hide their sign." Mace had calmed considerably and was now stalking around the area, looking for clues.

Jenet straightened and Drake joined the knight, nodding as he went. "And they're well within Draconia's borders. They knew someone would come after them on dragonback. It's like they wanted us to know who and what they were...and follow behind."

"Do you think it's some kind of trap?" Krysta asked astutely, coming up beside the men.

"Even if it is, we have no choice but to follow," Mace said, turning to her. "Securing Prince William's return is paramount. We can't turn back just because we fear a trap. But we go in with our eyes wide open and plan as best we can to avoid whatever the enemy may have in store."

"The other possibility is that they want us to find them so

they can make their demands. They may still want to negotiate for Prince Wil's return." Drake sifted some of the sandy soil through his hands as he studied the tracks and thought.

"Then why make us run the length of the land to find them?" Krysta wanted to know.

Drake looked up at her. "To bargain from their place of strength. They may have some sort of stronghold they believe sufficient to contain a royal black dragon. You must admit, there are few places that could hold him if he didn't want to be held. Mace and I both ran with Nico and Roland when they were about Wil's age and they already had the strength of ten men and magic to go along with it."

Mace nodded. "The gryphons are probably part of the reason we had to come south. They would have been seen and remarked upon had they ventured farther into Draconia than this. As it is, they probably flew at night to avoid detection. This is about as far inland as they could get in one night's work."

"But where did they come from?"

"Gryphon Isle." The dragons spoke in unison as the men turned to regard them with surprise.

Jenet stepped forward. *"It's a place of legend that the elders speak of only rarely, but we've heard the stories. It is part of every dragon's training to learn the history of what came before. Gryphon Isle is the place where Gryffid, one of the last of the wizards, fled when the end came for their race. It was he who created and nurtured the gryphons in the days before and he retreated with his children to his island when the end drew near for wizard kind."*

"Where, exactly, is this island supposed to be? And why have we never heard of it? Or this wizard Gryffid?" Drake stepped forward, curious. Apparently there were things dragons were taught that humans no longer knew—if they ever had.

Nellin moved next to Jenet protectively as Drake confronted them both. *"It is not for humans to remember the distant past, but we dragons must keep the memories alive against the coming days. That's what we've been taught. It is our role."*

"And why is this the first I've ever heard of this?" Mace moved to stand beside Drake. *"I thought there were no secrets between us, Nellin."*

Nellin's head shook. *"Not a secret, exactly. Just something you didn't know. Now you do."*

"There's more, but it's not our place to tell," Jenet said with quiet respect.

Drake grew intrigued. He'd had no idea the dragons were keeping—if not secrets—then their own counsel on certain things. Drake's eyebrow rose as he regarded the dragon he'd known all his life. He knew her...and trusted her. Yet it was strangely unsettling to find out there were things about her kind, unknown even to a knight.

He sighed deeply and made a quick decision, hoping he was right to trust his instincts—to trust her.

"Keep your secrets for now, sweetheart. I believe you would never withhold anything that could harm either Mace, Krysta or myself."

Jenet sighed in smoky relief. *"That means more than I can say, Drake. And it's the truth. Dragonkind is mankind's ally in this. If we have longer memories than you, do not fault us. It will be for your benefit in the long run."*

Curiouser and curiouser, Drake thought, but he'd leave it for now. They had little time to waste.

"We have to go." He shot a look at Mace and the knight nodded.

"But how do we track them across the sky? There's no trail

to follow anymore." Krysta followed Mace to Nellin's side and mounted.

"We don't need a trail," Drake called. "We know where they're going. Or at least, I believe the dragons do. Don't you, sweetheart?" Drake turned his words toward Jenet who hung her head almost bashfully. "You know where Gryphon Isle is, don't you?"

Slowly, she nodded. *"I think so. At least, we've been taught the signs by which to find it."*

Drake held her eye for a moment, then nodded. "All right then. Let's fly as quick as we can for Gryphon Isle." He mounted with a gentle leap and they set off almost before he was settled, Nellin, with Mace and Krysta, right behind.

Sometime around dusk they reached the coastline. This was the southern border of Draconia, a foamy turquoise sea and lovely wide beach. They'd passed a few villages and fishing huts on the way to this secluded spot, but the dragons were looking for signs only they knew and had brought them to a secluded cove between two large pillars of rock.

Drake looked up at the walls surrounding the cove and realized it would be nearly impossible for humans to reach this area other than by boat. The steep walls were too barren to allow for easy climbing and the monolithic rocks guarding the mouth of the cove kept all but the most intrepid away.

A few large caves were hidden on the inner walls, but none showed signs of human use. Still, there was something odd about the area...

A moment later, the little hairs on the back of Drake's neck stood to attention. Something was battering against him, but Jenet's loud trumpeting roar blocked whatever it was. And then Drake knew.

It was magic!

Gryphon magic, to be precise. He'd felt its flavor only once before, but that was enough to remind him of his first meeting with Taldor and Rulith, the gryphon pair he'd known in that far off land.

Drake turned, and there they were. Two mighty gryphons emerging from the largest of the caves. Their stance was adversarial and the dragons went immediately on guard. Mace and Nellin took the point, having more experience training and fighting as a pair, but Jenet moved to mimic Nellin's motions and Drake tried to follow suit, though he didn't carry a sword like Mace did.

Mace's sharp weapon was drawn and ready as he faced down the gryphons. Krysta, no doubt, knew enough to stay out of his way, her own hands occupied with weapons she'd had secreted on her person.

But Drake knew human weapons would have little effect on creatures such as these. He slid off Jenet's back and strode forward, facing the gryphon pair, his gaze steady and determined. He knew showing fear at such a crucial moment would spell his death. Gryphons were not to be trifled with, but luckily, he knew something of the creatures.

Jenet screeched at him in the back of his mind, but Drake tuned her out. This moment was too important for distraction.

Holding one hand up, palm facing the creature, he braced himself as he walked up to the female gryphon. She raised the blunt side of her front claw and he felt the jolt of her enormous strength against his hand. This was the moment.

If she meant harm, she would kill him now. If she were willing to parley, she would temper her strength to match his own, taking his measure.

Drake breathed an inward sigh of relief to find it was the

latter.

When the female pulled her foreleg back, Drake stood before her as tall and strong as he could. These creatures valued strength, skill and bravery above all.

"I am Drake of the Five Lands," he said loudly. "Plume bearer of Taldor, in hereditary service to the Doge of Helios. I've come for Prince William of Draconia."

"We have heard of you, Drake of the Five Landss." The female gryphon spoke with a clacking of her beak, her bird-like tongue making a hash of the letter s. Drake was used to it, though he hadn't heard gryphon speech in a very long time. The ones he'd known rarely talked aloud. Drake supposed this one did in deference to Krysta. It was interesting to note the gryphon evidently wanted all to know what was said.

Drake renewed his firm stance. "I've come for Prince William. Will you return him or must we battle?"

"He iss not ourss to give." The male gryphon stepped forward, his voice a little raspier than the female's. "You were expected." The male cocked his eagle-like head and looked at Mace and Krysta. "Though we thought it would be two, not three. Sstill, we will deal with you asss we were insstructed."

"By whom?" Drake asked, not backing down. It didn't do to show any weakness in one's first encounter with a gryphon. "Who took Prince Wil and why? Neither Draconia nor the prince have any disagreement with your kind. This act of aggression will not go unanswered."

The female bowed her feathered head in acknowledgement. "We are only messssengerss, but I can ssay that your prinsse will not be harmed. And he will be returned."

Jenet strode forward to stand behind Drake, her scales rippling with irritation.

"I want him back right now, do you hear me?" She was

155

shouting in a way Drake had never heard, truly upset. *"You had no right to take him! No right!"*

"Calm down, little hen," the male gryphon said almost disdainfully. "Your prinsse is ssafe."

Krysta watched the exchange with a strange mixture of awe, fascination and amusement. The dragons—Jenet especially—squared off with the gryphons. They were about equal in size and both species had sweeping wings, but where dragons sported a leather-like hide and glimmering scales, the gryphons had sleek wings of gleaming feathers the likes of which she'd never seen.

Jenet was clearly upset, facing down the gryphons and breathing smoke in her agitation. Even Nellin bristled as the gryphons replied to the dragon's silent speech, though he sat back and watched the exchange for the most part. Krysta could only hear the gryphons' side of the conversation, but it was enough to indicate Jenet was definitely giving the half-bird, half-cat creatures of myth a piece of her mind.

Krysta took up a position beside Jenet, wanting to stand united with the dragons and men. One of the gryphons cocked its head at her, as if questioning her presence.

"I wish I could hear what Nellin and Jenet are saying to you birds. I bet they'd make me proud."

The gryphon cocked his feathered head at her, his nimble tongue lolling while he clacked his beak. "Truly? It iss ssimple enough."

Krysta stood up straight as she felt the gryphon's incredible magic reach out to her. One feathered wingtip brushed her face and the last thing she heard before she collapsed was a roar of anger from the dragons before her head hit the sand.

When Krysta woke moments later, there was a cacophony of sound in her head and her senses were scrambled.

"You meddlesome bird. Now look what you've done!"

"Will she be all right?"

The first voice was gruff and angry. It sounded male, but like neither Mace nor Drake. The second was female and worried, if Krysta was any judge. Both were musical and rumbling, like the voice of a storm.

"Stop shouting." She sat up, holding her head with both hands as she struggled against the pain. "Please!"

Strong arms supported her back and she looked up to find Drake at her side. Searching for Mace, she found him confronting the gryphons, sword drawn. The gryphons didn't look too worried, though they backed away just slightly, giving them space.

"Did she bump her head? Check her head, Drake." Jenet craned her long neck over Drake's head, bringing her concerned, jeweled gaze into Krysta's line of sight.

Krysta tried to shrug him off as Drake ran his hand lightly over the back of her scalp. "Did Jenet just ask if I bumped my head?"

Drake stilled and all eyes turned to her. "How did you know?"

"Ssilly humanss." The male gryphon tossed his beak, ruffling the feathers around his neck.

"She can hear us." Nellin's voice was low and gruff, his giant face swam into her line of vision as he craned his neck to look at her. *"Can't you?"*

"Stars! I can," Krysta whispered, feeling Drake's hands tighten on her shoulders. "But how?" She looked to the gryphon who'd touched her. "Why?"

"It iss ssimple magic. Conssider it a gift to new friendss." The male gryphon tossed his head again as the smaller female moved forward.

"My mate hass a ssoft heart. We both like you, Kryssta. And your family."

"But more," the male spoke once more, "you are our alliess now."

Krysta stood with Drake's help, then moved out of his arms to face the gryphons. She held their gazes for a long moment. She realized what these amazing magical beings had given her and tears formed behind her eyes that she refused to let fall. Now was not the time for tears. Now was the time to forge new friendships that might see them through the tough times ahead. Krysta bowed low to each gryphon in turn, in the Jinn sign of respect, her gaze never leaving theirs.

"You honor myself and my clan." She fumbled for a moment trying to recall the traditional words, modifying them with a smiling shake of her head to fit this amazing situation. "I'm not certain I can ever repay this honor. Your gift of friendship is beyond measure and I am in your debt."

"Sshe sspeakss well." The female spoke as if to the male, but her words were clearly heard by all.

"Sshe doess," the male agreed, then nodded firmly. "Asss it wass foretold."

Krysta wondered at the gryphon's words. She got the feeling these magical beings were operating under their own agenda and somehow, she and her little band of dragons and men fit in with their plans. She could only imagine what would come next.

"I am Herorthor and thiss iss my mate, Llydiss. We give you our namess and now you have ssome power over uss. Do not sshare them with otherss."

Krysta put one hand over her heart. "I will guard your name as a secret."

"Sshe iss good at keeping ssecretss," the female, Llydiss, said with an amused feather ruffle. "You ssurprisse uss, Kryssta. We thought the sspymasster of the prophessy wass Drake."

"We don't know what prophecy you speak of, Lady." Drake came to stand next to her, and Mace was not far behind. He took up a position on her other side while the dragons stood behind them, united.

"We can tell you only part, for now." The gryphon began to recite:

Sspy, bard, dragon'ss brother
Comess on wing with another
Sseekss the sstolen, asss iss hiss right
Newly mate and newly knight

When winged brethren finally meet
On ssand, on sstone, on tired feet
There to sseek the sstolen prinsse
A wizard'ss ward they musst convinsse

New friendss, a common foe
Together they will go
Toward the easst and rissing ssun
Yet the quesst, jusst begun

"The resst will be told by otherss when you reach the

island. Asss we ssaid, we thought the sspy wass Drake, but it could asss eassily be you, Kryssta. Then the 'other' would be you, Ssir Mace." The female gryphon stretched her wings as if to fly, shifting backward to gain room.

"But I'm no knight," Drake objected, "newly mated or otherwise."

The gryphon clacked its beak as if in laughter, all but ignoring him. "Sstay tonight and learn to sspeak with your friendss, Kryssta. Bond asss you will need to. Tomorrow, sspeak our namess and we will come for you. Then we will go together to the island." The male moved off to join his mate, also stretching his wings in preparation for flight.

"Why can't we go now? Tonight?" Krysta asked.

"It iss not yet time. You musst bond fully to be protected from the magic of the island. Do that tonight. Or perissh tomorrow."

With that final admonishment, the gryphons leaped into the air, their great leonine hindquarters propelling them into the sky as their eagle's wings drew them higher. They were beautiful to watch, but their words were frustrating.

Krysta turned to the men and dragons beside and behind her.

"Well? What now?"

Chapter Twelve

Hearing the speech of dragons was a novel experience for Krysta. She had a hard time at first when the knights tried to teach her how to project her thoughts back to the dragons, but after an hour or so, she gained at least a rudimentary proficiency. Expertise would come with time, they all knew.

The dragons enjoyed speaking with her, glad to finally be able to express themselves fully to the woman who had come to mean so much to both Mace and Drake in so short a time. Jenet was a little reserved, but Nellin surprised Krysta with his droll observations and wit. She found herself laughing often at Nellin's wry humor as they prepared a quick dinner of fish the dragons speared with their talons in the shallows, and made a crude camp for the night on the moonlit beach.

The men gathered driftwood and the dragons provided the spark for a lovely fire. The dragons also settled down in a semi-circle around the campfire, allowing the humans to lean back against their warm bodies as they ate the fish and the crumbs of what was left in Mace's pack.

"Well, that's the last of my provisions. We'll have to forage from here on." Mace closed the now empty pack and replaced it with his pile of gear, settling down next to Krysta as they leaned back against Nellin's smooth hide.

"If the gryphons are to be believed, we'll be at the island

tomorrow. Maybe we can resupply there for the trip home."
Krysta tried to look on the bright side, but deep inside she
harbored reservations. Thy gryphons' rhyming prophecy had
lain heavy on her mind all day.

"I can't believe it'll be just that easy," Drake said from her
other side. He tossed a twig into the fire and the expression on
his handsome face was fierce. "They had to have a reason to
take Wil all this way. I can't see them just letting him go
because we flew down and asked nicely."

"I don't like that gryphons are involved. They're altogether
too magical for my comfort," Mace grumbled as he got more
comfortable against Nellin's warm flank.

"They are powerful, but the few I've dealt with in the past
have been entirely honorable," Drake said. "If they're anything
to judge by, I'd say we have less to fear from the gryphons than
we do from whoever lives on that island."

"Do you think it really could be a wizard?" Krysta's voice
was small in the darkening night. Wizards were to be feared.
They'd been banished from this realm for a reason. Some of
them were downright evil and the stories of ancient days told of
great wars between the evil ones who wanted to enslave all
creatures in this realm and the few who wanted to let the world
evolve on its own.

"I don't know. But there are a few in this world who have
wizard blood. The royal house of Draconia, the Black Dragon
Clan, and the Doge of Helios, for example." Drake tossed
another twig to the flames. "That's why gryphons serve in her
court. Magic seeks its own kind. Whoever we find on that
island, they will have powerful magic, indeed. Of that I have no
doubt."

"We can protect you," Nellin said softly from behind them.
"That's what the gryphons meant when they talked about our

bond. *Dragons are mostly impervious to magic, since we are creatures of magic ourselves. Mace's bond with me will protect him from whatever awaits us tomorrow."*

Jenet shifted her head on the cold sand to look at them. *"I believe it's why they gave you the gift of speech with our kind, Krysta. With that pathway now open, we can bond with you as we do with our knights. Our protection will extend to you."*

"But—"

Jenet sighed smokily. *"Don't fight it, Krysta. It is as the Mother of All wills it. You will bond with our knights and with us. I don't know why you humans must fight the will of the Mother at every turn."* Jenet shot a despairing glance at Drake. *"And now I'm sure you will make some argument about how you're not good enough to bond with me, though it's what we've both wanted deep in our hearts since the moment I hatched. Go ahead, Drake. Do your worst. But the fact remains. If you do not bond with me, you doom our mission. I would rather have had you willing, but at this point, my pride is in tatters. I'll take you any way I can get you."*

"Sweetheart," Drake's voice was as soft as Krysta had ever heard it.

Drake got up and went to the dragon, his long legs carrying him swiftly to Jenet's side. He tugged her sinuous neck into a loving embrace. Drake kissed the ridges of Jenet's eyes as tenderly as a lover and Krysta had to look away, lest the love she read in his every move stir her to tears.

"Never think that I'm not willing to bind my life to yours. I love you more than anything in the world, Jenet. I always have and I always will." Drake didn't care if his words carried. They should all know how much he loved this dragon who was his closest friend in all the universe. "I'm a stubborn ass."

He moved back and stared into Jenet's faceted eyes.

"I won't argue that point." Hope glittered in the depths of her miraculous gaze and Drake felt his spirits rise.

"Can you ever forgive me?"

"Are you willing to be my knight and all that entails for the rest of your days?"

His little girl was tough, but he loved her that way. Drake nodded solemnly and bowed his head, answering her in his mind as he knew it must be. He projected his thoughts to all present, knowing they needed to be witnesses to this most momentous of occasions.

"I don't deserve you, or your forgiveness for my many transgressions, but I love you, Jenet, my sister of the skies. I will be your knight and I will work the rest of my life to be worthy of you."

Nellin trumpeted his joy, his movements dislodging Mace and Krysta, who stood and came to Drake's side.

"Does this mean what I think it does?" Krysta asked breathlessly.

He pulled her close and kissed her while Mace laughed. "We've just witnessed the making of a knight. And about damn time, too."

Mace pounded Drake on the back and congratulated Jenet too, his eyes bright with what Drake suspected were tears. Drake knew there were tears of joy running down his own cheeks, but he didn't care. The moment was too special.

"Brace yourself now," Jenet warned, a split-second before the rush of her power hit him like a wave, cresting and breaking over him, reshaping his very soul. He felt the pathways that had always joined them snap into place even more firmly and blow wide open. He didn't know for a moment where she began and

he ended, so close was the bond between the dragon and himself.

Drake would have dropped to his knees if Mace and Krysta hadn't been there to prop him up. He was stunned by the well of power within the dragon, now shared with him in that blinding moment of revelation. He had only a glimpse of her vast strength and it humbled him. It was something he would remember all his life.

"Drake?" Krysta asked, concern in her lovely grey eyes.

"I'm all right. But I think I know a little bit about how you felt earlier when the gryphon's magic bowled you over. Damn, baby!" He turned to Jenet and hugged her with the arm that wasn't still holding Krysta. "You pack a wallop."

They all laughed then, joy bubbling over as the three humans hugged, surrounded and embraced by the dragons' twining necks.

"Now comes the hard part," Krysta said as their exuberance died down a bit. "How exactly do we all bond and what does it mean?"

"That's the easy part, my dear," Drake wiggled his eyebrows. "And the most fun. If you're willing."

"You mean—?"

Mace wrapped an arm around her waist. "The dragons will seal their troth. They will take to the air in a mating flight, bonding them—and us—fully, as we join them, by joining with you. Both of us, at the same time, will make you our mate."

"You want to marry me? Both of you?"

Krysta's breath caught in her throat.

"I know most women prefer to have the full ceremony, surrounded by friends and family, but I regret we haven't the option. If you bond with us now, we can always have a party later, when we return home, if you wish it." Mace was so serious, so earnest, she reached up to kiss him.

"You're forgetting, I'm Jinn. My family will give you a party whether you want one or not."

Drake joined in her laughter. "She's right about that. The Jinn will throw a party on any excuse."

"Then we can marry now, among ourselves, and seal our bonds." Mace was still serious, but that was his way. "I could not love you any more if we had a hundred witnesses to our vows."

"You love me?" Her heart nearly melted at the tenderness in the fierce knight's eyes.

Mace dropped to one knee before her. "That I do. Forgive me, but I didn't have the courage to tell you before. My heart is yours, Krysta, if you'll have it. For the rest of my days."

"Oh, Mace!" She reached down and kissed him, tears of joy mingling between their lips.

When she drew back, Drake was there, his expression sheepish. "I know it's sudden, and a giant step to take when we've never even been intimate—"

"You haven't?" Mace interrupted with a cocky grin.

Drake looked over at him, annoyed as Mace got to his feet. "No, we haven't. Not that it's any business of yours."

"Hot damn! I finally came first at something."

"Hey!" Krysta objected, but laughingly, at being a point of contention and competition between the two men.

"No disrespect intended, my dear." Mace was quick to assure her, though the grin hadn't left his face. "It's just such a novel experience."

"Would you shut up, please?" Drake shot Mace a pained

look. "I'm trying to propose here."

"What do you know? I beat you to that as well. My luck is looking up!" Mace shied away from the fist thrown negligently in his direction and wisely closed his mouth though his lips still curved in a wide smile.

Drake dropped to one knee, holding Krysta's hand in his. "I'm terrible at this," he muttered, "as I am at so many other things." The earnest look in his eyes sent a pang through her. "But in order to have Mace, it looks like you have to accept me as well. I want you to know that I've wanted you since the moment I first saw you. I've respected your skills and your heart, your compassion and your courage, for as long as I've known you. I'll honor you and cherish you—if you'll let me—and love you with all my heart. I don't know when it happened or how, but I do love you, Krysta. You've taken a place in my heart I never thought to have filled. I only hope you can find some room in yours for me, now that we're forced by circumstance to join."

Tears rolled down her face at his misunderstanding of the situation. She mustered the will to speak past the lump in her throat, knowing he needed to be set straight before they went any further.

"Drake," she swallowed hard, "I don't need to find room in my heart because you're already there." She saw hope light his eyes, but he still seemed skeptical. "I've been struggling with my feelings for you both. True, I made love with Mace, but I probably would have done the same with you, given the opportunity. But when Wil got kidnapped..."

"My seduction plans went out the window," Drake finished for her, seeming more confident now.

She nodded. "I've been so conflicted. I didn't understand how I could want two such completely different men—and at the same time. I worried about how to choose between you. And now I see, I wasn't meant to choose at all. I was meant to have you both, if you'll have me."

"If? Are you kidding? Krysta..." his voice dropped with emotion, "...I've never told any woman what I'm telling you now. I love you, Krysta Vonris, and I will love you, and you alone, for the rest of my days. Please say you'll be my wife."

She flung her arms around his neck and kissed him in answer. The joyful kiss turned passionate and only Mace's tug on her shoulders finally drew them apart.

Drake let her go, shooting his friend a dark look that promised retribution, but Mace only shrugged.

"We have to do this right, Drake. Vows first. Fun after." Mace took one of her hands and Drake the other. They stood in front of her, one on each side, facing her, their dragon partners looming over their shoulders.

"Do you, Krysta, take Mace and Drake to be your husbands?" Nellin spoke an approximation of the ancient words, but they were enhanced by his magic, making Krysta very aware of the power they held.

She took a deep breath.

"I do." Krysta felt bands of power snapping into place between her and the men, though she'd never experienced this kind of magic before.

"Do you, Drake and Mace, take Krysta to be your wife?" Jenet asked in a soft voice.

Each man answered with an "I do". The bonds that had started to form when Krysta gave her answer now widened and firmed, joining them together in a way she'd never before experienced.

"Now us." Jenet prodded the trio with the blunt edge of her

talon, nearly knocking them over as they broke apart, laughing. The trio faced the dragons, smiles on their faces.

"Do you, Nellin, take Jenet as your mate, to love, cherish and protect for all your days?" Mace asked.

"I do." Nellin replied.

"And do you, lovely Jenet," Drake embellished the words, "take Nellin to be your mate, to love, cherish and protect for all your days?"

"I do." Jenet rubbed her neck against Nellin's before they both trumpeted their joy to the skies. A moment later, they bounded into the air, circling each other playfully as they rose into the darkness of the night sky.

Mace and Drake swept Krysta back into their arms, taking turns kissing her breathless. She felt their bonds to the dragons through the mating bond and felt the fire in their souls. It was a heady experience, but she didn't have time to really savor it as first Mace, then Drake, kissed her in ways that made her knees falter. But they were there to catch her, wrapping her in their arms as they carried her to the soft sand in front of the campfire.

"It's going to be fast this time, Krysta, because of the dragons, but we would never hurt you." Mace drew away and fumbled in his pack, finally holding up a small jar as Drake grinned.

"Thank the stars one of us is always prepared." Drake took the jar from his new partner, placing it carefully beside him. "That's for later. First, we need to get naked." He glanced skyward. "Fast."

"Why the rush?" Krysta asked.

Mace turned her in his arms as Drake pulled off her boots, then tugged at the fastenings of her pants and tunic. "We are joined to the dragons. When they mate, so must we. Nellin and

169

Jenet have known for a long time that they would one day mate, but they have never been together. So they're...eager." Mace's expression was so adorably embarrassed, Krysta had to lean up and place a nibbling kiss on his jaw.

"Can't you feel it?" Drake asked, his breath stirring the hair by her ear as he knelt behind her and tugged at her laces. "Through the connection to us, you might feel a residual of their fire, their passion."

Krysta examined the new pathways in her mind and soul as Drake continued to undress her, startled to find passion feeding into her from somewhere outside herself. The men, she realized, and their dragons. The fire of their arousal was potent. It made her squirm as Drake slipped her tunic off over her head, leaving her naked. Mace thoughtfully made a blanket of her clothing and his own underneath them as Drake cupped her breasts from behind, teasing her nipples and pressing hot kisses to her neck. She was on fire!

Mace came back to them once he'd finished laying their bed, such as it was, and knelt in front of her. His gaze followed Drake's hands on her body, apparently liking what he saw.

"You are so beautiful, Krysta," he whispered. "I never imagined how hot it would make me to see Drake touch you like this."

Mace leaned in and kissed her, one hand going to the curls at the juncture of her thighs as the other grasped her leg, lifting and tugging until she was open to his exploring fingers. With Drake's hands still on her breasts, Krysta felt as decadent as a harem girl in Helios. Only it was the other way around. She had the harem, and they were concentrating on her pleasure. It made her want to purr.

Then Mace's fingers found her button and she whimpered instead. He moved back from her lips, his gaze appreciative as it wandered down her body, past where Drake still teased her nipples, to where his own fingers teased her clit.

"Ready for more, my love?" Mace asked.

She could only nod as one of his long fingers speared into her core, surprising her with his speed and sense of urgency. Then she felt the increased heat from the dragons through their shared bond and knew the men couldn't last much longer. Stars! She couldn't last much longer under this kind of pressure. The passion of the dragons washed over them all in waves of heat, firing her blood to a level she'd never before felt. Her body wept, spilling her excitement all over Mace's probing fingers.

He leaned in and captured a nipple with his mouth as Drake offered it up. Having one man hold her breast while another sucked on it was an experience she'd never even imagined, but it felt right. Being with these two was the most *right* thing she'd ever done.

"Try this one, brother." Drake's rumbling words tantalized next to her ear.

Mace grinned at her when he switched from one nipple to the other. Drake's fingers immediately teased the wet nipple, sliding around the point and making her moan.

"I think she likes it," Drake said, nipping at her earlobe as she squirmed. The heat from the dragons combined with the heat these two men generated to send her higher than she'd ever been before. Mace's fingers rubbed inside her, preparing her, inflaming her.

Mace sat back, letting her nipple go with a pop. "I think she does, Drake. I bet she'd like to have her clit licked, don't you?"

Drake's hands tensed around her soft skin and she knew Mace had surprised him. He'd surprised her too with his frank talk, but she liked it more than she would have thought.

Mace drew his fingers out of her channel, swirling around the button at the top of her thighs for a minute before pulling back. "Lay her down, Drake. Maybe you can use that golden tongue of yours on her."

She was lifted and placed down again on the bedding of discarded clothes, surprised to see Drake was naked too. He must've undressed while Mace had her otherwise occupied. Drake spread her legs with little consideration for any modesty she might've had, but she was too far gone to object. The dragon heat was really starting to affect her and she could see the dragons' fire reflected in the men's eyes as they gazed on her bare body.

Drake didn't ask, he merely swooped in, latching onto her clit with his mobile mouth. She felt his tongue licking patterns over her nubbin, making her come with little effort. She cried out as spasms seized her womb, a small completion that only set her up for more as the assault on her senses went on and on. There was no respite while the dragon fever heated them all, only pleasure and more pleasure, each touch, each lingering caress, building on the next in a spiral that grew higher and tighter with every movement.

Much as the dragons circling closer and closer to each other in the starry night above them.

Drake moved back with a satisfied grin as he rolled her to her side. Mace was there, facing her, as she settled on one hip, and Drake snuggled in behind her. Mace lifted her top leg, pulling it high and draping it over his hip, opening her in front and behind as Drake's slick fingers sought her back opening.

She'd been taken there only a few times in her life, back in her youth. She'd never really objected to the sensation, but never found even a hint of the pleasure she felt now, from the lightest brush of Drake's skilled fingers on her skin. She knew this night would be different from all others she'd ever known.

The jar Mace had given Drake suddenly plopped down into the sand above her head and she realized Drake had used some of the cream it held to make this easier on them both. She knew what was coming and now that the dragon fire had found its way into her blood, she was looking forward to experiencing these two men...together.

They couldn't wait much longer. The fire inside would not be denied. Drake's fingers speared inside her, well lubricated with the cream. With her passions running so high, there was no discomfort, only the driving need to have his cock replace those long fingers.

"Please, Drake!" she cried out as he removed his fingers.

"Yes, my love. Take us now. We cannot wait." Drake slid into the passage he'd prepared, making her whimper, while Mace's gaze held hers. She saw the fire leap in his eyes as Drake claimed her.

"Join with us now, brother," Drake encouraged. "We have little time."

Yet Mace held back, his cock head just teasing the slippery opening that wept for him. Krysta wasn't yet complete. She needed Mace to make her whole.

"Come on, Mace. I need you!" she implored him, tugging at his shoulders as he seemed to memorize her face.

"I love you, Krysta. For all my days." His rumbling words preceded his cock as it shoved home within her channel, the two men filling her as she'd never been filled before, the dragon fire lighting their way.

"Oh!" she cried out as they began to move. She could feel the dragons in the back of her mind, joining for the first time as they careened toward the stars. As the dragons became one, so did their human partners.

And as the dragons began to freefall in ecstasy, so too did their knights. A few thrusts and pleasure burst over all three of them, locked together in coital bliss. The men came as the dragons did, bringing Krysta along in a wave of pleasure higher than she'd ever known. She felt Mace tense as his cock swelled, releasing his seed in her womb. At the same time, Drake's long member spent in her back channel. She clenched and pulsed around both of them as they made her come as she never had before.

Tears streaked from her eyes, but there was no pain, only pleasure. A passion so great, it enveloped three humans and two dragons for a mindless moment in which nothing existed in the world but a pleasure so intense, it was all that mattered.

The dragons broke apart in the nick of time, their wings scraping the surface of the sea as they spread wide to resume flight. They were replete with the satisfaction of their first mating, the fire of their passion and the light of their love.

On the sandy beach, the human side of the family was feeling much the same.

Chapter Thirteen

Drake woke first the next morning, just as the pearly light of dawn rose over the ocean. He had the feeling that all was right with the world. Krysta was snuggled against him, between his body and Mace. Jenet slept at his back, her neck entwined with Nellin's, and his heart felt full for the first time in many, many years.

But all was not as it should be. There was a prince still to find and a nest of gryphons to figure out. Drake worked on the problem as he basked in the last few minutes of laziness before they would have to start another tough day on the trail, chasing after Prince Wil. Perhaps today they would find him and put an end to the quest. Or perhaps their dealings with gryphons would only bring more questions. Regardless, he would face the day a happy man. He had a mate whom he loved and who loved him in return, and he had a dragon partner of his very own. A childhood dream had been realized, though he still didn't feel worthy.

"Pish." Jenet's voice sounded through his mind, mocking him, but gently. *"You are the only knight for me. You always were, Drake."*

"I ruined you when we were little, sweetheart. That's all. If we hadn't been raised together, you would see my flaws as clearly as everyone else does. But I won't say I'm not thrilled to

have you in my life, Jen. I love you more than just about anything. You've always been the sister of my heart."

"And now you have a beautiful, smart, talented wife. All because of me." She preened, giving a smoky chuckle. *"You should listen to me more often, Drake. Things always work out for the best when you listen to me."*

He sighed dramatically, falling in with her teasing. *"I should've learned that lesson when we were children, but you may have noticed, I take after my stubborn father."*

Krysta turned in his arms, her eyes cracking open as she squinted against the faint light.

"Good morrow, my love." Drake leaned in to peck her cheek.

"Then it wasn't all a dream?" A teasing light entered her eyes.

"Afraid not." Drake's thoughts turned solemn. "Do you regret tying your life to two men—and two dragons?"

"I could never regret the dragons," she answered. "The jury is still out on the men. I'll let you know." She jumped away when he would have grabbed her and confounded him by running into the surf. Apparently she liked to play. Drake was glad of it. With his disposition, he preferred laughter in all things. That he'd married a woman who could see the joy in life was a boon to his spirit. He'd have to work on Mace though. The man had always been a little too serious, even as a boy, but they'd always gotten along. Mace had hidden depths and a wry sense of humor. It would be up to Drake and Krysta to help bring it out more often.

Drake prodded Mace's shoulder, waking him. "Our wife seems to be part mermaid," he observed, directing Mace's sleepy eyes to the ocean where Krysta was swimming like fish in the dewy morning light. Her slick body looked beautiful in the pinkness of dawn, sleek and wet, cutting gracefully across the waves. Mace sat up, rubbing his chin as he watched her.

Drake stood. "I'm going in. You coming?"

"I'm not much of a swimmer," Mace admitted, looking away from Krysta to shrug at Drake.

"Don't worry. After a few minutes, we won't be swimming." Drake's devilish grin communicated more than his words.

After a long, pleasurable "swim", the trio dressed and ate a skimpy breakfast. The sun was strong in the eastern sky when Drake called the gryphons' names. It was time to find Wil.

Feathery wings made rustling sounds as the gryphons flew into view a few minutes later. They landed with their padded back feet first, then sat, perched upright.

"It iss good to ssee you all sso happy. Congratulationss on your joining," Herorthor said.

"Thank you," Drake answered. "We are ready to see our prince. Will you take us to him?"

"We will," Llydiss replied. "Follow uss."

The gryphons took to the air and waited, circling, while they mounted and the dragons leapt into the sky after them. They set out across the ocean, making for some distant point only the gryphons knew.

"*I hope this isn't some kind of trap,*" Mace said in the privacy of their joined minds.

"*Gryphons are noble creatures. I don't think we're in any trouble trusting them, but keep your eyes open.*" Drake held Krysta in his arms this morning as she flew with him for the first time.

After an hour of flying, Drake realized the dragons were having a hard time of it. The air had thickened with magic that swirled in a miasma of color and shadow around them.

"*What is this?*" Krysta asked hesitantly.

"*Magic,*" Herorthor replied. "*The remnants of powerful time magic, to be precise. We cross over into the island's realm now. Brace yourselves.*"

The entire party felt a jolt as the air currents changed suddenly. A moment ago it had been early morning. Judging by the sun's position, it was now early evening. The red sun sank on the horizon as the cloud of magic cleared. The island rose in the distance, tall spires of rock and sandy beach. The dragons surged forward with a last effort to reach land, though all the riders knew they were tired.

They landed minutes later, and the humans dismounted quickly to give the dragons a break. Whatever they had flown through had taken all their strength and concentration. Jenet and Nellin were both panting as they sat back on their haunches.

A tall figure awaited them on the beach. He was dressed in black leather, his stance welcoming and his green eyes sparkling in the late sun.

"Jenet!" The young man strode forward to meet them, all smiles. "Don't you recognize me?"

"We've come for Prince William." Drake said carefully, his suspicion rising. The man walked confidently and he looked eerily like Roland had as a man at the brink of full adulthood. The swagger was the same, the hair, the build of a warrior, and those royal green eyes.

"I am William." The stranger stopped right in front of Jenet, seeking her out. "Don't you know me, milady? I know it's been a few years, but I can't have changed that much."

"Years?" Krysta asked. "The prince was kidnapped only days ago. We've been on his trail since the morning after his abduction."

"Are the others all right? Declan and Ren wouldn't let me go without a fight, bless their hearts." The familiar green eyes clouded with concern. "Arlis and Lilla were hurt too, I remember, but Gryffid assured me they survived."

"We do not know their fate, but Arlis and my father made it back to the castle to raise the alarm," Drake said. "They very nearly didn't make it and when I left, they were both still confined to their quarters and would be for many days."

"Your father?" The man switched his attention to Drake, surveying him with narrowed eyes. "Then you're Drake. You finally came back for Jenet? That's really great." A smile creased his face and a dimple appeared that made the younger man look just like Nico had at that age. Drake suspected the magic of the island had done something to the boy who was now a man.

"Jenet, my love, is this William?"

Jenet was suspiciously silent as she reached down to lick the man's cheek. Dragons often had the taste and scent of other dragons they knew. Being of the royal line, William was half-dragon, so if this strange young man was indeed the missing prince, Jenet would be able to say for certain.

Jenet retracted her tongue, blinking slowly as she considered. Shock didn't show well on draconic faces, but Drake knew every facet of her behavior. She was surprised.

"William? How can this be?" Jenet lowered her head to eye the man who somehow was the object of their quest. He reached up familiarly and rubbed her eye ridges, causing Drake to start in surprise. No one touched a dragon they did not know unless invited, yet this man seemed to know just what Jenet liked and she did not object.

"It's been five long years since I've seen you, milady. I've missed you."

Drake was even more surprised when the man threw his arms around Jenet's neck and hugged her close. That she allowed such treatment spoke volumes about her certainty that this was indeed the prince they had been searching for.

"I don't understand this," Krysta said.

"Ah, but you will. In good time." A strange voice interrupted and everyone looked up to see a tall man in a long coat standing on the rise of a sand dune, watching them. His voice carried on the evening wind, resonating through the air.

"Who are you?" Krysta moved in front, her curious nature warring with her upset at these strange circumstances. Drake could see the telltale tapping of her fingers against her thigh. She was uncomfortable with these developments—as were they all, if truth be told.

"Gryffid, please save the dramatics," the older version of William said with a sigh. "They are probably very tired after their journey."

The other man nodded. "No doubt you are right. Come, let us repair to the hall. We'll have refreshment and explanations there."

This was not quite the reception they had expected. Drake looked around and realized the gryphons had winged off elsewhere, leaving just the party from Draconia with these two strange men. The one on the dune turned abruptly and disappeared from sight behind the hill. The other man stepped away from Jenet and followed after, waving to them to catch up.

"What do you think?" Drake silently asked all four of his companions as they started after the two men.

"I think very strange magic is afoot on this island," Mace said with suspicion lacing his tone. *"We should be cautious."*

"Undoubtedly," Drake agreed. *"But do you think that young man could really be Prince William?"*

"It is William. Or at least, it tastes like Wil," Jenet said with confusion.

"His scent is that of Prince William," Nellin put in, *"and he has the looks of his brothers, and the power. That man is half-dragon. Of that I have little doubt."*

They crested the dune and saw a lovely old manor house, complete with a large, enclosed courtyard, outbuildings for animals and workers, what looked to be a garrison, and a very large tower rising from the main building. It was lovely, in a very eclectic sort of way, and it looked almost ancient in design, though very well preserved.

"That looks like a wizard's keep." Krysta spoke the thought that passed through all of their minds.

"Very good," came a strange voice, strong in all of their minds. *"It is in fact, my keep."*

"That man!" Krysta held her head, outraged at the intrusion. "A wizard?"

Drake thought about it. "I see little other plausible explanation."

"But they're all dead!" Krysta whispered emphatically.

"Or exiled," the man's voice came to them again, making it clear he could listen in on any sort of conversation they might have while in his domain. That was just unnatural. Nobody had skills like that...unless...

"William called him Gryffid," Mace reminded them in his quiet way.

"Sweet Mother of All!" Krysta kept moving, but her face was a mirror of shock. "The wizard Gryffid created the gryphons."

"And what better place for me to live than Gryphon Isle? Be

at ease, my new friends. My days of warring are over. At least for the moment."

They followed in silence, both weary from the journey and unwilling to let even more of their conversation be overheard. So far, Drake thought, the wizard—if he were to be believed— didn't seem hostile. Drake would wait and see.

He made note of every facet of his surroundings as they made their way to the hall. He noted his companions doing the same, looking around at the ancient stone battlements and noting the signs of gryphons everywhere. The place was teeming with them. Drake could count dozens in the distance, flying here and there around other parts of the large, rocky island. Several watched their progress from the rooftops and spires of the keep, their piercing eyes following the party's every move. Jenet's wings twitched in agitation and Drake put a steadying hand on her shoulder as he walked beside her.

Dragons and gryphons were well matched since their magic mostly cancelled each other out. Outnumbered as they were, the dragons were definitely at a disadvantage should these creatures turn hostile.

Jenet stopped just before the doorway when William paused.

"Do you not go in?" she asked him directly.

The man purported to be William shook his head. "I have a bit more to do outdoors while Gryffid explains everything."

"Then may I stay with you?" she asked, her tone both confused and hopeful. It hurt Drake's heart to hear her uncertainty. She loved William like a son—or perhaps a little brother. If this man was really the William she had lost only days before, Drake could understand her dismay.

Gryffid motioned offhandedly. "Certainly, stay and satisfy yourself that he is indeed William. I know this is a lot to take in all at once. For you, only a few days have passed."

"Do you mind, Drake?" Jenet blinked hopeful eyes at him.

"Of course not, sweetheart." He rubbed her scales fondly. "Stay and talk with…uh…William."

"I'll stay outside with my lady," Nellin declared and Drake wasn't surprised. The young male dragon would protect his mate. Always.

Drake turned, leaving them outside with the puzzling young man, and followed the wizard, Krysta and Mace indoors. He wasn't too surprised to see the doors and hallways of the keep were large enough for even dragons to navigate. It was clear the gryphons had the run of the place and in fact, the two who had escorted them to the island were waiting inside the great hall when the Draconian party entered.

Herorthor and Llydiss sat near a huge fireplace that was centered along one great stone wall. A large table stood before it, with several richly padded chairs. The entire place had a feeling of antiquity about it, but looked comfortable enough. Gryffid went directly to one wall covered completely in book cases. He pulled a large folio from one of the shelves and turned back to the group, standing very near the large table.

"Please, seat yourselves. I know you are weary from the crossing, but we have much to discuss." He opened the folio and sorted through a number of ancient-looking scrolls before setting two aside while they took seats around the large table.

"I have here something for you to read, Drake."

"How do you know my name?"

The wizard smiled coyly. "It is much more than your name, boy, it's what you are."

Drake sighed. Apparently it was true that wizards liked to speak in riddles. He tried to school himself to patience while the old man related his tale in his way.

"Draneth, Draco and the others. I knew them all, once upon a time, and called several friend. But then Skir started his rumblings and allied with other malcontents. They wanted war, so we gave it to them, but it was you—the sons and daughters of man—who suffered most. Then we hit upon the idea of creating Guardians. Powerful beings who could fight to protect the human race from our folly." He gestured toward the two gryphons lounging by the fire. "Draco was able to conjure little beings of fire that would flit around like birds, trailing flame from their wings and tail. They were formidable but lacked substance. That's when Dranneth got the idea for dragons, and you know the result of that experiment."

"So what has this to do with us?" Krysta asked.

"Patience, young lady. It will all come clear in time." Gryffid pushed one of the scrolls across the smooth tabletop toward Drake. "Perhaps this will help. Read it aloud, if you don't mind, young Drake."

Drake unrolled the ancient thing carefully, glad to see the writing was legible. He looked at his companions with a raised brow, then began reading, growing more concerned as he puzzled through the words.

"If you read this, you have at last found your destiny, my son, and dark days threaten the lands once more. Seek me in the forgotten places. Find me in flame. Hold fast against the frost and use what I have bequeathed as best you may. Do not squander your power, get of Draco. But use it as your forefathers once did. Let the dragons be your guide and protect them, sons and daughters of the flame made flesh."

It was signed, *Draco, Wizard of Fire.* After that followed a few stanzas of mismatched verse, much like what the gryphons had quoted the day before.

Burn bright fire light
Spark to blaze the dangerous gaze
Ember's glow, your inferno
Conflagration to save a nation

Thrice promised
The unexpected vow
Two will fly into forgotten realms
To fulfill the here and now

The vow to king
Prince and sire
Fulfilled five-fold
With untold fire

Flame rediscovered
Shared and passed
Kindled against evil
Magic meant to last

The Drake of Fire
Reborn and discovered
Partners in life
A weapon uncovered

Against the dark
Wield your purging flame

Judge with your heart

Live up to your Name

As he spoke the last word, Drake felt a tingling sensation in his palms that sizzled down his fingers. Little plumes of smoke drifted upward from the points where each fingertip touched the scroll. In those same places, the paper browned as if heated by open flame and Drake felt heat pool in his fingertips.

"What is this?" Drake looked from his fingers to the scorched page.

"Control your fire, son of Draco, or you will set my hall ablaze with your magic." Gryffid chuckled, making light of something that set Drake on his ear.

"I'm no mage. I have no power." He set the missive carefully on the table.

"Ah, there you are wrong, my young friend."

"You speak in riddles, old man." Drake felt his anger rising. Anger and something else, even more troubling—the tingling energy that somehow burned the paper. "I have never been able to use magic. The Jinn tried to teach me, but it was no use."

"But you always felt it there...just beyond your reach." Gryffid's eyes pinned Drake to the spot. "Didn't you?" he barked. "When the Jinn troubadours used their magic to sway people with their song, you felt the sting, the effervescence of it against your own." Gryffid looked at him with knowing eyes. "It's how the Jinn teach each other. How one mage schools another. Untrained magic will always rise to either caress or condemn its elders. Perhaps that's part of the reason you clashed so often with your blood-father."

"Is nothing unknown to you?" Drake's head was spinning.

Gryffid grinned, throwing him a half-lidded look over one

shoulder. It was neither a friendly glance, nor a combative one, but it spoke of...secrets.

"I have watched you. All of you." Gryffid reached out to include Krysta and Mace. "I knew sooner or later, separately or together, each of you would find your way to my island. When that part of the riddle was shown to me, I made it my business to watch you each from afar. Very entertaining, I might add." Gryffid winked at Drake, still smiling. Drake felt something cold crawl up his spine. Some spymaster he was. If the wizard was to be believed, he'd been spied upon his entire life and never been the wiser.

"You, Sir Drake, son of Declan, grandson of Darius, are also the son, many times removed, of my old friend, the wizard Draco. His magic runs true in you, though it has lain dormant in your forebears for many centuries. Your grandfather Darius was the first of your line to be chosen as a dragon's knight. It was his mother that was descended of wizards. She was a healer of some renown in her native land, but she left to marry two dashing young knights named Elias and Zach. They lived in one of the outlying Lairs, I believe."

Drake sat heavily. This was all starting to sound eerily plausible. "My great-grandmother, Delia." He paused, thinking back. "They say she could bespeak dragons."

Gryffid nodded. "And heal them too, of small wounds, at least. But her true gift was something quite different. Something she denied out of fear. She was a Firedrake, as are you." The wizard chuckled. "Oh, how I laughed at the irony when your parents named you."

"I'm glad someone is enjoying this," Krysta, bless her heart, interrupted the wizard. "What exactly is a Firedrake?"

"A flame wizard. Living fire. Your companion, like many of his forebears, has the gift of fire in a very tangible way. Is it any wonder his dragon partner is the color of glowing embers? Or his father's the color of the flaming sun? Darius's dragon partner was the red-gold of an inferno. It's rather poetic, actually." Gryffid seemed to enjoy his moment of revelation.

"What has Jenet got to do with this?" Drake's concern shifted to his beloved sister.

"Quite a bit, actually. I believe those three dragons sensed the hidden blaze in you and your forefathers. You have flame in common. And I believe—" Gryffid turned to watch Jenet enter the great hall at the far end, "—your dragon sister will be key in helping you find your fire. Though from what I've just seen, it is much closer to the surface in you than it was in any of your recent ancestors. Must be all that time spent among the Jinn mages."

"Wait. The Jinn really do have mages?" Mace asked from across the table.

Krysta shrugged. "Some. It's a closely held secret—" she shot a disgusted look at the wizard, "—but many Jinn minstrels have the ability to influence people with their music. If you'd asked me last week I would've thought Drake of the Five Lands one of the more magically talented of the Jinn troubadours, judging by his accomplishments, but now you say his magic isn't in his music?"

Gryffid tilted his head, considering. "Not entirely. Young Drake is descended of wizards and therefore some of our magic flows through him no matter what he does. I wouldn't say though, that Draco ever had musical leanings. Whatever musical talent Drake has is purely natural. I surmise his magic may have risen to flow with that of his teachers, though it could find no real expression in song. No, his brand of magic needs flame to express itself."

"That sounds dangerous."

"Only to his enemies." Gryffid's gaze sharpened. "Which leads to why he is here. I can set you on the path, Drake, with Jenet's help. Together you will rediscover the secret of your heritage and perhaps teach your blood-father a thing or two when you return home, eh?" The wizard's expression turned amused once more.

Jenet neared and sat behind Drake, all but cocooning him with her sinuous length twined at his back. Her head loomed over the table, then settled at his side while Drake reached up to rub her brow ridges. He was glad of her presence. She comforted him. She was his anchor in the swirling mass of uncertainty the wizard had stirred.

"Are you all right?"

"Did you listen in? Did you hear what he said?"

"I heard."

"And?"

"And I think he's right. There's always been something different about you. And about Papa Dec. I didn't realize it at first, but after knowing other humans, I can say whatever it is, it isn't present with anyone but you. And maybe a few of the Jinn." Jenet blinked her jeweled eyes at Krysta. *"It's magic, Drake. Only with you and Papa Dec, it feels so familiar, I almost didn't notice it."*

"It feels like fire," Gryffid cut in, clearly eavesdropping once again on a private conversation. "Doesn't it, little one?"

Jenet's head rose sharply to regard the man. She blinked once. *"It does."*

"Good. We can work with that. But for now—" Gryffid turned back to the other two who sat at his table, "—I wonder why you two are here." His mood turned pensive.

"I suppose Herorthor's actions play into your destiny

somehow." He gazed at Krysta searchingly. "You liked dragons before, but now you can bespeak them. That will change things. You may be able to put your skills to good use in the Lair and in the coming battle. If it comes to pass. Perhaps that is your reason for being here." Gryffid raised one eyebrow in her direction. "But you—" he turned to Mace, "—puzzle me."

"That is not my intent, sir."

Gryffid laughed at Mace's steadfast tone. "Oh, I believe you, Sir Knight. You've always played by the rules. You've worked hard to earn your place and you deserve it, but you've left joy behind somewhere. I think perhaps your new companions will teach you where to find it again though, so not to worry."

"I wasn't worried." Mace's dry tone wasn't lost on anyone. He was clearly uncomfortable with the wizard's scrutiny.

Gryffid sighed. "Ah, well, I will ponder your presence here, Sir Mace. I like puzzles and you represent a fine one. Now..." he turned to address Jenet, "...I assume you've checked William over from head to toe and are satisfied he is the boy you knew."

"I don't understand how, but it is Wil, just older."

"Oh, that's easy." Gryffid waved one hand in a negligent motion. "I accelerated time. Or rather, I let a bit of it catch up. This island is my refuge, but even a wizard cannot live forever. So when I went into exile, I slowed time on this island. I have lived only a few decades while centuries have passed in the outside world. When I sent for Wil, I let time flow again—just a bit faster than it does outside my island's boundaries so we would have more time together. Still, it's barely enough, but it will have to suffice."

"Time to do what, exactly?" Krysta asked.

Gryffid sat back. "To train him, of course. Wil has a destiny unlike any of his brothers. He will rule a far-off land, though I haven't told him this. I didn't want to burden him with the weight of his destiny. But I tell you now, so you'll understand my reasons for taking him."

"Nothing excuses kidnapping a boy and mortally wounding two dragons and knights," Mace pointed out in his quiet way.

"My apologies." Gryffid looked troubled as his eyes met Drake's. "I am truly sorry for what the hirelings did to effect Wil's capture. It was never my intent to harm anyone, especially not your fathers or their dragon partners. I hope you will accept my deepest regrets."

"If any of them die as a result of your meddling—"

Drake didn't get a chance to finish the sentence. Gryffid held up one hand, forestalling his angry words. "I can assure you, they are all well. Ren and Lilla made it to the Border Lair and were treated for their injuries. They will fly back to the castle shortly for reunion with Declan, Arlis and your mother. Oh, and you should know, I turned time to flow naturally once more on this island. You won't suffer the same effects of crossing my time barrier when you fly away from here. The outside world will not have aged much from when you left it and none of your family, Drake, suffered permanent injury, though it was a close thing."

"You'd better be telling the truth," Krysta warned.

"I have no reason to lie. Even if Drake here knew the full extent of his magic and how to wield it, he still could not damage me. He has only an echo of Draco's power, while I am a wizard." No conceit filled his words, just simple truth.

For the first time, Drake laughed at the absurdity of it all. There he was, sitting at a wizard's table, chatting. There weren't supposed to be any wizards left in the world. They'd all been killed or exiled after the wars they caused. But now, here was one of the ancient ones, still meddling in the affairs of man. Drake wondered how many others were still out there, quietly plotting. It was a frightening thought.

Everyone was watching him, but Drake couldn't fight off either the laughter or the fear. Relaxing back in his chair, he reached out for Jenet, the warm, reassuring heat of her grounding him.

"I'm sorry. This all just strikes me as odd. The youngster we were sent to retrieve is now a man. I'm suddenly a mage, sitting having a chat with a wizard."

"Put like that," Krysta said with a rueful chuckle, "it is a bit much."

Only Mace didn't smile of those seated around the table.

Chapter Fourteen

There was a bustle at the large doorway and moments later a striking woman entered the hall. She was stripping off her gloves as she approached with a wide smile on her lovely face.

"Ah, they've come then. Welcome, all of you!"

Gryffid stood and kissed the lady's cheek in greeting. "Let me introduce my granddaughter, Gwen. Gwen, this is Krysta, Drake and Mace. The beautiful lady behind Drake is Jenet and I bet you saw Nellin on your way in, didn't you?"

She smiled brightly. "It's why I came back early. A dragon above Gryphon Isle is a curious sight indeed."

The men stood and bowed formally to the lady as Krysta watched. The girl was about her age, she judged, with golden blonde hair and an angel's face. Krysta wanted to hate her for her perfect beauty, and the attentiveness of her new mates to the creature, but she found she couldn't. This Gwen seemed to have no idea of her effect on the men and as Krysta watched carefully, did nothing to encourage it.

Still, the way their eyes followed the other woman's every move annoyed Krysta. Her toe started tapping in agitation, but other than that, she kept her face schooled to calmness. It wouldn't do to let them see how jealous she was.

"I was out hawking, but it was growing dark so I headed for home. Then I saw the dragons in the distance." The blonde beauty walked to the fireplace and the waiting gryphons. She smoothed their neck feathers with obvious fondness as she threw her cloak and gloves over a nearby chair. "We seldom have visitors." She almost looked sad for a moment, but Krysta decided it must've been a trick of the flickering firelight. "I'll go down to the kitchens and see about dinner. I'm sure the entire keep knows about our visitors by now, of course, but I'll ask them to serve dinner a bit early. I can see you're all tired from the crossing." Her sympathetic gaze alighted on each one of them, ending with Krysta. A little nod of understanding passed between the women and Krysta suddenly realized the other girl wasn't totally oblivious to the effect she had on males of the species. Without waiting for comment, Gwen left.

Krysta had seen her kind of magic before. Every few generations, a Jinn woman would be able to channel her magic in such a way as to affect each and every male around her. Most thought it a fable, but Krysta knew from firsthand experience how dangerous a magic it really was.

She'd known just such a girl in her clan. The beauty had every man in the clan panting after her, but they protected her as well. She inspired fierce loyalty in every male she met, but that girl's selfish nature brought hatred from the other women. She brought divisiveness to a clan that had always been fiercely loyal to each other. Finally, the leader decided marriage to a reclusive nobleman would be the best solution. The girl had to be exiled for the good of the clan, but she didn't mind. She became a Duchess and quickly put her new, rich husband under her spell, along with all the menfolk in his domain.

This Gwen creature didn't seem selfish in the least, but Krysta was reserving judgment. She would watch and listen closely. She didn't quite fear losing her bonded mates to the beauty, but she certainly didn't like the way they watched her. Krysta had only just joined with them. Was she so forgettable that both Drake and Mace would begin to ignore her so soon? She almost expected it of Drake, with his rogue's reputation, but certainly not Mace. He'd always seemed so steady and stable.

Krysta must have frowned as she thought, for suddenly she felt two warm hands grasp both of hers, one on each side. She looked up from her depressing thoughts to find Mace—and Drake—each holding one of her hands, smiling at her in a comforting, loving way.

"She really can't help it, you know," Gryffid intruded on the shared moment. Krysta looked to the wizard who watched the retreat of his granddaughter. "It's her great-grandmother's power. Each of my grandchildren descended of my brief affair with Luna have been irresistible to humans of the opposite sex. Luna's magic is of the moon and the tides. She can also tug on the emotions, lust most of all. I'll admit, she ensnared me for a time." Gryffid shook his head. "We had a son, Rigel. He had— and still has—his choice of women, but he chose a human mate many centuries ago and when she eventually died, she broke his heart. Gwen is their grandchild. Luna's influence was strong in the girl so they sent her to me for her own good. I have few humans here on the island and most are impervious to her magic because I have bespelled them so. Rather ironic, that. Using magic to negate magic, eh? But it works."

They didn't have time to comment as a group of servants and Gwen herself arrived with a series of steaming platters and dishes. The servants were unlike any people Krysta had ever seen. They were tall, stately beings, with icy blond hair and perfectly chiseled features. They looked human—except for their delicately pointed ears.

They reminded her of Jinn fairytales and her heart sped a pace as she realized she was beholding fair folk!

"We'll start with this," Gwen said as she took a seat next to Gryffid, "and the rest of the household will join us shortly. I know the three of you are probably quite hungry after the crossing." A platter of bread with dipping oils and creamy butter was placed near the three travelers as the fair folk set the tables quickly and efficiently. They made little sound and smiled back when Krysta thanked them. They seemed friendly—not the powerfully scary beings of Jinn legend.

Krysta's stomach rumbled with hunger as she dug into the delicious breads. Some of the little loaves were black, some brown with spices and seeds of different kinds, but all delicious. She ate as daintily as she could, considering her ravenous hunger, but by the time she looked up, the entire hall was filled with tables, set with plates and platters of all kinds of things. People were filing in—more of the fair folk, for almost every single one had a fair complexion and varying shades of blond hair. They chatted amiably as they went to their tables and Krysta noted more than a few warriors among their ranks.

Nellin walked in behind William and two of the fiercer-looking warrior folk, heading straight for their table. William kissed Gwen on the cheek before he took his place on Gryffid's other side, and Nellin went to his mate, twining her neck with his as he settled behind Mace. Behind her, the two dragons made an impenetrable wall of protection for the three of them.

"Where did all those other tables come from? And the chairs?" Krysta finally asked, curiosity getting the better of her.

Gryffid's eyes twinkled. "Magic, my dear."

Two imposing figures stood at Drake's side of the table, waiting apparently for introduction. Both were fair folk, but of a more muscular tone than the servants she'd seen. Both wore leathers, and their hair was bound back in the style of warriors.

Drake and Mace stood, as did Krysta. She was a

Guardswoman and had been a warrior of the Jinn even before settling in Castleton. The fair warriors were male and female, a matched set. Krysta took the female's measure while her mates eyed the male, and she found herself filled with respect. These were not frivolous folk, wearing their leathers for show. No, she could tell at a glance, these were true warriors.

Gryffid rose to make the introductions. "My friends, these are my Captains of the Guard, Lilith and Gerrow."

"Two captains?" Mace asked, cocking one brow in question.

Gryffid laughed. "They are a mated pair. I couldn't let one outrank the other, now could I? Never let it be said that I was the cause of disharmony among mates." Both warriors smiled as Gryffid laughed and returned to his seat.

"I'm Drake." The bard offered a smile and a hand in the way of warriors, close to the other couple as he was. "This is Krysta, Mace, Jenet and Nellin." The dragons' heads rose over the backs of their chairs, blinking in acknowledgment.

"Well met," Gerrow's voice rolled over them as he bowed briefly to the dragons.

"We were foretold of your coming," Lilith said from his side, her voice higher pitched and every bit as musical, "but nothing could prepare us to see two such dragons over our island. They are a sight to behold." The pair took seats at the table and made themselves comfortable.

As far as Krysta was concerned, the woman was all right. No one could fake the admiration and awe in Lilith's voice, and anyone who admired Nellin and Jenet had good judgment in Krysta's opinion.

"We've had the pleasure of helping to train young William these past years. We'll be sorry to see him go." The male warrior dug into a platter, serving himself from the bounty laid on the table. The others followed suit.

"Then you're letting him go?" Mace addressed Gryffid.

"Yes, of course, Sir Mace. It was never my intention to keep him indefinitely. I only borrowed him for a few years." The wizard chuckled but Krysta watched William's face. He seemed troubled, though he kept his eyes down and his attention on his plate as the conversation flowed around him.

After the main meal was served, a place was cleared in the middle of the hall and a few of the fair folk brought out instruments. They began with soft tunes while the rest of the hall was cleared, warming up a bit as the last stragglers finished their meals and sweets were laid on each table for those who wished to partake.

Lilith eyed the minstrels then turned to Drake.

"Perhaps you would favor us with a song?"

Her mate, Gerrow frowned. "A bard? I thought he was a knight."

"Apparently—" Drake raised his eyebrows, "—I'm both."

Lilith put one hand over her mate's on the table. "Beloved, don't you recognize Drake of the Five Lands?"

Gerrow's fair face flushed. "Forgive me. Is this true? You are the famous Jinn bard?"

"One and the same. Being partnered with Jenet is rather new to me, so your pardon if I don't quite see myself as a 'knight'. I have little training in the ways of dragon knights, though I'm hopeful Mace and Nellin won't mind helping me learn my new role."

Mace almost cracked a smile as he nodded, though Nellin didn't stir from where he lay, neck entwined with his mate. The poor creature was besotted with Jenet, and who could blame him?

"We've heard many of your compositions, brought back to us from those who venture off the island from time to time." Lilith's eyes sparkled at Drake but Krysta didn't fear the beautiful woman would even try to turn his head. Lilith and she were equals. Warrior women who understood each other. That much was clear.

Drake looked uncertain. "I doubt I could entertain any better than your people. Fair folk are reputed to have the most beautiful voices in the world. I don't think I could compete." A sheepish smile softened his refusal, but Krysta heard the very real doubt in his words.

"What's this? Drake of the Five Lands, uncertain about his talent?" Gryffid scoffed. "You're a natural bard, my boy. Don't let these blond fools intimidate you. The ones who go abroad all return singing your praises and your songs." The wizard winked, smiling conspiratorially.

"Well..." Drake actually flushed, color riding his chiseled cheekbones, surprising Krysta, "...if you're sure. And if someone could loan me an instrument, I'd be happy to give you a song."

"It'll be more than one, if I'm any judge." Gryffid chuckled as Drake stood and made his way to where the minstrels had set up. Krysta watched him go with pride. She knew his reputation was well earned and she had even heard him perform once or twice in the distant past, though she hadn't heard him recently. She was looking forward to his performance, knowing this time, this special man was hers.

Drake walked the gauntlet of tables filled with fair folk. It was disconcerting to say the least, but their friendly smiles and encouraging looks were familiar. He'd seen just such looks on the faces of patrons the world over. They were eager for entertainment, eager to hear him sing and tell his tales through music. His only job was to not let them down.

He'd never doubted his ability. Not since he was a teen and just learning his skills. But he doubted now, though he fought not to let it show. The speaking voices of the fair folk had enchanted him. He could only imagine what they sounded like in song. He didn't think any human could hope to compete with such natural beauty, but he was damned well going to try. He would not bring shame to his own name or to his new family. He would give the finest performance any human bard could give and if he failed to please the fair folk, well, then, he'd given it his best.

The minstrels grinned in welcome and made a place for him at their center.

"I am Zarat," a darker-haired man introduced himself. He had golden blond hair, not too much lighter than Drake's own, though his skin tone was much fairer. "I'm honored to meet you. My wife had the good fortune to hear you play once in Helios when you were just a boy. Even then, she was impressed with your music."

"Thank you," Drake reached back in his mind for that long-ago trip to Helios. He'd only been about sixteen when his adopted Jinn clan had traveled to that distant land. Drake hadn't returned there until just a few years ago, so it must be that first trip of which the man spoke. "Hopefully I've learned a thing or two since then." Drake smiled, making an effort to charm the fair folk who listened to each word he spoke.

"My wife, Margan, will be up in a moment. She plays pennywhistle. She's just gone to fetch it from our home."

"I look forward to making her acquaintance," Drake answered politely.

"Which instrument would you prefer, Master Drake?" He swept his arm around the semi-circle of musicians who each held various instruments aloft in a signal they were willing to share with the newcomer. Drake was flattered by their offer. He knew what it was to let a stranger play a beloved instrument made just for you.

"A lute, if you have one. Though I will play anything you wish me to, if you have a preference."

Drake would come to regret those impulsive words later in the evening as one instrument after another was thrust into his hands, but he took it all in good humor. He started with the lute, checking the tune automatically and marveling at the sweet, mellow tone of the lower string and the sparkling clarity of the upper. This was far and away one of the finest instruments he had ever had the pleasure of holding.

"My compliments to the luthier," Drake remarked as he began a few warm-up fingerings and runs. The hall quieted as everyone listened. Drake knew he was the center of attention. He'd been in the position many times before, but this was special somehow. The air vibrated with waiting. He took his time, limbering up fingers that hadn't played in days.

When he was sure of himself, he began the introduction to one of his livelier compositions. It was a dance of sorts, though the lyrics told the story of an amorous young man and the fickle maiden who teased him. It sat well in his vocal range and was a particularly good warm-up. He knew he could sing it well, and if they wanted a second song after this, he would be in a good position to try something more challenging.

Drake launched into the lyrics, watching the faces of those around him. Smiles met his gaze, and toes were already tapping. So far, he was getting a good response. It wasn't just polite humoring, it was genuine enjoyment he read in their unconscious movements, the swaying of the crowd to the beat and the light in their eyes.

He was doing it. He was hitting his stride as the verses went on. At the humorous points in the song, the crowd laughed with him, caught up in the tale as so many had been before. When it came down to it, this audience was much like those he'd known before, just much prettier.

Drake relaxed as the tune ended with a flourish and was met with cheers from the fair folk. Zarat clapped him on the back, encouraging him to play another and Drake complied. This wasn't so bad, really. He'd been concerned, but it looked like the fair folk did appreciate a rough human voice. For certain, they appreciated his songs. They laughed at all the right places and tapped their toes. Several couples started dancing when he played a lively reel and the other musicians joined in, adding drums, bass, Margan's pennywhistle for trills and a score of other instruments all blending into a marvelous harmony of sound as the crowd danced.

They took a short break after about twenty minutes and Zarat introduced all the members of their impromptu band. Drake shook hands with each and every one, amazed by the welcome he read in their eyes. He'd never played with finer musicians. Each was an artist.

Zarat saved his wife for last, and she gave Drake an unexpected hug. When she pulled back, there were tears in her lovely, pale eyes.

"You're even more blessed than when I first heard you sing as a lad. Zarat didn't believe me when I spoke to him of the human bard who had impressed me so. He thought it must be a Jinn mage, but I knew better. There was no magic in your song, only pure, raw talent. I'm glad to see it's been nurtured and grown to such a level."

Drake was humbled by her words, especially since he knew her own talent was incredible. She'd sung lilting descant harmonies with him just moments ago that threatened to mesmerize him so much, he'd almost forgotten his own part of the song. She was a master not only of the pennywhistle, but of her amazingly delicate voice. That such a talented woman would compliment him meant more than he could say.

He told her as much, pleased when she blushed. "Oh, I've had more time than you'll ever know to perfect my craft. That you humans do so over such short lifespans never ceases to amaze me. But then, you're a knight now, your dragon will grant you longer than normal life, but still short compared to our own."

The thought startled him. His gaze shot to Jenet. *"How are you doing, sweetheart?"*

"We're good, Drake. Mace is his usual silent self, but your lady is befriending the warrior woman in between listening to your songs. I don't think they were prepared for how good you really are." The dragon preened a little over the heads of the crowd and Drake felt her pride in him.

"Would you play 'The Golden Beauty', Sir Drake?" Margan regained his attention. "It's one of my favorites that you've written."

"It would be my honor," he replied, as the minstrels sat. Everyone in the hall seemed to take that as a sign, and they settled down as well. Drake stood forth, in front of the group, addressing the crowd. "I've been asked to sing one of my favorite songs for you." He began to play the opening bars, instantly recognizable to those who'd heard it before. A hush fell over the crowd and eager faces turned to him. "But I think it safe to tell you, though only one other in all the lands knows this fact. 'The Golden Beauty' of whom I sing isn't a human woman, as all believe. Rather, she sits there, by the fire, with her mate. She is my sister, my fighting partner, my dearest

Jenet, the dragoness."

The crowd looked over as the stunning, peach-gold dragon blinked in surprise. She was so beautiful, even among the fair folk, she stirred hearts to tears. She winked at Drake and the crowd sighed. It was clear the beauty was enjoying every moment of their attention, as was her knight. They were well matched indeed. Drake blew her a kiss as he settled into the song. His voice rang pure and true as he sang of the beauty who'd claimed his love, though it broke his heart to leave her.

Drake was pressed to play almost every song he'd ever written and he switched instruments a few times as well. The minstrels seemed to want to test his limits, pushing to see how good he was with their instrument each time he switched to something new. A friendly competition Drake had experienced many times among the Jinn minstrels he'd learned from soon evolved and he felt more and more at home among these fair-haired beings.

"He has the voice of an angel," Lilith remarked, still seated at the head table while the band took a quick break. "Didn't I tell you, beloved?" Mace noted the way she squeezed Gerrow's hand as a teasing light entered her eyes.

"You did indeed, my dear. Tell me, where comes a human bard by such talent? He's better even than our best. Do you see the way they all look at him?"

"He learned from the Jinn, mostly, though they say he was already quite skilled when he was taken in by the Black Dragon Clan as a teen." Krysta turned questioning eyes to Mace. "Did he play much when he was growing up?"

Mace cleared his throat, thinking back to those early years. "He was always musical. His mother gave him his first lute and taught him to play it. Sir Ren helped too, though Sir Declan, his blood-father, never had much patience for music." Mace remembered the way Declan would scold his son for wasting time playing tunes. The older knight had been proved wrong and seemed to handle it well, but the fact remained, if not for the undue pressure he'd placed on his son, Drake would probably never have left home at such a young age.

"Who is his mother?" Gerrow's eyes narrowed.

"The lady Elena."

"And is she beautiful, by human standards?"

"Quite." Mace cocked his head, wondering where the fair warrior was leading him. "She is fair of face and form and has a lovely singing voice."

"I wonder..." Gerrow looked at Gryffid and as Mace turned, he realized the wizard was deep in thought. "He is descended of wizards, but what of our race? There is much about him that seems familiar."

"Alas, my friend, you stumble upon something I had only begun to suspect." Gryffid nodded. "I followed the bloodline of Draco to Darius, then Declan, and thence to Drake, but I wonder exactly where the fair Elena comes from? It could be she has fey blood in her somewhere along the line. That would explain much."

Mace felt his stomach sink. Would they never stop finding things to make Drake remarkable? How could a mere man ever hope to stand beside a being who proved more magical with every passing moment?

Hiding his worry behind his usual stony façade, Mace pretended to enjoy the evening. In truth, he did enjoy Drake's music. You'd have to be a stone statue not to enjoy Drake's skill with an audience, and seemingly any instrument he was handed. It was pleasant to watch, and when Krysta grabbed Mace's hand and dragged him into the dancing, he let go of his worries altogether, enjoying her vivacious zest for life and sunny laughter. He could learn a thing or two from her about how to enjoy the moment.

What had started as dinner turned into a party and though Drake was kept busy with the minstrels, Mace and Krysta enjoyed themselves as well. They danced a few times and listened with the others when Drake sang some of his more poignant ballads. Mace learned a great deal about his new fighting partner in those hours and he learned a lot about himself as well.

Try as he might to be angry or jealous of the boy he'd grown up competing with, those days of competition were long gone. Drake was an entity unto himself, as was Mace. They'd each followed their own paths in life and somehow wound up walking beside each other, with Krysta between them. Mace thanked the Mother of All for that miracle as Krysta teased him and made him laugh. She was a joy. She was his world—as much as Nellin, and now Jenet and Drake. Together they would find a way to deal with the puzzle Drake's background represented.

In those hours of fey celebration, Mace came to terms with his new family and the future that might await them. He accepted what he was—a damn fine knight of Draconia—and didn't begrudge Drake the new discoveries that set him apart from all other knights, and even his Jinn brethren. Drake was unique. But then, Mace could have told them that when he was just a lad. Drake had always had something special about him. It was why Mace had tried so hard to emulate him, in his way, but Mace accepted now he would never be able to do so.

"Why so quiet, Sir Mace?" Gryffid had come to stand next to him while he watched Gerrow dance with Krysta. "I know it is your usual way, but tonight you are very silent, even for you."

Mace regarded the wizard, still unsure how the man knew so much about everyone and everything. Finally he shrugged, just accepting...for now.

"It's a lot to take in."

"Ah." The wizard nodded. "I thought as much. But you seem to be handling all this rather well. Many other men would be raging or green with envy. I begin to see why you are here after all. It is clear a being of such light needs an anchor to the here and now. You and Krysta serve that purpose. But you most of all, Sir Mace. You will be his brother-in-arms, his fighting partner. It is for you to show him the way knights fight together. You will show him how to be part of a team, and part of a family."

"I honestly don't know if I'm up to that task, Sir."

"Nonsense!" The wizard laughed at him. "You are or the Mother of All would not have seen fit to put you in this equation. You must believe that. Without a strong tie to the land and the human race, I fear Drake will be lost. You are that tie to Draconia and humanity. Krysta is the binding to love and Jenet and Nellin will ground him in his fire. It is a perfect, delicate balance. A thing of beauty, indeed. Do not belittle it and do not fear it."

"I fear little in this world, Sir."

"That's the best thing about you, Mace. You don't show fear, but I know you are aware of true danger. You will not lead any of your new family into more than you can handle. That is your skill and your point of pride. Common sense that the others sometimes lack. Do not discount it."

Chapter Fifteen

Drake sang and played for several hours, but eventually he was able to break away from the minstrels as the fair folk began to retire for the evening. He found Krysta and Mace in a corner near the fire, surrounded by Nellin and Jenet. They looked comfortable, Krysta snuggled back in Mace's arms while they sat, watching the hall and the people within. The minstrels still played a mellow tune. He liked the way they looked together and didn't find any jealousy within his heart for their closeness.

Wil sat nearby, talking with Mace, telling him of his life in the past five years. Drake realized the boy he'd chased all the way across country was no more. William had grown into a man and he didn't know how the royal family would receive him when they returned.

"Sir Drake," William greeted him with a wide smile as Drake took a seat next to Mace and Krysta. The formal address jarred him a bit. He'd have to get used to this being a knight business. He could still hardly believe it, but Wil seemed to take it in stride. "Jenet talked about you quite often, but I had no idea you were so talented. I've heard your songs performed by others in my brother's court."

"Speaking of which..." Drake eyed the prince seriously. "You do realize that for us, you've only been missing a few days. When we get back—if Gryffid is to be believed—only days will have passed for us and your family, while for you, it's been years. I don't know how the king will react."

William shifted in his seat. "I've thought about this quite a bit. Roland will be royally angry at first, but he'll get over it. I think Nico will take it harder, as will the twins, now that I'm almost their age. Actually, I might even be a little older. Damn, I've missed them." Wil shook his head. "I mean, I understand why it had to be this way, and I'm glad for all I've learned here, but I really miss my family. It'll be good to be back with them, though they'll probably be suspicious of me at first."

"I'm glad you realize that, my prince." Drake liked the thoughtfulness of the young man's words. It demonstrated he had indeed grown from the impetuous boy who'd flown into the midst of battle with Queen Lana and Tor after Roland fell on the field. He'd shown bravery that day, but not a whole lot of intelligence. "I'd like to get going at first light. We've got a long way to go to get you back home safely."

"But you can't leave tomorrow," Gryffid interrupted.

"I thought we were free to go."

"You are, but not tomorrow. Wil's training is complete, but yours is not, Sir Drake. I'll expect you in the courtyard as the sun rises tomorrow morning, and I think Mace and Krysta would like to spar a bit with the warriors, if I'm not much mistaken. It would be good for you all to train just one day with Wil to learn what he is capable of. Your road back home will not be an easy one and you must prepare to face whatever comes together. You can leave the next day, though I wish I could keep you longer."

"We cannot delay returning Wil to his family more than we already have."

"I understand. I would slow time yet again, but it is not such an easy thing to do. Even for me. Time will flow normally on this island until the coming crisis is past. You can tell Roland that, with my compliments."

"I will."

"I'll be sad to leave you," Wil said quietly, watching the wizard. "I'm grateful for what you and your people have taught me."

Gryffid smiled in a fatherly way. "I know, my boy. I'm only sorry I had to take you from your family to do it. I regret that, you know, but I don't regret your presence here these last years. You've brought new life to us all and we'll miss you."

One of the more friendly servants showed them to a guest room that had been set aside for their use. The dragons were welcome to stay indoors in the great hall if they wished. There was nothing like the suites of a Lair on the island, for gryphons nested in rocky caves on the sides of the jagged peaks that covered the southern half of the land mass. Jenet and Nellin made do with their place by the fire in the great hall, while Krysta, Mace and Drake were shown to a sumptuously furnished room with a very large bed. It was hung with burgundy velvet curtains the likes of which Krysta had never seen before in her life.

"It's beautiful, isn't it?" Krysta observed as they entered. She tossed her cloak on a richly embroidered chair and plopped down on the side of the bed to tug off her boots. She was tired, but it was a good kind of tired. They'd found the prince and made new friends. A good meal had gone a long way toward settling her questions about these strange folk and now all she wanted was to be with her new husbands—though the idea still took some getting used to.

Being married was strange enough, but to two men? It boggled her mind and her senses. Especially when they both made love to her at once.

The dragons would not be flying tonight, so the human side of the family was on its own. If they chose to make love, it would be without the influence of the dragons to drive them mindless. Krysta rather liked the idea of taking her time making love to them, and the men taking their time making love to her in turn.

"These velvets are from the other side of the world, if what I've heard is true," Drake said, fingering the furry fabric. "But they're hung Jinn style. I wonder if the Jinn copied the fair folk or if it was the other way around?"

"Does it matter?" Krysta stood, barefoot now, and tugged Drake into her arms. She pulled him downward for a lingering kiss.

Drake didn't answer, too busy seducing her mouth with his talented tongue. She felt Mace come up behind her, bracketing her between the men's heated warmth. She loved the feel of them, even fully clothed as they were, but she knew it would feel even better naked. She pulled back and smiled over her shoulder at Mace.

"We have too many clothes on."

Mace grinned. "Easily remedied, milady."

Drake tipped her chin around with one finger and set about kissing her again, while Mace divested her of her clothing and his own. When he pressed against her again, they were both bare. She pulled back from Drake's drugging kisses.

"Your turn, Master Bard," she teased.

Mace tugged her onto the bed with him as she watched Drake undress. He really had the most amazing body. Tan and golden, he was more muscular than any bard had a right to be, but Krysta knew he was a fighter as well as a lover. He hid great talents under the bardic flair of his clothing.

He held her gaze as he bared himself, stroking his long, thick cock while she licked her lips. She wanted to taste him.

Mace's fingers were busy, stroking her clit and dipping within her channel to test her readiness. She'd never been so hot so quickly before meeting these amazing men, but now, it seemed, all they had to do was look at her and she was ready to take them any way they wanted.

Drake walked up to the side of the bed, his cock tantalizingly close to her lips. Mace seemed to understand what she wanted, for he lifted her by the hips, placing her on her hands and knees, her head in perfect position for Drake as Mace pushed into her pussy from behind. She whimpered as he filled her, eyes closing in bliss as he slid home.

But they opened even quicker when Drake pushed between her lips, sliding just as easily into her mouth. She looked up at him, her mouth filled almost to overflowing with his thickness as he grinned down at her.

"You feel good, wife. Damn, I think I'm going to really like being married." He stroked through her hair, holding her head at the angle he wanted while she let him guide her. Mace pushed into her from behind at a gentle pace, moving her up and down on Drake's cock as well. The slow rhythm stirred her senses by slow degrees, unlike the mighty conflagration of the dragons, but every bit as seductive.

They pulsed together for a few minutes, each enjoying the sensations the three of them created with each other. Krysta sucked at Drake, lifting one hand to cup his balls as his breathing hitched in a most satisfactory way. Mace moved a little more swiftly behind her, stroking her core with his warm hardness. He was a big man and he knew just how to wield that rigid cock. Krysta moaned as he hit that secret spot inside her again and again. She was close to exploding.

And just when she thought she'd gain the bliss just out of reach, Drake stepped back and Mace slid out. She could've screamed in frustration, but the men weren't done with her.

"You know," Drake said, kneeling on the bed as Mace moved her around like a rag doll, "I've never had her pussy. I think it's time we remedied that oversight."

"Don't complain, partner. I let you have her ass first," Mace griped as he spread her legs and settled at her side.

"And for that I thank you, brother. You'll find she's tight and eager."

"I won't be if you two don't stop talking about me like I'm not here," Krysta groused, playing along with their banter. The way they talked about her body was making her hotter—something she wouldn't have expected before meeting these two men. They changed every preconceived notion she'd ever had about what she liked and what would repulse her.

Mace reached out and pinched her nipple hard enough to make her squeak. "Pipe down, recruit. You'll do as we say. Do you understand me?" His fingers threatened retribution for the wrong answer, but his eyes sparkled with play she hadn't expected. Mace had surprised her yet again.

"Yes." She moaned when Drake settled at her other side, his long fingers diving into her pussy.

"Yes, what?" Mace grasped her other nipple between his thumb and forefinger. The grip tightened as he waited for her answer, and started to roll.

"Yes, sir!" She gasped as the pressure became unbearable, pushing her desire higher in a way she never would have expected.

"I think she likes her discipline, Mace," Drake observed, stroking her core with two limber fingers.

"I think you're right, brother." Mace plucked at her nipple, bending down to suck and nip gently at the other one. When he straightened, she was writhing on the bed. "We'll have to explore that some more later, but for now, I think you need to discover the delights of our wife's pussy. Fuck her, Drake. She needs it."

"I heartily agree." Drake grinned down at her as he positioned himself between her wide-spread knees and teased her clit with the domed head of his cock. "Do you want it, Krysta?"

"Yes!" she cried out when he pushed home in one hard thrust.

"How do you want it, wife?" He stilled above her, watching her face. "Slow?" He stroked into her a few times with agonizing slowness that only increased her desire. "Or fast?" He hammered home with rapid strokes that made her cry out with each assault.

"I think that was a yes for fast," Mace observed, watching them from the side. Drake sat up between her thighs and started a pounding pace within her as Mace bent to nibble at her breasts. The combination sent her into a fast and furious climax, but the men weren't done with her yet.

Drake pounded home as Mace sat back again. Drake came over her, gripping her shoulders while he kissed her, drawing back only to get more leverage, fucking her like she'd never been fucked before. This was a raw, earthy and sweaty kind of loving she'd never experienced. She felt his need for her in every movement of his body, every panting breath he took. It invigorated her, sending her up the crest of desire once again on a fast, perilous climb.

Drake tensed and she felt him come inside her, bathing her womb with his incredible heat as she joined him in a quick, powerful climax. He lay over her for several minutes, seeming to bask in the moment. She felt the same.

"Now you're mine." He spoke, for the first time, in the intimacy of their minds. Linked by the dragons, they could all communicate in ways most people would never know. *"I love you, Krysta."*

"I love you too, Drake." He kissed her sweetly before levering off her and collapsing at her side.

The flicker of his gaze over her shoulder was the only warning she had before Mace pounced. He flipped her onto her back and she marveled at the strength of these men, being able to toss her around as if she weighed nothing at all. She'd never felt petite, but these two brutes were doing a good job of it.

Mace smacked her ass, making her yelp. She hadn't expected that either.

"What are you doing?"

He slapped her other cheek. "What do you call me, recruit?"

She met his gaze, emboldened by the warmth she read there. Serious Mace was actually being playful.

"Sir?" she tried, licking her lips as his eyes followed the slow movement of her tongue.

"Better, recruit, but you're not out of the woods yet. I think you'll need to show me how sorry you are for disrespecting me. Sucking my cock ought to do it."

She lifted onto her elbows and smiled up at him. "With pleasure...sir." Reaching out with one hand, she balanced on the other, playing with his thick hardness until he was absolutely rigid. Only then did she lower her mouth to taste the glistening tip of his cock. She wasn't entirely unprepared when he drove into her mouth, expecting his forceful nature to override her teasing touches. Mace set a pace and she followed, eager to please this special man.

All too soon, he moved back, kissing the crown of her head as he positioned her on her stomach. A pillow was handed over her back—from Drake, no doubt—and Mace lifted her up with one hand around her middle, sticking the thick pillow under her hips. She thought she knew what Mace had in mind and was looking forward to feeling how he'd love her in this way. So far, every position they'd tried had been utter bliss. Mace was a skilled lover.

"Where's that jar?" he muttered and Krysta felt motion at her other side as Drake reached out with one hand. A moment later, she felt slick cream against her backside as Mace prepared her, interspersing forays of his fingers with slaps on her backside. The stark difference between pleasure and a hint of pain startled her and aroused her all at the same time.

She was whimpering by the time Mace left off and knelt between her thighs.

"Do you want it now, Krysta?" He bent over to growl in her ear. "Are you going to share your luscious ass with me?"

"Yes, Mace! Yes!"

She cried out when he slid home within her, the cream letting him easily inside. Though she'd never been overly fond of this kind of loving before, with Drake and now Mace, it had an appeal all its own.

Mace began a slow rhythm inside her, but then stopped, confounding her until he rolled them carefully to the side. Mace's cock was buried in her ass, tighter now in this new position, as she faced a randy and ready Jinn bard.

Drake winked at her when she dragged her gaze from his hard cock up to his face. She knew what was coming next, though she wouldn't have thought he'd be ready again so soon. Yet another thing to thank the dragons for, she guessed. Or maybe Drake of the Five Lands really was as good as his over-inflated reputation.

She'd soon find out for certain.

Drake lifted her leg over his hip and slid closer, rubbing his cock against her dripping core.

"Ready to take us both, my love? This time the dragons aren't pushing you to accept us. This time it's your choice, love. Do you want us?"

"Do you have to ask?" She was panting between words, more ready than she'd ever been. "Stars, Drake, just do it! Please! You're killing me!"

"As my lady commands." He winked again as he pushed into her. The position was tight as they both found a home within her body.

"You were right, Drake," Mace said from behind her. "This feels incredible."

"Much as I delight in hearing it..." she paused for breath, "...you two really need to start moving now." She squirmed between them, on the knife's edge of a pleasure so tantalizing she wanted nothing more than to come. But she needed them to move to bring it about.

"Haste makes waste, sweetheart," Drake teased her. "You'll get what you want, but we want to enjoy the feel of you for a bit before we speed on to that inevitable, pleasurable conclusion."

"Speak for yourself, Drake. I'm about ready to explode back here." Mace's voice rumbled from behind her, making her giggle at the frustration they shared.

Drake sighed dramatically and began to thrust. "As you both wish, then. But don't blame me if this is over too soon."

"Can't be soon enough for me!" She gasped as the men started a rhythm that soon caught her up in its swell.

Krysta actually screamed when Mace pulsed inside her bottom, coming hard against her, triggering her own magnificent release. Drake was only a step behind, drawing out her climax with his own pulsating need as he bathed her womb in his rich heat.

She'd never felt anything like it. Without the heat of the dragons to make her senses swim in a wash of pleasure that was theirs and the dragons' together, she felt the true depth of the experience. It was more than she'd ever dreamed she'd have in her life. She felt cherished, replete and so totally loved, she could never doubt their feelings for her ever again. The men pulled away and rested at her side, each breathing hard.

When she could move, she leaned over to kiss them both, one at a time, thanking them silently for the love they all shared.

The next morning, Drake was gone when Mace and Krysta woke sometime just after dawn. They went in search of breakfast and found a crowd gathered around the windows that looked out onto the courtyard. A quick query to Nellin confirmed the dragons were outside with Drake.

Mace and Krysta walked out onto the steps, watching the wizard and Drake, standing in the center of the large courtyard. The two dragons stood opposite the wizard, encasing Drake in a triangle. Mace listened in through his connection with Nellin, intrigued at the instruction Gryffid was providing.

"How is he doing?" Krysta came up beside him. Mace put his arm around her shoulders and drew her close to his side.

"Nellin says well. He says there's great magic in Drake, but it's so close to the dragon's own fire, he never realized it before. Plus, those years away, surrounded by Jinn magic must've brought it closer to the surface."

"And I bet a true wizard's instruction doesn't hurt either."

"No, our friend the minstrel seems to learn new talents and skills quickly."

"He's more than our friend." She turned to him and he felt the chastisement and query in her probing grey gaze. All his own turmoil rose and he knew the time had come to discuss his discomfort.

"He's our bondmate. Our family. I know that, but I have no idea what this new development will mean to us as a unit. How can I fight alongside a mage? I'm a simple soldier."

She touched his cheek. "A soldier you may well be, but simple? Never that." Reaching up, she kissed him gently. "The Mother of All has plans for us we cannot fathom. It's like Gryffid said. Each of us came to this island for a reason. We need only figure out what it is."

He hugged her close as they turned again to watch Drake's progress.

"I believe I was brought here for a lesson in humility." Mace smiled wryly. "All those years I strove to be the best. I had to work so hard to equal and only sometimes surpass what came to Drake naturally. But he never saw it. I never begrudged him his natural ability. But now..."

"Now he's a mage."

"There's no way to compete with that." Mace felt fear for the first time, but it wasn't fear of Drake or his abilities. It went deeper than that. "I'm afraid he won't need us now." His arm tightened reflexively around her as she snuggled into him.

"Time will tell, but I have hope the Mother of All knows what she's doing when it comes to the five of us. For one thing, you know Jenet will never let him go again, and I get the feeling she can be tenacious."

Her little chuckle warmed Mace's heart. "I believe you're right on that score at least, milady."

"Then we'll just have to see where this leads. Drake is a mage now. There's no turning back from something like that. We'll need to stand by him and accept him for what he is and what he can do, trusting him to believe in our love and accept it as his due."

Mace turned and hugged her close. "You're a marvel, my love. I don't deserve you, but I'll never let you go."

"Good." She smiled up at him. "Because I'll never let either you or Drake off the hook. You're mine now. Get used to it." The saucy wink she gave him belied her warning words.

In the courtyard, flames erupted around Drake's body, surrounding him in a pillar of fire, but all he felt was their warmth, none of the searing pain associated with natural flame. No, this was magical flame, and it came from within himself. He could hardly believe it.

"Good," Gryffid coached him from several feet away. "Now shape the power to your will. Command it and control it. Do not fear it, for it cannot harm you."

"Or us," Jenet said from behind him. She was on his right, Nellin next to her on his left. The dragons were there to help contain his fire, should it go out of control, but so far, he was able to master the immense energy that wrestled with his will.

"I was going to encourage you to let it all out, but I see I miscalculated your power, young Drake." Gryffid was laughing, apparently pleased with himself, though Drake didn't quite understand why. It was all he could do to retain control over the wriggling energies that vied to be let free.

With Gryffid's help, he'd learned to tap into the river of power that lay just beneath his soul's surface. It had always been there, but Drake was only marginally aware of it. Only at times when the Jinn power had been high had he felt the stirring, the rippling of energy current down deep inside him. He always felt itchy at such times—like something inside him was yearning to be free—but he hadn't known. No way could he have known the immense burning river that flowed beneath his surface, waiting for him to tap into it.

The feeling was like no other. The fire cleansed him. It burned him down to his simplest needs. Jenet was there, as always in the burning center of his soul, but so too was Krysta. Beautiful Krysta. Her love nurtured him and helped him bank his fire. Mace was there too, he saw, and Nellin, on the periphery, ready to protect him should he fail. It was a comfort he hadn't known since leaving his home.

They were part of him. Perhaps the best part. The thought of their love and care humbled him and gave him the strength to control the fire, to temper the flames. They were his world. His family.

Slowly the flames came to heel. He felt their submission with triumph. The inferno that surrounded him died down, but he knew he could recall it with the merest flicker of his will. It was a heady feeling.

"Magnificent!" the wizard cried, clapping his hands. "You're a natural, my dear boy. And more powerful than I would have imagined. Perhaps Draco's blood runs thicker in you than I'd first thought. This is good. Very good indeed!"

Drake felt the drain as he fought the magic for control and won. He was suddenly tired, but Jenet was there, the coils of her long neck supporting him when he swayed on his feet. Fire was the dragon's element, so Drake didn't worry overmuch about the flames that still licked at his feet hurting her.

"Is it all right?" he asked, just to make sure.

"Your fire can never harm me," she assured him. *"Just lean on me. You've had a startling introduction to your magic. It's bound to tire you at first, until you get used to it. I remember when I was just a hatchling. Managing the magic was even more tiring than learning to fly."*

"I think you have something there, Jenet." Drake chuckled wearily as he pushed the fire out completely. It wouldn't do to walk around all day with flaming feet.

Chapter Sixteen

Drake needed to lie down after his first lesson in magic. Mace and Krysta used the opportunity to take Gerrow and Lilith up on an invitation to train with their troops. The fair folk kept a fighting group the size of a small army ready at all times. Mace was surprised by the idea of such vigilance, but after watching them drill for just a few minutes, he understood these warriors were very serious about their calling indeed.

Punches weren't pulled. You either evaded or got hurt. Considering the fair folk were the next best thing to immortal, Mace figured that was a luxury of their training humans couldn't afford to emulate. At least not among lower-ranked warriors. Elite fighters often did train with no holds barred, but it was too easy for a newcomer to make a crippling or fatal mistake.

The men and women trained together, of which Mace approved. You could never choose the sex or skill level of your enemy in a real fight, so segregating your troopers for every facet of their training didn't serve them well at all. Krysta jumped in with both feet, joining her new friend Lilith with gusto as they moved through the figures of an intricate fighting dance. Krysta had no fear, he'd give her that, but Mace wanted to watch and learn more before he entered the fray. There was much to be learned from observing how these folk trained.

Perhaps some of their teachings could be used to better serve the knights or Guards of Draconia.

Eventually though, Mace felt he'd seen enough. The tang of battle was too tempting on his tongue and he joined in the fighting practice, glad when he more than held his own among the elite corps of fair folk. They weren't pulling their strikes for him, which he took as a compliment, and he returned the favor, scoring a few hits that took the fair folk by surprise.

Mace was just starting to really enjoy himself when William entered the courtyard, attired up for practice. He carried a foreign-style long-sword, like many of the fair warriors. Mace cleared to the side of the square to see what would become of the smiling challenge in the young prince's eyes.

He was not to be disappointed. Four fey swordsmen broke off from the main group—experts all, from what Mace had already observed. They faced the prince, each taking one side, while the prince stood ready. Krysta sidled up next to Mace as the entire group stood back to watch.

What followed was a blinding display of speed and skill the likes of which Mace had never seen. The elegantly curved swords flashed in the afternoon sun, swirling in patterns too complex and fast to see clearly. William was amazing. Once again, the expert swordsmen didn't go easy on the young prince, but he was faster than all four of them combined.

Mace realized he was watching magic at work. Somehow the prince had learned to tap into his dragon speed and strength even more than any of his line Mace had observed. No doubt, King Roland, Prince Nico and the rest of the royal brothers were able to call on the strength and the fire of their dragon half while in human form, but Mace had never seen nor heard of anything like this.

When the four swordsmen retreated—each having been

defeated—the prince wasn't even breathing hard.

"Now that—" Krysta nodded toward where Prince Wil was speaking with the warriors he'd just battled, "—was something I never thought to witness."

"Agreed." Mace would have said more, but Lilith tossed two shining metal objects straight at Krysta. They were long and slender, but somewhat boxy, in a shape that puzzled Mace.

Krysta, seeing them out of the corner of her eye, shot her hands out reflexively and caught the objects. They were each about a foot long. Surprise crossed her features, to be replaced with a huge grin. A moment later, two resounding snaps made Mace step back.

The objects were fans, but these were no mere lady's adornment. These were metal fans that had the distinct ring of steel, intricately patterned, to be sure, but tipped with sharpened, razor edges. They were weapons!

"Do you know the way?" Lilith seemed to challenge Krysta as the women squared off. Two more sharp snaps and Lilith was armed with her own set of bladed fans.

"I have danced the dance," Krysta answered with an almost gleeful glint in her grey eyes, matching the glint of sharpened steel she now twirled in both hands.

They didn't bow in the formal way of men, but rather did the graceful half-curtsy of noblewomen before engaging in a lightning fast swirl of bodies and blades almost too fast for Mace to follow. The battle was circular in form, with a great deal of pivoting and turning, long graceful sweeps of the fans that could be so very deadly if they made contact with tender skin. It was clear both women were expert with the amazingly odd weapons. Mace had never seen the like.

In a day of novel happenings, this ranked right up there with fireballs and wizards. The demure woman Mace had pledged his life to was more than the simple warrior he'd come to respect. She was some kind of weapons expert with knowledge of things he'd never even heard of. It was humbling, but also incredibly intriguing.

Mace settled in to watch the match as the women made graceful, arcing patterns with their supple bodies, their sinuous arms and those lethal half-circles of steel. The flash of light off the blade edges, as well as the patterns on the finely wrought metal, was dazzling and hypnotic. Mace was fascinated by the exaggerated movements needed to use such clever weapons.

The benefits of this kind of weapon were not lost on him either. Many women carried fans, as did men in warmer climates. A fan would not be remarked upon in places where folk could not go about armed with blades or bows. Social gatherings, for example, or intimate interludes. The sharpened blades of the fan could probably be concealed beneath a fabric covering until such time as the warrior was ready to strike. This then, was a perfect assassin's weapon.

And Krysta was an expert with it.

That troubling fact would require further thought but Mace saw the match between the women was drawing to a close. Both were breathing hard and as they stopped whirling around, Mace could see both had been bloodied by the battle. Krysta had several fine lines that welled with blood on her arms and legs. Lilith had fewer, but Krysta had held her own. Mace was proud of her showing against such a formidable opponent.

The four fans snicked closed as the women curtsied to each other a final time. Lilith closed the distance, a broad smile on her face.

"You're far better with those than I would have credited."

"Thank you. That's high praise coming from such a skilled warrior." Krysta turned the fans over to the fair woman. "It's been a while. Frankly, I'm glad to know I still have the knack, even if you were pulling your punches a bit."

"Not by much, Lady Krysta. I have never battled a human with as much fan skill as you. It was a pleasure."

"Likewise." Krysta grinned, but it turned to a grimace as she held one hand to a cut bleeding more profusely along her thigh now that they'd stopped moving.

Lilith must have seen it as well, for she called to one of her students and a young male rushed over. "Lothar will see to your injuries. He has more healing power than I." Lilith nodded and left the strange man facing Krysta.

"My sister is a little abrupt," the man began, moving closer. "I'm Lothar, youngest of the Eliadnae line. Lilith is my eldest sister. She's our best warrior of her generation, but not much on tact, I'm afraid. Please allow me to see to your wounds. Lilith's will heal momentarily, but you are human." He shrugged to punctuate the observation.

"It's nice to meet you, Lothar. I'm Krysta."

"Yes, I know. And Sir Mace." Lothar's gaze met Mace's, radiating assurance. Mace could see this man was much older than he appeared. The youthful face and eager gait to his step hid ancient eyes that held far more knowledge and power than a mere youth could, or should, have.

"I would be grateful if you could assist my lady," Mace said in the formal way of these people, nodding to the man.

"They're only scratches." Krysta tried to protest but Lothar was in front of her and Mace behind. She wasn't going anywhere until her wounds were healed.

"It will take but a moment, Lady." Lothar reached out one fingertip and drew it over the worst of the cuts—the one on her thigh. Mace felt a crackle of electricity along his skin as if the air itself reacted to the man's power. Mace stared as the wound healed before his eyes, sealing up as Lothar's finger passed over it. He did the same with the other small cuts on her arms and legs. In all, it took only moments, but the effects were startling. Krysta was as good as new, though a little bloodstained.

Mace had never seen the like. True healers often took long moments of concentration on their task for only slight improvement to their patient. Never had Mace seen a wound heal so completely, so quickly, with no apparent drain to the healer.

"Your power is amazing," Mace said, unable to keep the astonishment from his voice. "I thank you for helping my lady."

"It's always a pleasure to assist a lovely woman—" Lothar winked at Krysta, grinning, "—and a skilled warrioress."

"Thank you, Lothar." Krysta's voice was softer than Mace liked when she spoke to another man.

The fair rogue lifted her hand to his lips and kissed it before departing. Mace gritted his teeth and held back a growl, but Krysta must have sensed his mood. She turned to hug him, reaching up to kiss his cheek before twirling away to clean off the blood and get back into the ring.

Mace decided to work off his momentary anger in training and spent the rest of the day pummeling someone or being pummeled in return. It was an altogether satisfying day, spent learning from some of the finest warriors in all the world. Mace settled down to learn and felt, by the end of the day, he'd come out wiser.

Dinner that night was a quieter affair than the night before. The minstrels played for a shorter time, and most of their songs were sad. It was clear the fair folk would miss William when he left in the morning.

Some brought him little gifts as they left the hall for the

night, pressing kisses of farewell on his cheek and some of the more motherly women shedding a tear or two for his departure.

Several gave gifts to Krysta and her mates, and a few had things for the dragons as well. Most were small gifts that could be easily carried on their long journey, and some were practical gifts that they could use along the way. Krysta amassed a collection of colorful silk scarves, finely woven to the consistency of a spider's web. They were huge swaths of fabric, but folded up to mere nothings and would travel well. The weaving of the fair folk was reputed to be nearly indestructible as well as gorgeous.

The colorful silks gave her an idea she decided to put to use later, after they retired for the night. She asked Margan, the pennywhistle player of the night before, covertly, if the loan of a lute could be arranged. The woman was more than happy to assist with Krysta's little plan, promising a lute would be waiting in their room when they went to bed.

True to her word, the lute was lying across the covers when Krysta entered with her men. Drake saw it immediately and went to pick it up, strumming the strings contemplatively.

"What's this?"

Krysta shrugged. "Just a little something I arranged. Would you mind playing for me tonight?"

"You know I'll play for you anytime, sweetheart. Anywhere." The drawl of his voice fired her senses as she went behind the screen to set the stage.

"Good, then warm up a bit. I want your fingers to be nice and loose when you play the *velorania* for me."

Drake reclined on the large bed, smiling broadly. "We're in for a treat, Mace. Have you ever seen the Jinn veil dance?" He began warming up his fingers with a few runs on the lute, breaking into a soft, seductive tune as he helped his little Jinn warrior woman set the mood.

Mace shrugged as he sat on the other side of the large bed, removing his boots. "I've never even heard of it."

"The *velorania* is something special, my friend. Never performed lightly, and only shared among lovers—or so the legends say. I've only heard of it. I've never seen a true *velorania* myself, though all Jinn musicians know the proper tune. We play it for dancing, but the secret steps for the veil dance are known only to a Jinn female, and performed only for her mate—or mates—in our case."

Drake played the short notes that began the winding tune. It started out slow and sensuous, drawing higher and tighter, shorter and faster as the melody grew. He was in the first section of the seductive tune when Krysta appeared from behind the screen.

She stood before them clothed only in the brightly colored scarves the fair folk had given her. She was utterly, devastatingly, beautiful. Drake's fingers faltered before he gathered his wits and Krysta winked at him from under her veil. It was the sexiest thing he'd ever seen...but the night promised to bring even further delights he could only imagine.

The dance started slowly, and built. The first section, she'd been taught, was for Krysta to make her man more comfortable. She teased Mace, sitting on his lap for short moments as she danced around him, each time she came near, undoing a button or untying a knot that would eventually have him naked. When she had his chest bare, she dropped to her knees, swaying in time with the music between his spread legs. She brushed up against him in the moves of the ancient dance, using her fingers to free his thick cock from his leggings.

She dipped her head, letting her hair and the soft silk of the scarves trail over his erection, then moved away to dance for him as he took the initiative and shucked his leathers. She undulated her torso and shook her breasts under the thin veils, beginning the next section of the dance as she slowly pulled away the trailing veils. These were the smaller scarves she'd tucked in here and there among the longer veils she'd used to wrap her body. There were more layers than anyone would have guessed from looking at her, but the silk was so thin and transparent, it was deceptive.

She stripped off the smaller scarves, moving forward and back to tease the soft material against Mace's hard body. She wrapped them around his arms, his hands, his legs, and even his cock, using the gentle friction to drive him to a fever pitch.

The dance was working.

Soon she was left in nothing but the long veils she'd twined around her person in the ancient pattern. Now came the next part of the dance. Obligingly, the music changed subtly, growing faster and more intense.

Krysta drifted closer to Mace, holding out one corner of a scarf she'd untucked for him to take in his teeth. As the music increased slightly, she twirled out of the wrapping, uncovering a bit more of her skin to the night air and leaving Mace with the colorful silk veil in his lap. He discarded it quickly, reaching forward with his mouth for another of the strategically tucked scarves. This one was tucked in between her breasts. She covered his head with her hands as she snuggled his face between the soft mounds, allowing him time to nip at her skin under the soft veils, then drew away when he had the tail of the scarf between his teeth once more.

Spinning a little more quickly now, the veil unwound from around her body as Mace watched, transfixed. Oh, how she liked that look on his face. It told her the dance was working its magic. He was completely under her spell.

She glanced at Drake, glad to see him smile. Because he played the music, this veil dance was primarily for Mace, but she could tell from Drake's expression he didn't begrudge the quiet knight the treat, and Drake was enjoying the view as well, if the hard-on in his pants was any indication. She blew Drake a kiss as she coaxed Mace's hands to another tucked scarf point.

She spun away and more of her body was revealed. The music grew now, as she repeated the forward and back motions, each time she twirled away, removing another veil and coming closer to the climax of the dance. Mace was breathing hard now, his cock rising high against his belly.

Chapter Seventeen

The music wound to a final crescendo and Krysta stopped all movement, her final pose one of complete abandon. Her legs were parted, showcasing her moist folds, her arms thrown up and back, lifting her ripe breasts like offerings. Her mouth was open, lips pouting and wanton, and her eyes flashed desire at her mates.

Mace was too far gone by that point to do anything other than drag her down onto the bed. He mounted her swiftly, driving his cock home into her yearning passage. She cried out at the force of him, as keyed up from the dance as he was.

Drake placed the lute aside and watched, undressing as Mace pounded into their mate, enjoying the view. He'd participated in group pleasure several times before with the Jinn—most recently standing as witness for Nico and Riki's marriage—but this was so much different than the casual joinings he'd enjoyed before. This was forever. This was his woman, his wife. And Mace was his fighting partner, the only man in the world Drake would ever consider sharing Krysta with, for he knew if anything should happen to him, Mace would be there for her. It was a comforting thought, though Drake wouldn't have believed it before.

This joining was just for them. The dragons were not driving him and Mace with their lusts. The dragons lay by the fire in the hall, necks entwined as they suppressed their own desires in favor of sleep. They knew they'd need all their strength for the long flight tomorrow. It was tough on the newly mated dragons, but Drake had the feeling they'd all be making up for it when they were finally home and safe. Chances were, they wouldn't leave their suite for a week while the dragons flew almost non-stop, making up for lost time.

But this joining was special in another way. This was the first time Krysta had initiated intimacy. She was a powerful woman and this blatant display proved beyond doubt that this—her two mates—were her choice, and her pleasure.

She moaned as Mace increased his pace. Drake knew by looking at them, this first time would be quick. Drake was already hard as a pike as he shucked his leathers and drew closer to the bed. Kneeling on one side by Krysta's head, Drake felt his cock twitch with need when Mace lifted off her prone form to dig into her pussy with short, quick, deep strokes. Drake watched his friend's staff spear into their woman and felt himself tremble as Krysta's little hand reached around his cock and drew it to her lips.

Refocusing on her face, Drake saw she'd turned her head toward him, those pouty lips open and wanting as she tugged him forward. Drake went willingly, watching as Krysta's tongue peeked out to swipe at the tip of him. She smiled and he felt his knees go weak. When she opened her mouth again, she took him inside and Drake was powerless to control the thrust of his hips as she encouraged him to fuck her mouth as Mace fucked her pussy.

Judging by the pace Mace set, it wouldn't be long now. Drake reached down and palmed her breast, glad when his fighting partner worked in concert, raising one hand to tug at Krysta's other nipple. She moaned around Drake's cock, the vibrations shooting right up his spine. She followed that with a hard suck that almost made him shoot his load right on the spot. Drake stilled, his cock loving the warm, wet place and agile tongue stroking it.

"You do that too well." Drake's voice was full of admiration. The Lady had truly blessed him when She'd brought Krysta to him—in so many ways. Not the least of which, at the moment, was the fact she was some kind of sex goddess. Drake held her gaze as she blinked up at him, temptation in her gorgeous grey eyes.

Mace groaned, drawing his attention and Drake looked over to see the knight gasping as his crisis drew closer. Mace held both of Krysta's legs up and out now, pushing into her from a sitting position that allowed Drake to watch every thrust. It made his mouth water and his dick twitch.

Krysta was near the edge, but not as close as Mace. Drake could see it in her lovely eyes, hear it in her whimpers of pleasure. She needed a little something extra if she was going to come with Mace. Luckily, that's where Drake could help.

He reached down and stroked his fingers through the sparse curls at the juncture of her thighs. Like most warriors, she trimmed herself there. How Drake would enjoy helping her the next time she felt the need to barber herself. But that thought was for another time. Right now he had to concentrate on ratcheting her arousal up another few notches, so she'd be ready to fly when Mace was. Judging by the look of the man, that would be any time now.

Drake withdrew his cock from the hot cavern of her mouth and got down on his stomach, partially over her as he kissed her sweet lips. Their tongues dueled as her body shivered with Mace's pounding thrusts. Drake left her mouth, using his hands and lips to trace down her body, pausing for a delicious moment at her breasts.

He sucked her nipples into his mouth one by one, plumping and teasing her with nimble fingers. His teeth nibbled gently on her delicate skin as her breathing increased. One hand strayed downward to reclaim the womanly curls at her apex. Dipping lower, Drake ran one finger down into her folds as Mace hesitated only briefly before continuing his assault on her feminine core.

Drake turned his head to look up at the knight. Mace nodded shortly, his expression one of fierce concentration. They were of one mind in that moment. Mace didn't want to come until Krysta had. And Drake was just the man to help them both.

Delving deeper, Drake found the hard nubbin of flesh that made Krysta squirm with excitement. Palpitating it with one long finger, he turned back to watch her eyes dilate and felt an increase in her slick fluids near his fingers. Mace groaned as Drake smiled.

"You like that, Krysta? You like my fingers on your pussy while Mace fucks you senseless?"

Her dazed eyes opened and stared up at him. It was a look he'd never forget. "Yes!"

"Would you like it more if I licked you while Mace fucked your pussy?" They both stiffened slightly. "I'm not sure how our friend Mace would like it, but I'd do anything for you, Krysta. Anything at all."

He tugged on her clit then, using two fingers and coming close to touching Mace's thick cock as he made short digs into her warm body. He rode the razor's edge.

Drake tugged rhythmically on her clit and bent to whisper in her ear. "My tongue on your clit while Mace's cock strokes in deep. What do you say, Krysta?"

"Yes!" She exploded then, writhing in his arms as Mace

stiffened. Drake kept his hand on her clit, stroking her through the powerful climax while Mace drove home and stayed, his cock spurting within her hot depths in a series of pulses. Drake could feel it all through his fingers as they climaxed together.

When Krysta finally came down from the high plateau, Drake patted her pussy a few times in praise before withdrawing his hand. Mace caught his eye as he withdrew also and dropped down at Krysta's side on the wide bed. Mace turned her away from Drake as Mace kissed her gently, his hands stroking down over her soft skin as if in thanks.

Drake could be patient while they cuddled, but only to a point. He was a man in need and he knew he could bring Krysta up to that peak of pleasure again. In fact, it was his new mission in life. He'd see to it she was stuffed with cock every moment of the nights they shared together, screaming their names as she creamed around them and came at least ten times a night. It was a goal to work toward, and one he'd spend his life enjoying.

When he could wait no more, he tugged her hips backward, breaking them apart just enough to place her on her knees, ass in the air. She had a lovely ass. Muscular and round, smooth and firm, she was perfectly formed for long riding and double penetration—a good thing in the wife of a set of knights.

But Drake wanted her pussy now. It was slick with Mace's come and her own juices, an easy glide for his abused cock. He'd been hard for hours, it seemed, and he knew it wouldn't take much for him to shoot his load, but he wanted her to come with him. He'd hold out as long as he could to make that happen.

Drake pushed in with little resistance, glad of the welcome of her tight body. He began a languid rhythm, wanting to stoke her fires slowly, to bring her to peak with him.

But Mace had other ideas, apparently.

Mace lifted her to her elbows, positioning his head beneath her body so he could suck on her hanging nipples. Drake paused only a moment to lean over and see what the other man was up to and received a cocky, satisfied grin in return. Drake had never seen the sober knight smile in just that way and it boded well for Krysta's pleasure this night.

Drake thrust into her with renewed energy, knowing Mace was there to help him as he'd just helped Mace. This partnership business had unforeseen benefits, indeed.

Krysta's excitement built as Mace worked her nipples with his tongue, teeth and lips. Mace slid the fingers of one hand into Krysta's curls, seeking her clit, much as Drake had done, only this position put the other man perilously close to Drake's own arousal. He didn't mind. He'd done this before once or twice with drunken Jinn, but this was the first time he'd been part of this kind of excess with two people who really mattered in his life. Two people he'd spend the rest of his days with— living and working side by side. The thought was staggering.

Mace did something that made Krysta clench and Drake looked down to find they'd readjusted their position. Mace lay to her side now, one hand pinching her breasts, the fingers of the other on her clit, his hard cock sticking up near her mouth. Even as he watched, she lowered, increasing the angle of her pussy on Drake's cock as she took Mace into her hot mouth. The thought of that wet heat had Drake picking up the pace. He was close now. He could feel his balls draw up, his seed boiling inside.

"Pick it up, Mace," he ground out between clenched teeth.

Krysta came hard around him, clenching and tugging at his cock with her powerful, inner muscles. Drake came a moment later, spewing inside her.

As they calmed, Mace turned on the wide bed, making room for Drake to collapse, which he promptly did after long, long moments of bliss inside his woman. When Drake was finally spent, Mace was there to take Krysta in his arms, and place her gently on the bed. Drake was glad. The will was strong, but his flesh was weak. She'd wrung him out and left him nearly unable to move.

"Sweet Mother!" Drake whispered his shock at one of the best orgasms of his life.

Krysta rolled to her side, snuggling into him as he lay on his back. He brought one arm around her shoulders, enjoying the feel of her next to him.

But Mace wasn't done. He cuddled behind her, stroking one hand between her legs as Drake propped up on one elbow to watch. Mace drew their wetness from her pussy back to the tight hole of her ass and Drake's gaze shot up to Mace's.

"I want to come from behind this time."

Krysta wiggled in renewed arousal at Mace's possessive words.

"As you wish, brother." Drake wasn't going to argue. Mace was on a roll and Drake didn't mind following his lead one bit.

What followed was a long night filled with what could only be termed debauchery. They tried all sorts of positions and combinations, free from the dragons' influence. The dragons enhanced their pleasure, to be sure, but also directed their actions on some basic levels. Without the dragons' pleasure riding them, it was purely up to them and Drake was amazed to find Mace had some rather creative ideas on how to pleasure their woman. The knight definitely knew how to operate as part of a team.

They took her together and separately, used the scarves to tie her to the bed frame in various positions until she screamed in ecstasy.

The early morning light bounced off waves as they rolled ashore on Gryphon Isle. A small party set out for the beach. Two dragons, two knights and their mate, two fey warriors, a set of gryphons, the prince and the wizard Gryffid.

Lilith and Gerrow would fly on Herorthor and Llydiss's backs as far as the shore of Draconia as honor guard. They would not trespass on Draconian soil, but would turn back for home as soon as they saw the dragons reach their homeland. From there, it would be up to the small party to make their way safely back to the capital city and William's family.

Lilith and Gerrow took their leave of William first, then passed a few words of farewell with the Draconian party. In particular, Lilith presented Krysta with a set of matching, incredibly beautiful fans. They looked normal enough at first glance, but when opened in a certain direction, they could be lethal. The intricate metal work was breathtaking and Krysta thanked Lilith profusely for the thoughtful gift. The fair warriors took their leave and positioned themselves near the gryphons, ready to fly when the dragons were.

Drake had mixed emotions about leaving. On the one hand, he needed to return to the castle, to fulfill his quest and his promises to Roland, Nico and especially to Declan. On the other hand, a whole new world had opened up to him and Drake wanted to explore it more fully under the wizard's tutelage. The magic mystified him, but it also intrigued him. Now that he knew it was there and how it felt to access it, he wanted to do it more often. He wanted to master this new skill and experiment with ways to use his fire.

But that would come, in time. Gryffid had been clear it was

a matter of practice now that Drake was aware of the magic. Jenet had promised to help, as had Nellin, and Drake was looking forward to his next attempt to call his hidden fire.

"Practice, Sir Drake." Gryffid walked up and clasped him on the shoulder. "Your fire is your birthright. Be wise in its use and learn to temper its ferocity and you should do well."

"Thank you, my lord. This has been one of the strangest, and most enlightening few days of my life."

Gryffid laughed at that. "You started on your quest a simple bard and return home a hero, a knight and a mage. I think you should write a song or two about your travels before some of your former colleagues get their hands on the tale and start to elaborate."

Drake laughed, knowing just what the wizard meant. Bards were known for taking a tale and twisting it so that it seldom resembled the actual facts. Drake was careful to stay true—as much as he could—to actual events when he wrote his songs, but others were far less circumspect.

"Thank you for everything, my lord." Mace came up beside them. "Most of all for returning Wil to his family."

"He was never mine to keep, Sir Mace," Gryffid replied. "I only wish I hadn't had to do it this way. His family will be displeased, I fear, but there was no alternative. Please express my regrets to the royal family. I was an ally of their progenitor and that alliance stands firm. I and my fellows will stand with the dragons and knights of Draconia, and all the descendants of our ancient pact, should the worst come to pass."

"We'll do all in our power to prevent that, Gryffid." Wil put his hand on the old man's shoulders. He'd taken his leave of the fair folk and now moved to say goodbye to his mentor. Drake moved back, giving them some space.

Wil hugged the wizard tightly and Krysta was touched to see the genuine affection on the wizard's face as he returned the gesture.

"That's just amazing." Krysta marveled as the black dragon took to the sky. She'd never seen the change before, though she'd known about the shapeshifters of the Black Dragon Clan for some time as spymaster for the Wayfarer Clan. They'd acted as her conduits on occasion for information to pass between her clan and the leaders of all Jinn.

"You're not too surprised, though, are you?" Jenet's head butted Krysta companionably in the back as her voice sounded through all their minds.

"No. I've heard about black dragons before, though I've never seen them with my own eyes."

Krysta turned to face the dragons, expecting more questions, but Drake scooped her up and threw her onto Jenet's back without so much as a by-your-leave and the moment was lost. The dragons didn't seem too concerned with her knowledge, though Mace wore a bit of a frown between his dark brows. Drake took pity on the knight and explained.

"The Black Dragon Clan has quite a few shapeshifters among its ranks, Mace. Our mate is one of the best spies in all of the Jinn clans. I'd be disappointed if she didn't know about them—and a whole lot else. I have a feeling her knowledge and contacts will come in handy in the years to come."

Krysta reached back and kissed him. The confident words and the pride she felt from them bolstered her heart.

"She's a spy?" Mace asked.

Drake nodded. "A master spy."

"Sweet Mother," Mace groused good-naturedly as he mounted Nellin's back, *"I'm surrounded!"*

They laughed as they took to the skies after Wil, sparing a moment to wave to those left behind on land. Two gryphons took to the air nearby, with Lilith and Gerrow on their backs.

As they neared the shore, the gryphons veered away, the fair warriors on their backs waving in farewell. They made no sound, probably to preserve what little stealth the dragons could claim as they made their way back to their homeland. Drake wasn't sure what dangers might await, though the wizard seemed certain the return trip would not be as easy as it seemed.

Gryphon Isle lay off the shore of the mainland, at a point that rested on the border of Draconia and Skithdron. They were very near the border even now, which wasn't the safest place to be, but it would take some travel before they were deeper within the border of Draconia.

Drake kept an eye out for anything that might look suspicious, but he was not trained for aerial reconnaissance. He'd never thought to accept Jenet's offer of knighthood, and left home before he could do any training at all.

"I'm counting on you, my friend," Drake broached the topic, bridging the gap to Mace's mind and including the rest of their party in the conversation. *"I've never trained for this kind of work."*

It was a hard admission to make, but Drake needed to be up front with them. They all knew he wasn't a trained knight, but they'd been too kind to point out his deficiencies. It was about time he faced facts.

"Don't worry, you more than make up for it, Drake. I haven't written any songs or lobbed any fireballs lately." Mace's tone was dry, but Drake felt the humor in his words.

"That may be, but right now I feel at a distinct disadvantage

not knowing what I'm looking at from the air."

"Nellin and I will keep watch with Mace and Prince Wil. If we see anything," Jenet assured him, *"we'll point it out. It's the only way you will learn."*

"Ah. We are home." Nellin's deep voice communicated his satisfaction as they crossed over the point where the sea ended and the beach began. The dragons began their descent. They'd all agreed to take a quick break when they reached the shore, even as close as they were to the winding border with Skithdron. The flight between Gryphon Isle and the mainland was a long one. The dragons could have gone farther of course, but it was better to let their riders dismount and stretch their legs a bit every few hours.

Plus, it was nearing midday and the fair folk had given them more than enough provisions to make their way back. It would be good to eat something before they began the next leg of their long journey.

The inhabitants of Gryphon Isle also gave them warm cloaks and kitted Drake out with a spare shirt and leggings as well as a pack to keep them in. The garments and tack, made by their best artisans, were of the highest quality.

Drake had felt odd accepting such costly gifts at first, but the people had insisted, gifting them all with matching bags. Krysta especially loved the delicate designs on the leatherwork. She'd preened like a sparrow when she saw one of the packs was meant for her and thanked their hosts effusively.

The riders dismounted and Wil changed form so he could join them for a bit of lunch. They didn't spend a long time at it, but ate well and quickly, stretching their muscles before remounting.

"It's good to be back on Draconian soil," Wil said contemplatively as he lingered over his last bite of seed bread. "I feel the land welcoming me. It's a good feeling."

"I know what you mean." Drake nodded. "I returned last week after fifteen years. I was dreading the meeting with my family, but still it felt good when I crossed that last border. Even though I knew I had to face my fathers." Drake laughed wryly at his own fears.

"I feel some of that. I'm a little worried about how Rol will react," Wil admitted with a shrug, "but all in all, it's good to be home."

"On the way down we camped, but I think we can stop in the town of Bayberry Heath for tonight," Mace said. "As I recall, they had a nice inn with good food, for all that it's close to the border."

"I think the royal treasury would cover that," Wil said with a facetious grin. "Or Drake could always sing for our supper."

Drake laughed. "Most landlords will cover my own room and board in exchange for a few songs—maybe my lady's too— but the rest of you are on your own."

"Now is that any way to treat your brothers-in-arms?" Wil nudged Mace in the ribs, grinning. Mace even cracked a smile, making the ribbing all worthwhile.

"Regardless, I still have some coin that ought to cover a decent bed and a hearty dinner."

"Nellin and I have been to Bayberry Heath before. It's a nice little town, though it was attacked when the Skithdronian army came through a few seasons ago. They've rebuilt well since then and they have accommodation for dragons. They're used to patrollers from the Border Lair stopping by every week or so. We might be able to get news of what's been going on since we left."

"It's a good plan," Drake agreed.

After lunch, they all remounted and Wil transformed back

into the black dragon that was his birthright. They launched from the hard-packed sand and took to the sky as the noon sun started its slow descent toward the horizon. They would have an hour or so of light left when they reached Bayberry Heath.

Krysta rode with Drake, for which he was grateful. He liked having her warm body next to him. Liked being able to touch her as they flew along on Jenet's back. He just liked everything about his new life, though he never would have imagined it when he'd left home so many years before. Here he was now, a knight, married to an incredible woman who was his match in almost every way, and partnered with a man he'd respected and liked since they were boys.

Life couldn't get much better.

Chapter Eighteen

"Do you see that?" Mace's thoughts rang urgently through all their minds. *"Skith sign, and lots of it. Heading for Bayberry Heath."*

"Damn!" Wil's tone was filled with anger as he put on a burst of speed. Black dragons were faster than all others, though Jenet and Nellin did their best to chase the prince down.

"Prince William!" Drake called after him. *"Think about what you're doing. I doubt this is a random attack. Could be they're just waiting for you. The threat from Lucan still stands. I had good intelligence before you were kidnapped that he was aiming to capture one of the younger princes. I doubt that's changed in the time you've been gone. You can't just rush in there!"*

"Dammit, Drake! This is my homeland. My people. I can't just let them die."

"An admirable sentiment," Mace reasoned, *"but a wise warrior never attacks without a plan."*

"I have a plan all right. I'm going in. Follow or don't, it's up to you."

They neared the town and could see the black dragon descending, flaming as he went, lighting fire to the trees and the skiths below. But there were a large number of soldiers waiting there as well. This had to be a trap, though how they could have known exactly when their party would arrive was a mystery to Drake. Still, Lucan had devious ways of using magic for his own ends. Perhaps some kind of magic was afoot here.

Too late, Drake saw the machine hidden in the trees. A spear launched toward William's black hide, piercing his wing as the black dragon cried out so loudly, it reverberated through the air, the trees and the ground itself. Nellin and Jenet trumpeted their distress as well, watching from the distance, just not fast enough to keep up with the prince.

William went down in a ball of black fire, flaming everything around him as he fell to the ground, teeming with enemy soldiers. The townsmen were trying to fight as well, but were sadly outnumbered.

"Jenet, stay clear of the crossbow. They've got those diamond-bladed spears." Mace rattled off instructions, though he knew Nellin shared his mind as they'd been trained to do. Already the dragon was angling in for the perfect approach. With time and training, the four minds would work together, but for now, they had to make do.

Nellin slowed marginally, dropping down under the fire. Mace could see that Wil had transformed and was swinging those twin sabers of his in lightning fast arcs, though his back was bleeding profusely. He wouldn't last for long, even as skilled as he was.

As he hit the perfect position, Mace dove headfirst, arms out to clobber a warrior who was aiming a deathblow to William's unprotected back. They went down in a tumble of arms and legs as Nellin veered off, riderless. Mace dispatched the enemy warrior quickly, then placed his back to Wil's, fighting with the prince, holding off all comers until help could arrive.

First the dragons would take out that infernal machine. Drake and Krysta could be of some use as well. Though he hated to see either of them in any danger, Mace knew Krysta was a skilled warrior, as was Drake.

Sure enough, seconds later, Krysta joined the fray on the far side of what Mace realized belatedly was the tavern yard. She moved quickly, Drake at her side. Mace noted flickering flames out of the corner of his eye and knew Drake had called his fire. Armed with balls of white hot flame, Drake lobbed his magical missiles at the enemy soldiers one by one, causing little damage to the surrounding area, but sending soldiers scrambling for cover.

Two skiths slithered in and all the Skithdronian soldiers stepped back to let the evil creatures do their work. Drake moved forward, a fireball in each hand that grew bigger and hotter as Mace watched out of the corner of his eye.

When Krysta's short sword was knocked from her grasp, she was forced to use the fan blades Lilith had given her. She wasn't sure just how strong the delicately patterned metal was. She hadn't had a chance to test the blades yet, but they were better than nothing. She used the edges to slice her way through the enemy and the flat of the fans were excellent for blocking as well as shielding. More than one arrow bounced off their glittering surface and several blades were repelled by their deceptively beautiful strength.

All in all, Krysta was well pleased with the thoughtful gift. They'd come in handy already. She fought at Drake's side until he called his flame. She gave him room to maneuver as he began to lob fireballs at the enemy, and when the skiths slithered in, she backed away to as safe a position as she could find.

The enemy soldiers retreated, probably expecting the skiths to take care of them, but they hadn't reckoned on Drake—or rather the FireDrake. The dragons did their part too, cutting off any line of escape.

Dragon fire was deadly to skiths, but it took some doing to roast them. Apparently Drake's fire was even more potent. The first skith went down in a ball of writhing flame that flared, but did not spread to the surroundings. The flame enveloped only the skith, not igniting the surrounding buildings no matter how close the burning carcass came to the tinder dry wood.

The flame began to engulf Drake and he faced the remaining skith with renewed fire. Krysta watched, mesmerized as the fire spread, hissing in the spitting, acidic venom released by the skith as it fought back. Drake's fire increased, forming an impenetrable shield around him as he advanced on the skith.

No one advanced on a skith. No human, at any rate. Krysta realized she was witnessing something never before seen. Drake was braver than any man she'd ever known, facing down a skith with magical fire as his only protection.

"That fire is something," Mace said. He'd come to her side as she watched Drake, Wil beside him. With their backs to the only stone building in the square, they were reasonably well protected from enemies, though most of the soldiers had fled. They apparently preferred to let the skiths do the work, and gave them a wide berth to do it in.

Although, to give them credit, between the humans and the dragons, they'd taken out more than half the enemy fighters. Only a few were left to scamper away from the skiths.

And scamper they did, as more skiths showed their ugly maws near the center of the action. Drake fried the skith he faced in short order. It was easier this time—at least it looked that way to Krysta—and another skith slithered in to take its place. The dragons each faced skiths and flamed everything in the creatures' paths, but more replaced the ones going up in flames.

Mace had to restrain Wil, though if the dragon prince had really wanted to shift, nothing would have stopped him. But Wil was still bleeding, injured too severely to put up much of a fight.

"You keep watch, I'll see what I can do for Wil." Krysta switched places with Mace, doing her best to field dress Wil's seeping wound while Mace stood guard.

"There are too many of them," Mace said just barely audibly. Krysta looked up to see even more skiths had arrived, but the dragons were holding their own, as was Drake.

His fire flamed brighter and higher than any natural fire she'd ever seen. It got to the point where all Drake had to do was lob a swath of his magical fire at a skith and it would immediately burst into showering, cleansing flame.

Slowly, the dragons and Drake gained the upper hand, frying the skiths until there were none left. Only remnants of their acidic venom and acrid, burnt heaps of ash remained all around the inn yard. Drake took care of the dangerous acid by skipping magical flame from one area to the next. All around the inn yard, puddles of acid burned away until they were gone, the earth itself cleansed of its taint.

Mace stood on guard, but it soon became evident that the few enemy soldiers left had run fast and far away. He leaned against the stone wall next to Krysta as Drake took care of the last of the cleanup.

"Something's wrong." Krysta watched Drake with wide, worried eyes.

251

Mace looked over at Drake, startled by the fire that still surrounded him. Drake's hands battered against forces only he could see. As Mace watched, Drake's expression went from anger to despair and Mace knew he had to act quickly.

"Jenet, Nellin, can't you do anything?"

"We can hold the fire away from others, but we can't send it back to its source. We are creatures of fire, we can't banish it." Jenet was clearly worried.

"Drake has to do that himself." Nellin sounded unsure.

Mace stepped right up to Drake, pulling back quickly when the flame surrounding him flared hot in his direction. Mace could feel the heat of the fire, but it didn't burn him. Guessing Drake didn't have long before the fire consumed him, Mace stepped forward into the living pillar of flame.

It hurt like hell, but it didn't injure. Mace grabbed Drake's forearms when he tried to move back. They held each other elbow to elbow in the way of warriors, grounding each other.

"Come back, brother. Control your magic and bring it to heel."

"I don't know if I can, Mace. Let go. I don't want to take us both down."

"You won't. We're partners now. Where you go, I go." Mace gripped Drake's arms, squeezing hard. "Master the fire, Drake. It's what you were born to do."

Mace held Drake's gaze steady as he struggled to conquer the flames and quell the inferno he'd called. Little by little, the licking tongues of fire dissipated, caressing now rather than consuming. Mace gritted his teeth against the pain, but held firm to Drake's arms, imparting his strength to his new brother.

This then, was what Mace had to offer their partnership. Drake was a creature of air and light, flame and magic. Mace was here to hold him steady, to anchor him to earth and to the partnership.

"Thank the Mother of All that you came to help, my lords!" A stout man approached them from the tavern, wringing his hands and smiling in welcome. "You've saved my inn and our village. Thank you!"

A cheer went up from the villagers. Many had stood and fought for their homes, but the old and the very young were just emerging from scorched buildings to tend the wounded. Wil was still bleeding, but even before Mace could comment, the first of the dragons from the Border Lair landed. It was carrying two—a knight and a lady. The lady approached quickly.

"I'm Belora." Her green eyes were curious as she regarded the prince.

"I'm William."

"William! But you're..." She trailed off, seemingly at a loss for words.

"He's hurt, is what he is." Krysta stepped forward. "I know it seems strange and we can answer all your questions later, but he really is Prince Wil. Ask the dragons if you don't believe us."

Belora cocked her head to the side as if in thought. A moment later she strode forward, placing her hands on William's shoulder.

"I don't understand any of this, but I can help. Turn around now and let me see to your wound."

Mace watched yet another flagrant display of magic as the young woman—famous throughout Draconia for being one of the lost princesses of the House of Kent—laid delicate hands on Wil's injured shoulder. Within moments, the wound began to knit as her special brand of magic took form. Mace could actually feel it.

Something was different now. He'd seen skilled healers do their work before. In fact, he'd witnessed both Queen Alania and Princess Arikia heal dragons and knights alike in the Castle Lair, but he'd never felt this tingle of magic before. He'd seen Princess Belora from afar as she visited her sisters, but he'd never spoken to the youngest of Adora's daughters.

The innkeeper stood back, watching with just a bit of awe on his round face. Villagers began the grisly business of cleaning up and trying to recover. All the while, the small woman worked healing magic on William's deep wound.

"We all heard your distress call. We came as fast as we could. I knew a dragon was in trouble so I made Lars take me along." Belora spoke soothingly as she worked her healing.

"Thank you, cousin. I know this seems odd to you, but I really am William. I'm just a little older than you expect. To you, I've only been gone about five days, but to me, it's been just over five years."

"I don't understand it, but Kelvan is sure to be getting the story out of your dragon friends as we speak. He doesn't like me to say it, but he's a terrible gossip," she teased, even as Wil winced. She had to manipulate his arm in order to reach the deepest part of the wound and was talking, Mace noted, to help distract Wil from the pain. "Who are your companions, Wil? Shall I guess?" She didn't wait for an answer. "We were told a minstrel named Drake and a Guardsman had taken off with Jenet, Nellin and Sir Mace."

"I'm Drake." He nodded wearily. "Did Ren and Lilla make it to the Border Lair safely? Are they well?"

"They are doing better each day, though it was a close thing. My mother stayed behind to look after them when I insisted on coming here. So you're the minstrel? Funny, I could have sworn I saw you throwing fireballs. I'd have said you were some kind of mage." She winked, smiling as she moved Wil's arm again. He was in less pain now, Mace could tell from Wil's expression. The princess was truly gifted. "And I suppose you're Sir Mace. I don't think we've ever met officially though Kelvan talks about his friend Nellin from time to time. I met Jenet when I was at the castle last."

Mace nodded politely. "I'm glad to meet you, Princess Belora. Thank you and your mates for coming to our assistance."

"Towns up and down the border have been having trouble the past few days. We've been on even higher alert than usual."

Sir Gareth walked into the tavern yard at that moment and headed straight for Mace. They shook hands in the warrior way and exchanged grim expressions as he looked at the carnage all around.

"My lady is right," he said to the group. "Something's stirred up the skiths and King Lucan's soldiers these past few days. My bet is, you're the reason."

"You'd win that bet, Gareth." Mace nodded grimly.

"We had intelligence even before Wil was snatched that Lucan is after one of the younger princes. He must have heard about Wil's abduction." Drake stepped forward to meet the knight.

"It's been the talk of the land," Gareth agreed.

"I have to get back to the castle," Wil said as Belora finished up. "Thank you, cousin."

"You should rest for the night at least," Belora admonished him. "It will you do no good to reinjure the wound I've just managed to heal."

"We'd planned to stay the night in this town anyway," Mace added.

"Now that we know what's stirred the hornet's nest..." Gareth eyed William thoughtfully, "...we can help. You'll have company as you make your way toward the castle. Hopefully you can avoid any more incidents like this until after you get a chance to see the king."

"Thank you, Gareth." Mace felt his burden ease. "That would be much appreciated."

The tavern owner approached once more after having gone off to help some of the wounded villagers. "I have a few rooms and accommodation for your dragons, sirs. Please stay the night with us. I think it would make the entire village feel more secure."

"We will be happy to stay." Drake turned his charm on the man. "We'll need three rooms. One for Sir Gareth, his partner and his lady, one for Wil and one for us." He pointed from Krysta to Mace and back. We'd like Wil's room to be between the other two, if that's possible." Drake spoke in low tones so that only the immediate company could hear his plans. The innkeeper nodded agreeably. "We can arrange that, sir. No trouble at all. Interior room, with no access except from the hall. I know how you knights like your security. I'll set my girls to fixing the rooms up right away."

Drake walked off with the tavern owner and Wil and Belora followed slowly after. It was clear the prince was still in a bit of pain and the lady watched over him. Krysta followed as well, shaking her head at how Drake charmed the innkeeper.

Mace felt Gareth's eyes on him. Gareth was older than he and Drake, but Mace had trained with him for a year after being chosen by Nellin, and knew the man well.

"So what's this? Nellin's taken a mate?"

"He has. Lady Jenet."

"But she's been pining away for some poet for the past

decade or more, so they say."

"You just met him." Mace started walking toward the inn and Gareth fell in beside him. "Have you ever heard of the bard called Drake of the Five Lands?"

"Who hasn't? He's played for every monarch but our own. He's the most famous of all Jinn bards."

"He's also Jenet's knight partner. Newly chosen and in need of training." Mace slowed his pace just before they reached the door. "He's also, I'm sure you saw, a mage of great power, newly discovered. Something called a Firedrake. He can call magical fire at will and it only burns what he wishes it to burn. Go easy on him. This has all happened in the past three days. It's been a bit of a shock."

"To you as well as him, if I don't miss my guess." Mace fought not to wriggle under Gareth's scrutiny. "Why are you so easy with this, Mace? How can you partner so easily with a stranger?"

"He's not a stranger." Mace felt his heart rise to defend his fighting partner. "We grew up together. He's Sir Declan's son."

Gareth whistled between his teeth. "I heard Dec was so hard on his only boy, the kid ran off." He looked to the doorway and back to Mace. "Declan is a great knight and he's mellowed over the years, but he's always been a ball-buster. I always felt sympathy for his son, though I'd never met the lad, but he's turned out to be quite a surprise, hasn't he?"

"You can say that again." Mace shook his head. "Drake's taken all life has thrown at him and he always comes out on top. Give him a chance. I know you'll like him. He's even more talkative than you are." Mace said the last with a mocking grin. Gareth was a garrulous sort and though Mace liked him very much, he got along with his fighting partner, Lars, better. Lars spoke even less than Mace did and the two men understood each other well.

"Congratulations on your joining, Mace." Gareth stopped him with a warm hand on his shoulder. "Once we get Wil to safety, we'll celebrate it properly."

"I look forward to it." Mace led the way into the dark interior of the tavern.

The wounded were given a place in one of the large private parlors that served as a sort of hospital when needed. Princess Belora organized the villagers to patch up folks as best they could, while Drake, Krysta and Mace went off with the men to help the villagers set up watches and deal with the aftermath of the day.

After she'd reorganized what was left of the village Guard, Krysta left the warriors to see what she could do inside the inn. She wasn't much of a healer, but she could wrap a bandage properly. She also set herself the task of watching over Princess Belora and the wounded. If further attack should come, Krysta would be on hand to defend them until help could arrive, if needed.

They spent long hours putting the village back to rights. Many had been injured, but when the princess finally told Krysta to seek her bed because she was swaying on her feet, she went. The dragons had bedded down in the tavern yard where a pool of sand had been set aside for their use. Drake escorted Krysta to the room that had been assigned them. Mace was already there when they entered and stopped short.

Mace lay sprawled on the bed, sitting up against the headboard. In his right hand, he toyed with a small ball of flame as if it were nothing out of the ordinary. His usual stoic expression was replaced by curiosity as he regarded the fire bouncing merrily in his palm.

"Sweet Mother!" Drake swore.

The flame winked out as Mace closed his fist.

"How can this be?" Krysta asked, astonished.

Mace stood. "I have no idea, but..." he paused, clearly uncomfortable with his thoughts, "...when I walked into the fire, I felt something..." Again he trailed off as his thoughts jumbled. "I felt something open up between us. And between me and the fire. It's there now. I can feel it deep within me, very near the place Nellin and I share in our souls. It comes when I call and it leaves when I close the connection."

"It's like a river of fire beneath your feet, only it's not one of substance, but of pure energy." Drake moved into the room. "Isn't it?"

"That's a good way of putting it. But this isn't my power, Drake. I've had some time to think about it. The only reason it's accessible is because of you. It exists in the same place in my soul that's joined now to you, through Krysta and then to Jenet. It's a convoluted path, but it's open now, as it's never been before. I think the only reason I can use this power of *yours*," he emphasized the last word, "is because we're bonded partners now."

"But that's great!" Krysta started forward, hugging him. "Isn't it?" She pulled back, enthusiasm gripping her. "I mean, that makes two Firedrakes instead of just one. Think of the tactical advantage if you can both work the fire magic."

"She's got a point." Drake leaned back, watching them both.

"And if you can show your father how to access his fire," Krysta went on, addressing Drake. "He might possibly be able to share it with Sir Ren and then there will be four of you. We can use every weapon we can get if all these portents are to be believed. This is a good thing."

"If you say so." Mace looked uncertain.

Chapter Nineteen

Gareth and Lars, along with Belora, Kelvan and his mate, Rohtina, escorted them back to the castle. It was quite an honor guard for one black dragon and a newly joined family. Word spread quickly and Drake wasn't surprised to find a crowd gathered on the landing platform when they arrived. Jenet and Nellin landed first, making way for Wil between them. They weren't taking any chances with his safety. They all knew what a shock it would be for his family to find him so changed.

Drake helped Krysta down from Jenet's back and Mace met them, flanking her other side as they faced Roland. The king was understandably confused.

Drake bowed. "My liege, we found your brother, but he's a bit..." Even the golden-tongued bard was at a loss for words, it seemed.

"I'm older than they expected." Wil's voice carried from behind the trio. Drake moved aside to allow William—now clad in black fighting leathers—to walk forward and face his brother. William didn't bow, but he did nod his head in respect to his king, his brother. "I know it's shocking, but for me, five years have passed, while for you it's been five days."

"How in the world?" Roland looked to Mace for an explanation. Mace was the steadiest of the lot and stepped forward, making his bow as well.

"We traveled to Gryphon Isle and met the wizard Gryffid." The dragons gathered all around hushed, as did their knights. "He had your brother abducted in order to train him with his army of fair folk."

"What you're telling me sounds like a fairy tale," Roland said with disbelief clear in his voice as he gazed at Wil.

Mace nodded. "I know, my liege. But every word is true. And there's more, but I think it should wait 'til we are more private." Mace shifted his eyes to the attentive audience all around and Roland sobered.

"Good idea." Roland stepped forward to face the tall young man clad in scarred black leather. "Wil? Is it really you?"

William nodded, clearly choked up. "It's really me, Rol."

Roland reached out to his little brother, cupping the side of his head. A flare of power from each of them met and held as they recognized each other. Roland knew the flavor of his brother's magic and knew in that moment—somehow—his brother had grown up.

"I've missed you so much," Wil said, breaking the silence.

"Sweet Mother!" Roland whispered his amazement as he drew his youngest brother into a crushing embrace. "It is you!"

They gathered in a private chamber, big enough for Nellin, Jenet, Kelvan and Rohtina to join them and give their version of events. Roland, Lana, Nico and Riki listened to every detail of the chase and discovery of William on Gryphon Isle.

"I spent five years there, training with the fair folk—" Wil took over the narrative, "—and learning the legacy of our line. Rol, there's a lot we didn't know—a lot the dragons were charged to remember for us—and Gryffid thinks the time is coming when we'll have to settle the ancient feuds once and for all. That's why he took me."

Roland's eyes narrowed. "He could have asked. He didn't have to kidnap you and grievously injure two of our best fighting pairs in the process."

"He did apologize for that," Drake said with a raised eyebrow. "Apparently the mercs he hired to do the job got a little overzealous. Still, I agree, he should have just asked. Then again, would any of us really have believed one of the wizards still lived?"

"Good point." Roland nodded in his direction. "So what's the dire news from your wizard friend?"

"There's a place in the far north. It's called the Citadel." The dragons perked up as Wil spoke.

"I've heard of it. Recently, in fact. Salomar was giving King Lucan of Skithdron safe passage through the northern wasteland for his search parties in exchange for diamond blades to take down our dragons. They were looking for the Citadel."

Wil's expression grew dark. "So Gryffid feared." Wil took a moment to gather his thoughts. "When the wizards left this realm, some stayed behind. A few, like Gryffid, voluntarily exiled themselves. Some were exiled by force—imprisoned in the ice at the top of the world—in the Citadel. It's likely that our neighbor, King Lucan, is looking to free the worst of the worst of our enemies from the ice. Probably hoping they'll reward him for his efforts. Roland—" his voice dropped low with deadly seriousness, "—the wizard Skir was imprisoned up there after he created the skiths."

Silence reigned for a long moment while everyone digested this awful news.

"And the dragons knew this?" Roland looked to the dragons

gathered behind the human party. Four large heads nodded.

"So we were taught," Jenet responded. *"It is our place to remember where our human friends do not. It is our task to be ever vigilant and ready to defend the lands should any of the entombed wizards seek to escape their punishment. Ours, and the Guardian's."*

"What Guardian?" Roland demanded.

"We know not," Jenet said sadly. *"We only know there is a Guardian in the North. A being of great power, born to watch over the Citadel."*

"A hereditary Guardian, then. A human?"

"Perhaps a human born of wizard blood," Nellin mused, *"like you. It would make sense."*

"That's only a theory," Jenet groused.

"But a good one, I've always thought," Nellin countered.

"You two bicker like a married couple." Nico's voice was laced with suspicion.

"That's because we are," Jenet answered, sticking her tongue out at the Prince of Spies, much like a human child would.

"My congratulations to you!" Nico walked over to Jenet and touched her neck, now entwined with Nellin's. "I'm very happy for you both." He turned to the human part of the new family. "And you three as well." Nico winked and slapped both men on the back. "It's about time you claimed your birthright, Drake." He hugged Drake and gave Krysta a kiss as the others added their congratulations.

It was a joyous moment, but it was overshadowed by the serious issues they had yet to discuss. Nico moved back, taking his wife in his arms and pulling her back against him so they faced the rest of the discussion together.

"So you found Wil on Gryphon Isle..." Nico prompted so they could resume the story.

"We met Gryffid and his army of fair folk." Drake shifted uncomfortably.

"And Gryffid advised Drake of his heritage," Mace said. "Seems he is descended of the wizard Draco, through Sir Declan's line and possibly the fair folk, through his mother's."

"You're joking." Riki's eyes widened.

"I'm afraid not, milady." Mace was serious, as always. "More than that, the wizard Draco gifted his descendants with fire magic, and through our new bond, I seem to have gotten some of it too." Mace opened his fingers to display a plume of flame, conjured in his palm.

"Sweet Mother!" Lana breathed.

"Firedrake!" Kelvan said with awe.

"What in blazes is a Firedrake?" Roland wanted to know.

"Apparently, I am, my liege." Drake smiled ruefully. "As is Mace now, and perhaps my blood-father too, if we can show him how to tap into the flame."

Mace closed his fingers, making the fire wink out. "Drake has already used this magic in battle against skiths in the village of Bayberry Heath on our way back from Gryphon Isle. As a weapon, it is formidable."

"And a little uncontrollable at the moment," Drake admitted. "I need a lot more practice, I'm afraid."

"Astounding," Roland said. "And it's effective against skiths?"

"Burns them to ash quicker than dragon fire. And Drake can selectively target what he likes. He can flame the skith and leave everything else unharmed."

"Now that sounds familiar." Nico turned his gaze to his

wife. "Riki can do that too."

"Only against evil," she reminded her husband, then turned back to the group. "I did it once, when I was cornered by a skith. I can't call flame in my fingers like Mace just did."

"Drake becomes a pillar of flame," Krysta added with some pride in her voice. "It's very effective."

"I bet." Roland looked over the newly made knight with interest. "So you're more than a pretty voice and glib tongue, eh?"

"I pray I prove to be, my liege. I know..." Drake hesitated briefly. "I know I'm not exactly knight material, but now that the deed is done, I vow to do everything in my power to live up to the expectations of knighthood."

Roland chuckled and shook his head. "You already have, my friend. You were ever blind when it came to your own stature. You are the best—the only—partner for Jenet. We've all known it for as long as we've known you both. As for being worthy of being a knight..." Roland grasped Drake by the shoulder. "You've always been worthy, Drake. Your love for Jenet, your loyalty to the land and people of Draconia—even as you traveled far and wide—your honor, your courage. All of those things make you one of the champions of this land. You found Wil, as you promised. You're more than worthy. You're one of our elite, just like Mace. A better matched pair, I've never seen."

The men shared a moment of respectful camaraderie before Roland turned to Krysta. "Welcome to the family, Krysta. Your brother and I had a long talk while you were away. We'll be glad of your skills in the coming days."

"Thank you, my liege." Krysta bowed, keeping her gaze on Roland's in a show of respect.

Hours later, Drake, Mace and Krysta had a hastily prepared wedding celebration and their dragons flew in a mating flight, long anticipated since that first time they'd been together. The party was a mix of Jinn and Lair traditions, with Prince Nico and his wife Riki standing for them as witnesses, though all agreed neither Drake nor Mace needed any guidance in making love to their wife as was custom for newlyweds in many of the Jinn clans.

They were given a small enclosure on the battlements traditionally used for such celebrations so the dragons could stay near their human counterparts until the very last moments before they took to the sky. Only this time, the enclosure was festooned with Jinn tapestries in bright colors, donated for the cause by Krysta's clan. There would be a party the following night with the entire Wayfarer Clan as well as those of the Black Dragon Clan who were already living in Castleton to celebrate the joining of Krysta and Drake. Mace would be adopted into both clans and made Jinn by marriage as well. Krysta figured that party would last for days.

As the dragons trumpeted their joy to the heavens, coiled together in bliss, so too were the human partners in the family. Krysta and her men were swept up in the driving pleasure spurred on by their bond with the dragons. Golden sparks of fire enveloped the three, heating their blood but harming none—a magical display of Drake's power brought on by intense emotion.

The first joining was hard and fast, with few words but a wealth of emotion passing between the three humans and the dragons whose lust pushed them. Now that Wil was home safe, Jenet and Nellin had warned Krysta that she would get little sleep that night. She'd thought it a joke at the time, but after the second, intense round of dragon-inspired lovemaking, she began to wonder.

Drake lay panting on one side of the soft bed, Mace on the other. Krysta crawled over to a low table near the entrance to the small enclosure and began to nibble on the delicacies that had been prepared for them. If they were going to keep up this pace, she'd need some nourishment. A grin passed over her face as she ate, watching her two gorgeous husbands watching her.

"What puts such a devilish smile on your face, lovely Krys?" Drake beckoned to her with one finger. She took a small plate of pastries back with her as she rejoined him on the mattress.

"I was just thinking we should eat while we can. One cannot live on love alone, after all."

"Says who?" Mace sat up to nibble on her shoulder. "Personally, I find you delicious and very invigorating."

Krysta felt the dragons stir in the back of her mind. Joined as she was to the men, she had felt echoes of the dragons' passion in her own body even as her men drove her higher with their love. Judging by the passion just passed, the dragons were gearing up for a third round of aerial love.

Placing the plate on the small ledge behind Mace, she leaned over him, only to be caught in his strong arms and pulled down for a kiss. The kiss turned to a thorough exploration that made her senses swim. By the time Drake came up behind her, she was ready for anything these two might want from her.

Mace drew back and pushed her head downward. She knew what he wanted. She wanted the same.

As the dragon fire burned hotter, she took Mace's thick cock between her lips, playing with him at first, before sucking him deep. At the same time, Drake lifted her hips off the mattress, settling behind her as she rested on her knees. He entered her slick channel, pushing her forward onto Mace's cock. He drew out and pulled her back. He repeated the motion, increasing his pace, essentially fucking them both as his motion pushed her back and forth on Mace.

Gazing upward, she saw Mace's head drop back on his shoulders, his eyes shut as pleasure swamped him. Drake increased his pace yet again as the dragons spiraled higher, trumpeting to the heavens along with their fellows. Many knights and dragons were celebrating in pleasure with them this night.

As the dragons reached their peak, so too did their human counterparts, Mace coming in her mouth while Drake's seed flooded her womb. Krysta's whole body clenched in bliss, riding the waves of ecstasy for long moments as the dragons rode the air currents toward the earth far below.

The Jinn party did indeed last for days. Krysta was excused from her duty as a Guard while the knights enjoyed the usual respite from their work as well. Newlyweds were given a week to enjoy their married state before having to go back to work.

For Drake, the end of their honeymoon signaled the beginning of a new life for him. He'd never expected to be welcomed back to Draconia in such a fashion—being partnered with Jenet was a boyhood dream come true and being married to Krysta was every fantasy he'd ever had. She was inventive in the bedchamber and a true partner in the life he saw unfolding before his eyes. It was a life he'd never expected, but one that promised great joy.

The rest of the Lair kept their distance during that initial week, though both sets of parents had contributed to the basic decoration of the set of rooms assigned now to Mace, Drake,

Krysta, Nellin and Jenet. Krysta had brought a load of gifts from her family as well. Her brother had attended both ceremonies— the public part of the Lair wedding and the full Jinn ceremony performed a day later. Unexpectedly, Drake discovered the new leader of the Wayfarer Clan, a lovely grey-eyed woman named Malin, was also Krysta's sister, the eldest of the three siblings.

Rulu, the aged former leader of the Clan, was her father, and he delighted in giving both Drake and Mace dire, half-hearted warnings about how to treat his baby girl. The Jinn weren't used to three-partnered marriages, but were more open-minded than other peoples, having traveled in all lands and seen all kinds of customs and traditions.

During that week, the dragons had mated almost continuously every night, making up for lost time, they claimed when they paused long enough to speak. They all slept deep into the morning, only stumbling out for sustenance around noon each day to the teasing grins of the Lair folk. A few times, the human side of the family would have to go running for their chamber when the dragons unexpectedly took to the sky. They didn't always make it, but the Lair folk weren't easily shocked. Dragons were exhibitionists after all, and more than a few of the knights took after their brethren of the skies.

Nico and Riki came upon them in a darkened hall as Drake fucked Krysta's mouth while Mace plowed into her from behind. Nico grinned and settled in to watch the show, fondling his mate through her blouse while he met Drake's eye. It was only fair, he realized, since Drake had stood as witness to the royal's Jinn wedding ceremony, even helping in the marital tent later that night, as was custom.

The dragons peaked, bringing all three mates to completion as the royal couple watched, though only Drake knew they were there—until Drake, Mace and Krysta broke apart, all three of them righting their clothing. When Mace and Krysta turned toward the arch to the stairs, they stopped short, seeing Nico and Riki standing there, smiling at them.

"Felicitations on your union." Nico winked as he held his wife against him, both arms around her waist as they faced the red-faced trio. Well, Mace and Krysta were blushing, but Drake knew he'd gone well past the blushing stage with this particular couple. Nico was like a brother to him and Riki was a very special woman he would protect with his life, though his heart was fully Krysta's now. "Don't mind us," Nico went on, "we were just on the way to our quarters."

"My liege—" Mace halted, confusion clear on his face. Drake stepped in to save his brother-in-arms.

"We hope you enjoyed the entertainment." Krysta gasped as Drake bowed mockingly low and both royals laughed at his antics.

"You always were a showman, Drake. I'll give you that." Riki's voice drifted to them as Nico turned her away, back toward their apartments. "Thanks for the reminder."

When Nico and Riki were out of earshot, Krysta turned on Drake. "Reminder? Please tell me you haven't bedded the Jinn queen! I knew you were a scoundrel, but honestly, Drake!"

"Sweetheart." Drake tried to take her shoulders in his hands, but she evaded him, turning to Mace instead. "Please try to understand. I was part of their mating ceremony. Their *Jinn* ceremony." She seemed unconvinced. "I never actually bedded Riki," he mumbled, knowing this was something Krysta might never forgive him for. Already, they were off to a rocky start.

But Krysta surprised him, taking his face in her hands and kissing him soundly. "You don't know how glad I am to hear that. I don't think I could compete with a queen."

"Sweetheart." He kissed her back. "There is no competition. You're the only woman I will ever love, the only woman I will ever bed. And it's been that way from the moment I first saw you."

"You do have a silver tongue." She smiled as she stepped away, taking one of his hands in her own. She took Mace's hand as well, leading them toward their chamber. "Now let's find a bed so you can show me again just how talented it really is."

Drake looked over her head at Mace. The knight's expression held a mixture of shock, envy and rekindled passion as Krysta dragged them along, but they were of one mind when it came to their wife. Mace nodded at him and they each took one arm and one leg, lifting Krysta off her feet and running the last few steps to their chamber door.

The dragons were flying again.

Epilogue

Drake of the Five Lands stowed his wagon and hung up his minstrel's garb—for the time being at least. One never knew when the bard's persona might come in handy once more, but Drake of Draconia had to learn how to be a knight first. He spent every day training with Jenet and Mace, welcomed home at night into Krysta's loving arms.

She'd changed her work schedule to the day watch, and continued to work, though she too, had much to learn about Lair life. She wasn't the typical lady of the Lair and before long, she'd inspired many of the other women to start some basic training in arms as a way to keep fit and prepare for any contingency. All the knights thought it was a good thing, though they didn't communicate their worries about impending war too broadly.

Krysta led classes for the women, teaching them simple ways to defend themselves. A few were more gifted and she invited them to study with the Guards when it was her turn to teach. All in all, they were settling in to a beautiful life in the Lair.

Then came the magic training.

Drake relied on Mace to temper his volatile emotions when dealing with Sir Declan. Nico, and even Roland, sat in on those first few sessions when Drake began to call on his fire, hoping to show Declan how to do the same.

Dec wasn't the only one astounded when the fire came much easier to the older knight than it had to his son. Declan was a natural and the dragons confirmed what Drake was astounded to learn. Declan's fire was much closer to the surface than it had been in Drake. It explained a lot about Declan's temper and the tight control under which he'd always lived.

Now that the fire was released, Declan's disposition changed as well. He was much more easy-going than ever and began to see the humor in life as well as the struggle. It was a positive change for them all.

Drake took his place at his fathers' sides as a close counselor to the king. Declan and Ren had always been valued advisors, but now with magic more prevalent in the kingdom, Drake and Mace were called upon to offer their expertise as well. They spent part of each morning with Roland, often with Nico and some of the other royal princes present as well, going over communiqués and talking strategy.

It was on one such morning when a near breathless messenger arrived from one of the southern cities. He rushed into the throne room, then fell to one knee before Roland.

"My liege." The man breathed hard, as if he'd run all the way from Tipolir to Castleton. "News from the south. A flight of gryphons with mounted warriors heads this way at a slow pace, though they can't be more than a few hours behind me."

"From whom did this news pass?" Roland asked

"The news started with a messenger from Tipolir, thence to Bayern, Hallowet, Sewell and on, but I saw them myself, my liege. They overtook me on the road and shadowed me for a time but let me pass unmolested."

"How many would you say?" Nico helped the man to his feet, handing him a glass of water since the poor man looked well worn from the hard ride.

"A dozen that I saw. The reports stated twice that many, but I only saw twelve gryphons—each with a mounted rider, though the riders blended so well with the gryphons' golden plumage, they were hard to make out. My liege, I never thought to see the like."

"Thank you for making haste to give us this news," Roland said, calmer than Drake would have credited. He signaled to Nico and the Prince of Spies led the man from the room, questioning him quietly as he led him to the great hall where he could rest and have a meal. Drake also saw Nico pass the man a few coins for his trouble. Nico had never skimped on paying for good service. It's what made him such an able spymaster.

Roland turned to Drake and Mace, a raised eyebrow enough to make Drake share his thoughts.

"I think it's safe to bet these could be some of Gryffid's folk."

Drake sent a quick message to Jenet. *"Sweetheart, are you with Wil?"*

"He's flying out near the southern edge of the new town with some of the others. He's safe."

"Gryphons are coming, Jen. They're close to Castleton."

"My brother Wil is flying to the south," Roland confirmed, informing the rest of the gathered advisors. "I've asked him to wait, but I doubt that will hold him." Roland stalked toward the door. "If your partners are near, mount up and fly with me. I'm going out to meet them."

Drake, Mace, Ren, Declan and several others of the king's advisors were hot on his heels. The knights raced for the ledges where their dragons waited, ready to fly. Roland, Nico and a few of the other princes shifted and took to wing as black dragons, the large contingent heading south to meet the wizard's emissaries.

About the Author

A life-long martial arts enthusiast, Bianca enjoys a number of hobbies and interests that keep her busy and entertained such as playing the guitar, shopping, painting, shopping, skiing, shopping, road trips, and did we say...um...shopping? A bargain hunter through and through, Bianca loves the thrill of the hunt for that excellent price on quality items, though she's hardly a fashionista. She likes nothing better than curling up by the fire with a good book, or better yet, by the computer, writing a good book.

To learn more about Bianca D'Arc, please visit www.biancadarc.com. Send an email to Bianca at BiancaDarc@gmail.com or join her Yahoo! group to join in the fun with other readers as well as Bianca. http://groups.yahoo.com/group/BiancaDArc

An abused woman has the power to unite werefolk, fey and vampire against an evil that would see them all dead—if she can learn to love again.

Sweeter Than Wine

© 2007 Bianca D'Arc

Christy lies near death after a brutal beating by her estranged husband. Her preternatural friends reach a desperate conclusion: The only way to save her is to turn her. Sebastian steps forward to take on the burden of being her Maker.

For him it's no burden at all. She draws him as no other woman has for centuries. With the help of a werecougar friend, Sebastian teaches Christy about her new life and abilities, making certain she is as strong as he can make her. Only then can she face her abusive ex-husband and put her old life behind her. But Christy's ex-husband is involved in something more dangerous than any of them had guessed.

Vampire, were, and even a fey knight must work together to put an end to the threatening evil. To overcome her past, help keep the darkness at bay, and fight for a new life with Sebastian, Christy must draw on all of her new-found strength.

Will it be enough?

Warning, this title contains explicit sex, graphic language, ménage a trois, hot neck biting and werecougar stroking.

Available now in ebook and print from Samhain Publishing.

GET IT NOW

MyBookStoreAndMore.com
GREAT EBOOKS, GREAT DEALS . . . AND MORE!

Don't wait to run to the bookstore down the street, or waste time shopping online at one of the "big boys." Now, all your favorite Samhain authors are all in one place—at MyBookStoreAndMore.com. Stop by today and discover great deals on Samhain—and a whole lot more!

GREAT
cheap
fun

Discover eBooks!
THE FASTEST WAY TO GET THE HOTTEST NAMES

Get your favorite authors on your favorite reader, long before they're
out in print! Ebooks from Samhain go wherever you go, and work with
whatever you carry—Palm, PDF, Mobi, and more.

Samhain
publishing LTD

WWW.SAMHAINPUBLISHING.COM